"Perhaps it is my presence that makes you blush so."

Julianna's mouth opened and shut with a snap. "Of all the arrogant, conceited—"

His smile enlarged to a grin.

"And another thing, my lord," she said, eyeing him smolderingly. "I would appreciate it if you would, in future, refrain from pressuring my mother to talk about me—"

"But you mistake, Miss Cresston," he interrupted smoothly. "Your mother requires no urging to talk about you. Come. Dance with me."

"I will not!" she hissed.

"Miss Cresston," the earl said, favoring her with his most attractive smile. "Let us cry friends for one dance. Waltz with me."

"Well—if you promise not to be disagreeable."

"I promise," the earl told her, taking her hand and sweeping her out onto the floor, his arm firmly circling her waist in a way that seemed to contribute greatly to the heat already present in the room.

To her surprise, Julianna did not object when the band struck up a second waltz, and he swept her out into the whirling couples again.

Trust her mother to be right—the earl was a beautiful dancer.

"Highest rati_____ delightful romp."

_____ *Confusion*

ALSO BY JUDITH NELSON

The Merry Chase
Kidnap Confusion

Published by
WARNER BOOKS

JULIANNA

Judith Nelson

WARNER BOOKS

A Warner Communications Company

WARNER BOOKS EDITION

Copyright © 1989 by Judith Nelson
All rights reserved.

Warner Books, Inc.
666 Fifth Avenue
New York, N.Y. 10103

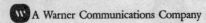
Printed in the United States of America

First Printing: March, 1989

10 9 8 7 6 5 4 3 2 1

❧ Chapter 1 ❧

It was not the first marriage proposal Julianna Cresston had received from her cousin Jonathan, and perhaps that was why she was not attending.

Her mind was occupied by much more important matters—in particular, the knot that had worked its way into her embroidery and showed no signs of working itself out again—so she ignored the eager young man standing—for effect—before the morning room fireplace, his elegant head cradled interestingly on one well-manicured hand, his elbow resting comfortably on the mantelpiece.

Another gentleman, of a more observing nature, would have noticed that the lady before whom he was outlining the glorious deeds, plans, and actions he desired to undertake to ensure her happiness seemed remarkably unmoved. But Jonathan, never the most observant of fellows, was intent on the verbal flights and flourishes so dear to his heart, and which he believed incumbent on any marriage proposal, and was lost in his own long periods.

When, at last, he eagerly inquired, "Well, Julianna, what do you think?" the young viscount was surprised to find he had to repeat the question; Miss Cresston was at that

1

moment particularly engaged in disentangling that trouble-some knot.

At his second "What do you think?" Julianna raised her clear green eyes and said, with more feeling than tact, "I think that embroidery is one more of those foolish pastimes invented for women by men who did not like them very much!"

He goggled at her.

"You think—*what*?"

"I *also* think, Jonathan," she said, surveying him criti-cally as she reached in vexation for her scissors, "that you should go home at once and change that ridiculous waistcoat!"

Her cousin's face, so eager a moment before, stiffened alarmingly; too late Julianna realized that she had been neither diplomatic nor—she was sorry to say—kind. She tried to palliate her faux pas with a smile, but Viscount Bushnell was having none of it.

"Go home—and change—my *waistcoat*?" he repeated, astonished at her criticism. Like many of his friends, the viscount considered himself complete to a shade, and was used to being praised for the style in which he carried himself and the way his tall frame set off the most daring of apparel to advantage. He tried to remember the last time someone had had the audacity to criticize his choice in waistcoats.

It had been . . . it had been . . .

He frowned heavily. It had been several years ago. And the critic then, as now, was Julianna.

Miss Cresston, unaware of this sudden and regrettable improvement in her cousin's memory, nodded.

"Something not as—bright," she offered, turning from the large green and yellow stripes he wore as if they pained her. "Perhaps something in dark blue. Dark blue becomes you, Jonathan. Or you could wear claret. But those stripes—" She shook her head reflectively, sighed, and snipped the frustrating thread.

Her cousin's face flushed, and Miss Cresston changed her mind about his wearing claret.

"I lay my heart at your feet, and you talk to me of embroidery, waistcoats, and the selection of *colors*?"

His high tone was spoiled when he added, a moment later, in the voice of the thirteen-year-old boy who had found his eleven-year-old cousin particularly tiresome, "And I will have you know, Julianna, that this style of waistcoat—and these colors—are *particularly* favored by the Regent!"

Julianna, who had her own opinions of the Regent as an arbiter of fashion, believed that even *he* would blink, could he see her cousin now. One look at Jonathan's face suggested that it would be wise to keep such thoughts to herself, however, and she did, starting to smile. "It is more sensible to talk of embroidery and colors and waistcoats than it is to talk of laying your heart at my feet, Jonathan! You have never done so—"

"I have!" he protested. "Time out of mind—"

"Oh!" Julianna smiled again. "You have proposed to me time out of mind, to be sure. But what has that to do with your heart, my dear?"

Thrown off stride, her cousin glowered at her. "I don't know what you mean," he said stiffly. "If not my heart, then what?"

She shook her blond head, so close in color to his golden curls, and her voice was soft. "I think, dear Jonathan, that your proposals have much more to do with laying your hands on my fortune than laying your heart at my feet."

Viscount Bushnell, who had attained his title three years earlier upon the untimely demise of his sire, and who had, ever since, been busily dissipating the inheritance left him by that careful man, had the grace to blush.

"No, dash it, Ju, I'm very fond of you," he protested. "Always have been—"

"But you find it easier to be fond of me when I have substantial holdings than you would if I had—shall we say—one thousand pounds a year?"

"Well..." Her cousin, realizing the outcome of this proposal would be no different from that of his last twelve, grinned ruefully at the companion of his childhood. "I'd still be fond of you if you had only one thousand pounds a year, coz. Even if you had none at all!''

"Yes." Her deep green eyes surveyed him tranquilly. "But I doubt your fondness would prompt you to marriage. You must be badly dipped again.''

"Yes, well . . ." Jonathan shrugged philosophically, as aware as she that his proposals of marriage were always linked to certain pecuniary embarrassments. "I shall come about again. I always do.''

It was true so far, she knew; he had always come about, escaping—or postponing—the fall of an ever increasing load of debt by a lucky wager, or backing himself to do some shocking—and often dangerous—deed.

But she worried—and she knew his mother did, too—that one day the right horse wouldn't outrun the field, or the right card wouldn't turn, and Jonathan would find himself with nothing.

Genuinely fond of this cousin with whom she had grown up and who bore her such a familial resemblance that many people, upon first seeing them, believed the two to be brother and sister, she reached forward to clasp one of his hands as he stood near her, saying suddenly, "Do you know what you ought to do, Jonathan? You ought to find yourself a nice girl who knows how to hold house and retire to Bushy. My father was always used to say it is a very good estate, and I'm sure that if you put your mind to it, and practiced a few economies for a while, you could soon have it back in shape to provide you with a quite comfortable . . .''

Her voice trailed off as her cousin stared at her, his bright blue eyes wide, his eyebrows raised in real surprise. "Retire to the country, Julianna? *Me*? You must be joking!''

She was not, but his shocked gaze made her laugh, and she let go his hand with a playful slap, telling him that if he were wise he'd do so before he found himself completely in the basket.

Jonathan, who at his particular stage in life thought the basket preferable to his ancestral dwelling, told her with feeling that she was a good one to talk, what with her London home and her Paris hôtel, and her choice of several estates in various parts of the country to visit whenever she was feeling restless or peevish or in need of a change of scene or pace.

"Seriously, though, Ju"—he continued; for a moment she thought he was going to renew his petition for her hand and, surprised, she waited—"about this waistcost... Do you really think I ought to go home and change it?"

He was startled when her richly vibrant laugh bubbled up; it amused her that, after all this time, thoughts still darted in and out of his head as they had when he was nine. Jonathan was a man not given to brooding on a refusal that might have been expected to cut up all his hopes! She would not tell him why she was laughing as she assured him, with as much solemnity as she could muster, that the waistcoat did not become him.

"But dash it—" he protested. "I just had it made. Wore it especially for you. My tailor said it was all the crack."

Julianna studied the waistcoat one more time and closed her eyes. "Your tailor," she informed him gravely, "lied."

"Yes, well—" Jonathan ran a distracted hand through his curly hair and disposed his lanky frame in one of the leather chairs to her left. "Daresay you're right. Bunch of plaguey tradesmen—I know they lie about their bills, because the amounts they say I owe them are not to be believed, while as for—"

He broke off suddenly, realizing his cousin was watching him intently, and he straightened slightly to grin at her. "You wouldn't care to change your mind, would you, Ju?"

She said she would not, and he shrugged.

"Can't say as I blame you," he said candidly. "Daresay I'd make a devil of a husband. Would try to do things right, you understand but—well..." He grinned boyishly. "I do rather like to have things my way."

"You and every other man I know," Julianna said, returning his grin.

"Yes. Well, then!" The lighthearted insouciance that always characterized him came to the fore, and he rose. "Guess I'll be off. No use cooling my heels here if—" He realized the infelicity of that remark, and grinned at her again. "Sorry, Julianna. Didn't mean I wouldn't like to stay, but—"

"But you have better things to do," she supplied.

"Yes," he agreed, unaware that he had again blundered. "I do." He bent to kiss her cheek and gave her a slight pat on the shoulder. "Be seeing you, old girl."

"Next time you're temporarily at a stand," she suggested, and he smiled. When he had reached the door she stopped him by asking if he needed a loan, and he turned a scandalized face toward her.

"Dash it, Julianna!" he said. "I can't borrow money from you! You're my cousin! And a woman, besides!"

"Yes, but, Jonathan," she reasoned, rising to walk toward him, her hand outstretched, her rose silk gown rustling as she walked, "if I were to marry you, I'd still be your cousin and a woman, and you wouldn't have any problem at all taking my money—not just a loan, but all of it!"

"True," he agreed, "but then you'd be my wife. A man can take from his wife; every man takes from his wife. It's expected! But it's a pretty scurvy fellow who takes from his cousin."

Julianna did not understand his reasoning, and said so. She told him she liked being his cousin, but did not at all wish to be his wife, and she would rather give him money as his cousin than have him take it from her if they were wed . . .

Her voice trailed off as the expression on his face told her it was pointless to discuss with him the fine line between a cousin who is a wife and a cousin who is only a cousin. Instead she shook her head and asked, "Is this one of those male codes of honor you're forever telling me about, Jonathan?"

He said it was.

"It is all very strange, I think." She sighed.

He regarded her with a lofty wisdom that seldom sat upon his tall shoulders. "That, my dear, is because you ain't a man." And with that irrefutable rejoinder he walked out the door, leaving his cousin shaking her head.

* * *

Jonathan was right in that at least—Miss Cresston was not male. And while she did not herself take what was said too seriously, she was used to hearing herself described both as graceful and statuesque. From the time of her come-out it was apparent that Miss Cresston had her own style. It set her apart and made her, if not a diamond of the first water, sufficiently out of the ordinary to inspire her own vociferous and loyal group of admirers, one of whom had even been moved one night, when she was looking particularly lovely and he was more than a little foxed, to write a sonnet to her left ear—an ear that still burned whenever Miss Cresston thought about it.

Julianna was likely to put such offerings as that absurd sonnet down more to her considerable fortune than to her actual ability to inspire poetry.

Perhaps it was her cousin Jonathan's constant offers of marriage whenever he was in financial difficulties; perhaps it was her former governess's admonishments that "beauty is as beauty does"; perhaps it was the warnings against fortune hunters that her late father poured into her ears, along with the advice that she had enough money to please herself, and didn't have to worry about pleasing anyone else; perhaps it was a certain shrewdness and judgment of character that lay behind her smiling eyes that made Miss Cresston take such flattery with a large grain of salt. Perhaps it was because she did not care about them—at least, not very much—that all such appeals to her vanity did not long turn her head.

Whatever it was, she had, since her come-out six years earlier, at the tender age of seventeen, received many offers of marriage similar to Cousin Jonathan's, all with the same result—she remained unwed, smiling tranquilly at the world and refusing to accept its dictum that a young woman who passes through several seasons without being married is on the shelf.

Of course, the world made allowances for such a rich young woman as Miss Cresston. Her admirers obviously did not consider her on the shelf and, while Julianna did not think it would have troubled her in the least—although she was not sure she wanted to find out—she saw no diminution in the crowd of gentlemen who gathered around her at the parties and dances she chose to attend.

Nor was her mother one to urge her to marry (despite her many aunts' loud and persistent advice and opinions on the subject), that good woman saying only that she wished Julianna to be happy, and Julianna herself was the best judge of what would accomplish that. When Julianna's Aunt Sephrinia so far forgot herself as to cry, "We are not talking about happiness! We are talking about *marriage*!" Julianna's mother had actually laughed, and said that she hoped *her* daughter, at least, would find the first if she chose the second.

The look on Aunt Sephrinia's face made it apparent she considered the combination of marriage and happiness neither likely nor necessary, but a quick glance at her sister-in-law's face had kept her from doing more than rolling her eyes.

Now Julianna sat, thinking deeply about her cousin Jonathan and his latest visit, and her brow furrowed slightly. He was still the easygoing companion of her childhood, but for all his smiles, and the way his blue eyes lit up when he was amused, for all his wild starts and carefree ways, there hung about him now some subtle air that was different, some worry that seemed to settle on him when he sat silent for a moment.

Next to her mother she considered him the best of her relatives, and she loved him as she would love a brother, had her parents been blessed with a son. It was Jonathan, two years her elder, who had taught her to jump a horse (in a neck-or-nothing style her aunts deplored, but she found exhilarating), and (although neither her aunts nor her mother knew this) to shoot a pistol until she could cup at least as many wafers as her cousin at twenty feet. Jonathan had undertaken her education in driving, too, until her father firmly stepped in and said that he had no desire to see his daughter overturned in every ditch between their home and London, and he would teach her to handle the ribbons.

He had taught her so well that if Miss Cresston were

male—something her cousin had so truthfully pointed out she was not—she would have been a likely candidate for the Four Horse Club. To his very great chagrin, Jonathan was not, the rattling great rate he affected too often landing him in trouble for the taste of those so-strict champions of driving precision.

She worried now that perhaps the latest in his series of financial difficulties was more serious than the rest, and she wondered if there was any way—short of marriage—that she could extricate him from it. She pondered the matter for some time, but had reached no solution when, an hour later, her abigail entered the room to complain that she had been waiting in Miss Cresston's bedchamber the better part of half an hour, and that now Miss must hurry along if she wished to change her dress and not keep her mother waiting for dinner.

Miss Cresston rose at once and dutifully hurried.

One must always dress.

੩৯ *Chapter 2* ੩৯

It was ten days before Miss Cresston saw her cousin again, and she could not honestly say that he and his troubles had fully and solely occupied her thoughts in all intervening moments.

He had, from time to time, been on her mind—especially when a morning visit from Aunt Sephrinia prophesied a dark and ignominious future for the young viscount, if he did not at once change his ways. But then, thought Miss Cresston fairly, Aunt Sephrinia was always prophesying a dark and ignominious future for someone.

It bothered Julianna that when she *did* think about her cousin's problems, she found herself no closer to a solution as to how she might best aid him than she had been before. Once or twice she thought wistfully of the days when Jonathan's biggest worries were hiding the fact that he had eaten all of Cook's just-baked tarts, or that he had inadvertently peppered the gardener's shed and broken a window after taking out a gun without leave.

These days, there were many reasons Miss Cresston could not give her full attention to her cousin. One of them was the *al fresco* party given by Lady Witherton for 450 of her nearest and dearest confidants. That was followed by the Seftons' ball, and in due course by the opera, and the theater, and a charming performance by Kean to which she and her mother had been escorted by one of Julianna's oldest and best friends, Lord Wafton.

There had been a time the betting men at Watier's were laying odds that it was Wafton who would lead Miss Cresston to the altar, but in the end even the most optimistic of the gamblers had had to concede that the relationship between the two was friendship, nothing more, and had had to pay up and look elsewhere for another interesting topic on which to wager and recoup his losses.

And there had been the morning calls, and the afternoon drives in Hyde Park. The *ton* would have thought it odd indeed had several days passed without the sight of Miss Cresston in her high-perch phaeton *(a bit unusual a vehicle for a lady, perhaps, but oh, my dear, a woman with more than twenty thousand pounds a year! If she wants to drive something usually left to the sporting gentlemen, what is one* really *going to say?)* at the time of the fashionable promenade.

. So it was that when Miss Cresston spotted her cousin as she was going down one of the country dances with young Mr. Harrington shortly before 11 p.m. at Almack's, she experienced two emotions immediately. First—and most predominantly—came shock at seeing him in a place he had numerous times castigated as abominably flat, and had gone to great lengths to avoid, categorically and vociferously refusing to take her there when she had more than once asked him to serve as her escort.

Shock was followed closely by concern, for she thought there was a worried look in his eyes and a tenseness about his person that was gravely at odds with his usual carefree nature.

The mystery of why he was present was quickly solved, as the viscount stepped aside and Miss Cresston saw their redoubtable Great-Aunt Elizabeth behind him, with a pale and rather dowdy girl in charge.

Miss Cresston almost put a hand to her bosom; had she known Great-Aunt Elizabeth was to be present, she would not have allowed her dresser to put her in this gown for the evening. She knew even before the words were uttered that its décolletage was enough to bring her aunt's criticism down upon her head.

Not that it was *that* revealing, she comforted herself; but Great-Aunt Elizabeth would not let the fact that over half the ladies present wore gowns that were even more daring deter her from giving her niece her oft-repeated and totally unsolicited opinion on the disgraceful ways of the present-day generation.

Drat, thought Miss Cresston as she replied very much at random to young Mr. Harrington's nervous pleasantries. Why hadn't Jonathan warned her the dowager duchess was coming to town?

The reason, Miss Cresston discovered as she met her cousin in the refreshment room where Mr. Harrington escorted her in search of a glass of lemonade, and to which Jonathan soon fled on the pretense of securing something to drink for the ladies in his charge, was because the viscount had not himself known.

"Dash it, Ju, do you think if I'd known she was coming, I'd still be in town?" he said disgustedly, his voice low so those around him could not hear. "I'd have posted down to Bushy, or off to see old Harold, if I'd known. But no—it's just like her. Ran into her in Bond Street this morning; taking a toddle on the town, you know, not paying much attention to what was around me—for I can tell you, if I'd seen her carriage before she saw me, I'd have made myself scarce!—when I heard someone calling me. I looked

up, and there was Great-Aunt Elizabeth. Gave me a nasty
turn, Julianna, I can tell you!''

His face reflected the memory, and Julianna smiled in
spite of herself.

"Oh yes!'' he said, frowning at her, "it's all very well
for you to smile, but let me tell you, dear coz, you're next.
She's got some poor little dab of a girl with her—says she's
her goddaughter, and a more tongue-tied little mouse I've
never seen—and dragooned me into bringing them here
tonight.''

"You should have told her you had another engagement,'' Miss Cresston said calmly, ignoring the viscount's
dire warning and accepting a glass of lemonade from Mr.
Harrington with a smile. She told her young admirer that
her cousin would see her back to the ballroom, and Mr.
Harrington cast the unheeding viscount a look of wistful
envy before bowing regretfully and moving away.

"I did tell her I had another engagement!'' the viscount
said indignantly. "What kind of sapskull do you think I am?
But would she listen? Not Great-Aunt Elizabeth! All she
would say was, 'I do not believe it can be more pressing
than the need I have of you tonight, Jonathan'—all the time
looking down her nose at me like she did when I was seven
and we snatched the blackberry tarts. Do you remember?''

Miss Cresston did, and smiled. They had spent several
glorious summers at Great-Aunt Elizabeth's estate in Kent
when they were children, chasing their aunt's peacocks and
whiling away hours playing masquerade as they rummaged
through the old trunks in the attic that she put at their
disposal.

Julianna loved and admired Great-Aunt Elizabeth, and
thought it wonderful the way the woman spoke her mind on
everything. It was just that Great-Aunt Elizabeth, who had
been her father's father's sister, and who had married first a
baron and then, later in life, a widowed duke—to the
amazement of her entire family, and the disgust of his—was
one of those people easier to love and admire at a distance....

"So you came with her,'' Miss Cresston said.

"As if I had a choice!''

Miss Cresston smiled again. "Did you think she was going to take you by the ear if you disobeyed?" she teased, remembering their great-aunt's early methods of gaining her cousin's attention.

Although he thought it possible she still might try, Jonathan denied that in the face of Julianna's evident amusement, and said instead that it would have been dashedly unchivalrous of him to persist in his excuses when their great-aunt's goddaughter was sitting there in the carriage blushing, and telling the old lady that she didn't really care about attending Almack's that evening, even though they had been given vouchers, and begging her godmama not to impose on the viscount—entreaties to which their aunt turned a deaf ear, the viscount added indignantly.

"Oh?" Miss Cresston's interest was sparked. "She had the girl with her this morning, too?"

"Yes," the viscount said, nodding glumly. "And that reminds me—that's why she wants to speak with you."

"What?" A close acquaintance with both Great-Aunt Elizabeth and the mischievous sparkle now seen in Jonathan's blue eyes made her sense danger. "What do you mean, she wants to speak with me?"

"I think," the viscount said ominously, enjoying her rising color, "that it would be better if you heard it from our esteemed aunt yourself."

"Jonathan—" Miss Cresston put her hand on his arm. "Dear Jonathan, tell me . . ."

Her cajoling might have worked if their aunt, having grown tired of waiting for her lemonade, had not chosen that moment to enter the refreshments room in search of her great-nephew. She had her young protégée in tow, and she bore down upon her guilty young relations looking, Jonathan whispered irreverently, for all the world like a ship in full sail. Her stiff purple gown rustled as she walked, and each movement sent an assortment of scarves and shawls billowing about her.

"Great-Aunt Elizabeth!" Miss Cresston cried, slanting a reproving glance at her cousin as she moved forward to meet their relative and dutifully kiss the rouged cheek offered her. "What a pleasant surprise!"

The old lady snorted, eyeing her knowingly. "A surprise, anyway, Julianna, I'm sure!"

She pulled forward the young girl standing a step back to her right, and said, "Want to make you known to my goddaughter, Miss Marley."

Julianna held out a hand to the blushing Miss Marley, her friendly smile bringing an answering look of gratitude to that young lady's face. "I'm pleased to meet you, Miss Marley—" Julianna began, only to be interrupted by her great-aunt.

"Well, of course you're pleased to meet her!" the old lady said, shaking her head in such a way that the purple feathers she had lodged in her hair seemed in imminent danger of floating away. "Stands to reason. Nice gel. My goddaughter. Know you'll be happy to do all possible to make her feel at home here in London—help her know how to go on."

"Of course—" Miss Cresston said, not sensing the danger ahead, conscious only of wanting to put the uncomfortably blushing girl before her at ease.

"Thought so." Satisfaction was apparent on Great-Aunt Elizabeth's wrinkled face and in her brightly snapping eyes. "Tomorrow you can take her out and dress her."

"*Dress her*?" An astonished Miss Cresston repeated the words as her cousin grinned and winked knowingly at her, every inch of him seeming to say, "I told you so."

Great-Aunt Elizabeth fixed Julianna with a minatory eye.

"Not *dress her*, Julianna—not literally. Just *dress* her— take her about with you to the shops, pick out the clothes that will best become her. I'd do it myself, but all that racketing around . . ." She left the sentence unfinished, delicately giving them all to understand that it was her advanced age that kept her from such "racketing."

Julianna thought uncharitably that it was more a desire to be spared tedious hours of waiting while materials were chosen, patterns were discussed, and fittings were made, and glowered, even as the dowager duchess spoke again.

"Because I will say this for you, Julianna, you always have had impeccable taste; get it from your mother, I'm sure. Not," she added, tempering the handsome compliment by fixing a critical eye on that portion of her great-niece's bosom exposed by the diaphanous blue dress Miss Cresston wore, "that that gown is a prime example of your taste, with its low-cut—"

Julianna saw the grin growing on her cousin's face and, knowing they faced a twenty-minute lecture on the deplorable style and manners of today's young people, hastily averted it by saying that she would be most happy to take Miss Marley about.

"Thought you would," Great-Aunt Elizabeth said, nodding in satisfaction, as Miss Marley blushed again and uttered several disjointed sentences in which she said she did not wish to bother Miss Cresston—or anyone, for that matter—and if it was inconvenient . . .

"Nonsense!" Great-Aunt Elizabeth brushed aside any inconvenience to Miss Cresston with a careless wave of her hand. "No inconvenience at all. Do her good to be of use to someone."

Her last statement brought a chuckle from Jonathan, a chuckle quickly squelched when Great-Aunt Elizabeth turned to lead them back to the ballroom, telling her great-nephew that it was time he danced with Miss Marley.

Julianna, watching the stricken faces of both the young lady and the young gentleman before her, found that despite her indignation at her great-aunt's high-handed interference in her own life, she had to grin.

It was a grin that turned to laughter when, a short time later, Miss Cresston watched her cousin trying manfully to shepherd Miss Marley through one of the country dances. Dancing had never been the viscount's forte, and when his ineptitude was coupled with an inexperience as great as that of Miss Marley, only disaster could result.

"Oh, dear!" Miss Cresston said unexpectedly, as she saw her cousin tread on his partner's hem. Lord Wafton, who had claimed her hand as soon as she'd reentered the ballroom, looked down inquiringly.

"What is it?" he asked, glancing around, and Julianna was obliged to point out the young couple.

"Poor girl!" Lord Wafton said after critically surveying the viscount's desperate attempts to stay off Miss Marley's toes. "I doubt she'll be able to walk at all, tomorrow! What a bungling fellow Jonathan is, to be sure!"

"He rides well," Miss Cresston said in defense of her cousin. Lord Wafton pointed out, with just the tiniest twinkle in his eyes, that the two qualities were not interchangeable, especially not at Almack's. Just then Miss Marley looked up and happened to meet Julianna's smiling eyes, the despair in her own so apparent that Miss Cresston was moved to ask Wafton if he would squire the young lady through her next dance. The good-natured earl agreed, and Miss Cresston led him toward the flustered viscount and his equally flustered partner.

"Miss Marley," Julianna said, smiling down into the girl's flushed face and wide brown eyes, "may I present Lord Wafton to you as a desirable partner for the next dance?"

"Oh, no!" Miss Marley breathed involuntarily and then, seeing the surprise on the faces of the three before her, flushed even further and said that it wasn't that she didn't appreciate—it was just that—she'd made such a mull with Viscount Bushnell. . . .

"No, no!" Lord Wafton said soothingly as the music began and he took her hand. "That wasn't you! Jonathan has two left feet." He paused, and his eyes teased Julianna's. "He does, however, ride well."

"I'm sure he does," a confused Miss Marley agreed politely, even as she was swept away in the dance. After giving her a few moments to mind her steps, Lord Wafton told her gently that she danced very well, and was rewarded with such a grateful smile that it occurred to him fleetingly that she was not the little mouse he had first thought her.

Watching them whirl away, Jonathan morosely offered to partner his cousin, his martyred posture making it apparent that he had nothing more to lose that evening. She declined with a laugh, telling him that she valued her toes much too much to let him tread on them, and suggesting that they sit the dance out instead. Soon they were seated near the dance floor, Miss Cresston's eyes thoughtfully following Lord Wafton and his charge around the room.

"I wonder what this latest start of Great-Aunt Elizabeth's is," she mused, watching the dancers. "Who is Miss Marley? It seems to me I've heard the name somewhere before . . . a long time ago . . . but where . . ."

Roused from his own abstraction, Jonathan's eyes flitted indifferently over the girl. He sighed and gave it as his opinion that she was just their great-aunt's latest ploy in a long line of ploys to make their lives difficult.

Miss Cresston rapped him with her fan and told him he was being unfair—Miss Marley seemed like a very pleasant girl—

'And pleasant is totally out of Great-Aunt's line," he finished for her. "I think so, too."

"You're sure she didn't say where Miss Marley is from?" Julianna inquired. "Because those summers we spent in Kent, I don't recall a Marley family, do you?"

Jonathan did not, and did not seem to care. Julianna dismissed Miss Marley from her mind and turned her full attention to her cousin as she asked if he was feeling quite all right?

Of course he was, he told her; it was just that—well— Almack's was so cursed flat, and Great-Aunt Elizabeth such a—well—

Julianna laid one of her gloved hands on top of his. "Are you in trouble, Jonathan?" she asked. "Because if you are, I'd like to help. You must know my offer of a loan still stands—"

He shook her hand off, sending one of his own to run through his carefully pomaded locks, an action that would have seriously shocked his valet, had he seen it. Muttering that he would come about—it was nothing, really, and she wasn't to worry her head about it—Jonathan was relieved when the music ended and Lord Wafton restored Miss Marley to them. With alacrity the viscount rose to lead the young lady back to her godmama, and Julianna soon real-

ized that her cousin was taking great care to see that they
had no opportunity for a further chat. Her brow furrowed,
and she did not object at all when Aunt Sephrinia, in whose
party she had come to Almack's, approached her shortly
thereafter to see if she was ready to leave.

But it was long after she'd been delivered home and had
retired to her room that Julianna, tired as she was and with
much to think about, was able to make her mind quiet
enough to allow her body to sleep.

❧ *Chapter 3* ❧

When Julianna joined her mother at breakfast at the early
hour of nine the next morning—early, at least, for members
of the *ton* who had danced the night away—it was to find
that that good lady knew of Great-Aunt Elizabeth's arrival
in town, and had even had the pleasure of meeting her Miss
Marley, whom she spoke of kindly as "very prettily be-
haved, although painfully shy."

Julianna stared at her in amazement, the piece of toast she
held halfway between table and mouth forgotten. Since her
mother had forgone an evening at Almack's in favor of
other entertainment last night, that meant . . .

Hmmmmm . . .

"You—met—Great-Aunt Elizabeth, and Miss Marley?"
Julianna asked cautiously.

Tranquilly her mother said that they called yesterday
afternoon, when Julianna was out driving in the park.

"Well, you might have told me, Mother!" Julianna put
the toast down and picked up her cup of tea instead, the
better to stare broodingly at her mother over the cup rim.
Mrs. Cresston laughed into the younger pair of eyes so like
her own in color.

"Now, Julianna—I didn't want you crying off from your Aunt Sephrinia's party last night!" she teased. "Which you very well might have done, had you known you'd encounter your Great-Aunt Elizabeth there! Besides"—Mrs. Cresston put her own cup down and took a small spoonful of her egg before smiling once more at her daughter—"Elizabeth particularly desired me to keep her arrival in town a surprise."

"Oh, she did, did she?" Julianna grumbled, picking up her toast again, her brow furrowed as she thought. "I wonder why . . ."

She gazed inquiringly at her mother, but that lady only shook her head and said that she couldn't imagine, except that Elizabeth seemed to like to keep people off balance, when she could, and it probably afforded her a great deal of amusement to pop in and see her great-niece's face.

"And Jonathan's," Julianna added. Her mother raised an inquiring eyebrow.

"She commandeered Jonathan to escort her and Miss Marley to Almack's!" Julianna supplied. "It was not a request that endeared him to her—or brightened his night."

Mrs. Cresston said that it did not hurt Jonathan to bestir himself on someone else's account now and then—a statement that made Julianna, having heard it said about herself only last night, squirm—and added thoughtfully that if Jonathan would spend more time at Almack's, and less at his clubs and the races, his poor mother might not worry so much. Julianna stared at her in surprise.

"Have you—heard—about Jonathan's—ah—" She searched for the right word, eyeing her mother cautiously; out of loyalty to her cousin, she had never discussed his pecuniary embarrassments with any of their other relatives before. "His—excesses—then?" she finished cautiously.

Her mother, aware that she probably knew much more than her daughter about Jonathan's expensive habits, regarded Julianna with amusement. "Heard? My dear, one cannot be within twenty feet of your Aunt Sephrinia, and not hear! Not that I would regard her so much, but my last letter from Emilia made me think that—"

Julianna's Aunt Emilia was Jonathan's mother, who resided most of the year with her married daughter in York, and Julianna waited in respectful silence to hear what her favorite aunt had to say about her erring son. Mrs. Cresston seemed to decide against continuing the conversation, however, for she simply smiled at Julianna and said that perhaps it was nothing, after all, and they would have to wait and see.

"Jonathan asked me to marry him," Julianna offered, watching her mother's face for further clues.

Mrs. Cresston laughed. "Again?"

Julianna nodded. "Almost two weeks ago. I forgot to mention it earlier."

"Poor Jonathan!" Mrs. Cresston shook her head, and Julianna noted affectionately that her mother's locks, so near the guinea-gold color of her own, were only slightly flecked with white. Many of her mother's gallants liked to tell Mrs. Cresston that if they did not know better they would believe Julianna to be her sister. "He does so lack originality! You'd think he would give up by now!"

"Oh, no!" Julianna protested with a sudden insight that surprised her mother, and made that lady think fondly—as she often did—that she had raised a very remarkable daughter. "I think he offers for me because he is sure I won't have him. I'm sure the poor boy would be quite upset if I said that I would! I think it's just when he's feeling excessively pressed by his debts, he offers for me, decides he has done something in an effort to rectify his situation, and goes off feeling much better. You know how Jonathan is!"

Mrs. Cresston nodded. Having spent twenty-five years as his aunt, she certainly did.

Mrs. Cresston was about to go shopping, a becoming chip straw hat perched at a rakish angle of her head, its ribbons exactly matching the green of her eyes, when she saw her daughter again. As she stood in the hall pulling on the gloves that were a lighter shade of green, she looked up to see Julianna descending the stairs wearing her riding habit of soft rose, with epaulettes à la Hussar, a high, lace-trimmed collar with matching lace ruffles at the wrist, and a carefully tied cravat of snowy linen. Her tall-crowned hat of a deeper rose sat loftily atop her curls, its trailing ostrich feathers tickling one shoulder. Mrs. Cresston's eyebrows lifted.

"I thought you were promised to take Miss Marley shopping this morning?" she questioned.

Julianna said that that was set for several hours later; she believed that if she hurried, she had time for a ride before Miss Marley arrived.

"It won't do to keep Great-Aunt Elizabeth waiting," her mother warned as they walked out the door together, and Julianna smiled down at her. Miss Cresston had inherited all of her coloring from her mother, but her height came from her father, and Mrs. Cresston stood a full head shorter than her daughter.

"I won't," Julianna said before moving to where a groom walked her lovely Bess, and the hack he would ride when accompanying her to the park. "Bess and I will have just one good gallop, to shake the fidgets out of both of us, and then we'll be back—before the cat can lick its ear!"

"Not a gallop, Julianna!" Mrs. Cresston objected, knowing from the mischievous look in her daughter's eye that her protest would do no good. As she watched Julianna ride away, the groom in close attendance, she hoped that the last of her daughter's statement was correct, and Miss Cresston would indeed return before the dowager duchess and her goddaughter paid their visit.

If not . . .

Well, Mrs. Cresston would see to it that her own shopping kept her out until Great-Aunt Elizabeth could be sure to have departed!

Morning rides were a favorite with Julianna; when she was in the country she was almost always up early for a glorious canter through the green rolling hills where, because she was on her own land and very much at home, she often dispensed with a groom, and rode off by herself.

In town, of course, she knew she could not do so. But she had long ago trained Thomas to drop far back on their morning rides once they arrived at the park—if, she reminded herself conscientiously, there was no one else around—to give her, she told him, "room to breathe." In actuality it was room to think, to enjoy a few moments of solitude. That was something she treasured, and found little of in London.

She could almost always find the park empty—or practically empty—at this hour of the day. There were a few nursemaids about, with their charges, but most of the *ton*, who would have thought it odd to see even the rich Miss Cresston defying convention by *galloping* down one of the many paths that dotted the park—for galloping in the park was simply not *done*—could be depended upon to be still abed.

This morning proved no different, and she had left Thomas far behind as she and Bess skimmed over the ground, Julianna relishing the speed and the feel of the wind in her hair, and bent on putting all the puzzles of the last few days—of Jonathan and Great-Aunt Elizabeth and the unknown Miss Marley—to flight. As she and Bess shot from the trees into a clearing Julianna found her horse nose to nose with another well-bred beast that took instant exception to her abrupt entrance. The other horse rose alarmingly on his back legs, neighing loudly before starting to plunge and turn. He was doing his best to unseat the man whose loud, "What the devil—" had apprised Julianna of his presence even as she strove to control Bess. Her own horse, startled by the other animal, also had reared and turned, and now stood trembling, obedient to her mistress's command.

The quieting of her own mare gave Julianna time to appraise the horsemanship of the stranger upon the large gray stallion, and she found herself favorably impressed as the rider, his grip firm and his voice steady, swayed in the saddle, letting the animal express its disfavor with this interruption, even as he made it clear he was only tolerating the horse's antics. He was a tall man, and dark, his broad shoulders encased in a coat of the first quality. He had an air of command, giving the impression of one very used to going—and having—his own way. And there was something about his dark face and those heavily hooded eyes that would, Julianna thought, be dangerously intriguing to many women—but not, of course, to someone as level-headed as she.

"Well done!" Julianna exclaimed when the stallion had at last been brought to a stand. "Your horsemanship is exceeded only by the excellence of your mount—"

The compliment died on her lips as cold brown eyes met warm green, and proceeded to rake her from head to foot. Unused to such behavior from the gentlemen of her acquaintance, and suddenly conscious of the way the wind had been whipping her hair for moments past, Julianna put up a hand to tuck what strands she could reach back under her hat, and flushed.

"I beg your pardon," she said, wishing she had not left Thomas quite so far behind. "I should not have been riding so—"

"No," the stranger agreed calmly. "You should not."

Julianna stiffened. It had been a long time since she had been addressed in such a tone, as if she were an erring schoolgirl in urgent need of a lecture. Experience had taught her that the general run of man, confronted by a flushed and acknowledged beauty, was apt to reply in a much different voice.

"I did not expect to meet anyone—"

"Obviously." His cold indifference, as well as his apparent acceptance that it was she who was in the wrong—even though it *was* she who was in the wrong, and she was quite willing to admit it, as soon as the stranger very politely said that *he* was the one to blame—heightened her color even as she tried again.

"I do not believe we have met, Mr.—"

He ignored her obvious fishing for his name as he said he had only recently returned to England after a long absence, and would not be known to many people. "When I left, however, it was not the custom for ladies to ride unattended in London. Unless, perhaps, you are not a . . ." He let the sentence fade, and his eyes mocked the angry color now flooding Julianna's cheeks.

"I am not riding unattended," she flashed, "and let me
tell you, sir, that your manners—or lack of them!—make it
abundantly clear that you are *no* gentleman!" She drew
herself up haughtily, and tried her best to look down her
nose at him—no small feat, since he sat much higher than
she. "Be so good, sir, as to ride on!"

The last was said in her most icily civil and imperative
tones, which had been known to send more than one
gentleman who had displeased her bowing himself away as
best he could. This man remained unmoved.

True, he did bow, his iron hand controlling the fidgeting
of his horse without difficulty. But it could not be said that
his was a bow of civility or abject embarrassment. In fact,
there was a hint of irony and—yes, amusement!—about the
action that made Miss Cresston's lips tighten further.

"Perhaps," he said, ignoring her command to ride on, "I
have merely failed to spy your attendant." He gazed around
the clearing with exaggerated scrutiny, and she had the
oddest feeling that he was minutely aware of every leaf and
every blade of grass surrounding them. "Perhaps he is
very small. Or even—invisible?"

Miss Cresston was not used to being mocked, or spoken to
just so, and her chin tightened and her eyes sparked as she
looked at him. "My groom will be here shortly," she said.
"I have asked you before to be so good, sir, as to ride on."

But that the stranger would not do. He said with exaggerated civility—and a pointed emphasis on the word—that as
a *gentleman* he could not leave her unattended—for the
safety of the others in the park, as well as for her own.
Seeing that that impertinence had gone home, he smiled
silkily, adding that he would ride with her until her lost
groom was found.

Miss Cresston said coldly that she would not dream of
troubling him so, and they sat, each eyeing the other until,
with an angry sound, she turned her horse and started riding
slowly back down the way she had just come. The gray
stallion moved at her side, always a step ahead, the tossing
of his mane making it apparent that he considered her

suddenly decorous pace poor sport and entirely beneath him.

"He really is a beautiful horse!" she said suddenly, her admiration for the animal overcoming her disgust with the man.

"Yes," the stranger replied calmly. "He is."

Miss Cresston met his eyes, saw the amusement there, and gnashed her teeth, wishing she could stuff his murmured "Quite"—an acknowledged understanding of her anger—down his throat. From then on she stared pointedly ahead, not turning in his direction but extremely aware of his powerful frame, his saturnine grin, and the small scar that ran from just below his right eye to the middle of his cheekbone. She was considerably relieved when a worried Thomas came into view, volunteering the information that he had lost sight of her and had taken the wrong path.

"Ahhh," said the gentleman at her side. "I told you he was lost."

Miss Cresston's eyes flashed fire at the stranger even as, to quiet the uneasy Thomas's mind, she turned and thanked him stiffly for the escort. The man bowed, saying gravely that it was the least a gentleman could do for a lady.

Thomas did not know why he emphasized the words "gentleman" and "lady," but Julianna did, and her color rose again.

"I apologize again for startling your horse, and I am glad you were not hurt," she said with stiff civility as she prepared to take her leave of the man.

His sardonic, "You will find, my dear, that I am remarkably hard to wound," spurred her pace.

Even on horseback it could be said that Miss Cresston gave a decided flounce as she rode away, followed by the anxious Thomas and the annoying sound of a deep male chuckle.

❧ *Chapter 4* ❧

Julianna's color was still high when she arrived back at her London home, and her temper was not improved by the sight of her great-aunt's carriage sitting outside her door, or the reproving glance directed at her by her aunt's elderly coachman as she rode by.

"I believe my great-aunt is early." Julianna reined in and smiled at the coachman, whom she had known since she was a child. She regretted instantly that she had tried to justify herself; he shook his head sorrowfully and remarked to the world at large and Julianna in particular that there was plain folks' time and there was duchess's time, and them that was smart wound their clocks to duchess's time—if they knew what was good for them.

Miss Cresston would have liked very much to snap at him for his trouble but realized, even before the words were out of her mouth, that the person she *really* wanted to snap at was, for all she knew, still scolding unsuspecting damsels in the park. She tightened her lips and rode on. As she dismounted she told Thomas to have her carriage brought round in twenty minutes, then strode up the steps to confront the ancient lioness.

It was an apt description of the coming encounter, for no sooner had she walked through the door than Broughton, the excellent butler who had been with the Cresston ladies ever since Julianna's father's death seven years earlier, hurried forward to whisper in her ear that her great-aunt was in the morning room with a Young Lady and quite—ah—distressed not to find Miss Julianna awaiting her. His warning had barely been uttered when Great-Aunt Elizabeth's voice was heard through the partially opened French door to what was normally one of Julianna's favorite rooms, asking loudly if the shutting of the front door signified that Julianna had come at last.

Feeling that she already had had more than enough to bear that morning, Julianna smiled at Broughton and walked quickly toward the morning room. There she found her aunt, comfortably regaling herself with several glasses of the best sherry, while Miss Marley sat perched on the edge of a salmon-colored satin-covered sofa, her feet barely touching the floor as she nibbled absently on a macaroon while her large eyes surveyed the room with awe. She seemed particularly taken with the large Dresden figure on the mantelpiece, her glance returning to it again and again, and she started self-consciously as Julianna entered. Miss Marley blushed, and Miss Cresston smiled at her before stepping forward to greet her aunt.

"You're late," Great-Aunt Elizabeth said accusingly as Julianna bent to place a quick kiss on her cheek. "You've kept me waiting."

Smiling determinedly, Julianna replied that No, she was not late; her aunt was early. She added that she was sorry they had had to wait, and she'd just stopped in to greet her guests before hurrying upstairs to change her riding dress for something more suitable for venturing out in search of the modish apparel desired by Miss Marley.

"Oh, pray—do not hurry! It isn't me that desires—that is— Godmama and—someone else—seem to think..." Miss Marley was lost in a tangle of sentences as she strove to disabuse Miss Cresston of the quite horrifying thought that she minded waiting the least little bit, or that she wanted in any way to be a burden to her new acquaintance. "I do not mean to inconvenience you, and we truly are early—I daresay very early—"

"Tush!" said the dowager duchess, waving her charge's breathless comments away with one hand. "*I* am *always* on time."

"Dowager duchess's time," murmured Miss Cresston, thinking of the coachman's statement. Her great-aunt regarded her suspiciously.

"What was that, girl?"

Julianna smiled. "I believe, dear Aunt, that you have a perception of time different from that of the rest of us lesser mortals."

Elizabeth shrugged and helped herself to more of the sherry. After a moment's thought she agreed that what Julianna said might be true—it was amazing how many times others were either several hours early or several hours late for appointments with her, while *she* was always on time.

The sparkle in Julianna's eye suggested that she was about to carry the discussion further when she happened to glance at Miss Marley, who appeared genuinely distressed by the conversation and the possibility of a growing argument between the other two ladies. Julianna's brows rose.

Like the infuriating stranger she had encountered in the park that morning, Julianna considered her great-aunt remarkably hard to wound and, in her present mood, would have greatly enjoyed sparring with her. However, she did not want to be rude to Miss Marley, and if such conversations upset the child that much...

With a shrug Julianna excused herself and hurried up to her room to exchange her riding habit for a gown of lavender crape, and the most modest of the many hats in her wardrobe, believing that neither the dress nor the bonnet was likely to bring her great-aunt's censoriously delivered opinions down upon her head. When she descended the stairs she felt herself tolerably composed and entered the morning room again with a bright smile, only to find it empty.

She turned an inquiring eye toward the second footman who stood in the hall; he volunteered the information that the old la—he meant, he said, conscientiously catching himself up at the last moment, and glad his superior, the imposing Mr. Broughton, wasn't there to hear and soundly lecture him—the dowager duchess had departed some ten minutes earlier, and that Mr. Broughton had taken it upon himself to escort the young lady to the—ah, kitchen—her being so desirous of speaking to the chef, and not wanting to trouble him to come upstairs...

"Departed?" Julianna repeated, unable to believe Great-Aunt Elizabeth was gone, and she had put on the lavender crape for naught.

"*Kitchen*?" The second half of the footman's speech penetrated her brain, and her brow furrowed. Why on earth . . . ? "Did you say—the kitchen, Harry?"

Harry nodded.

"I see." Julianna put a hand to her head and wondered if it was she, or if it truly had turned out to be a most unusual morning. "Well, then . . . I'll just go—join her. In the kitchen."

Which she did, entering that warm and cheerful room that smelled faintly of rising bread dough and the morning's breakfast, to find Miss Marley deep in conversation with Miss Cresston's excellent chef, while Broughton and Mrs. Bentley, the queen of all of London's housekeepers, looked on benignly.

It was Broughton who saw Julianna first and hastily straightened; his action made Mrs. Bentley look around and rise quickly from her place by the fire to drop a respectful curtsy.

Miss Marley, glancing up inquiringly, was immediately remorseful and cried, "Oh, Miss Cresston! Have I kept you waiting? I am so sorry! I thought we would only be a moment, but I wanted to step down and thank your chef for the excellent macaroons, and then—we began to talk about recipes—"

Her distress at keeping her hostess waiting was so apparent and so real that Julianna smiled soothingly, saying that it was quite all right and acting for all the world as if all her guests found it incumbent upon themselves to visit the kitchen to compliment the chef—something they most assuredly did not, and something she felt she would have to convey to Miss Marley at a not-too-distant date if the young lady was to go out in society with Julianna's great-aunt and the Cresstons.

On the other hand, Julianna could picture the faces of several of London's best known hostesses if a guest were to ask in all innocence to be directed to their kitchens, and it was almost worth . . .

The picture made her face light up and Miss Marley, much encouraged, came forward after shyly thanking the denizens of the Cresston kitchen for their time. Mrs. Bentley told her kindly that she was welcome there always.

Her statement was seconded by the Gallic genius who presided over Julianna's stove and oven—an honor that almost staggered Julianna in its enormity. Her chef was not known to welcome intruders into his private and autocratically ruled domain. Miss Marley seemed unaware of the compliment that had just been paid her as she thanked them again before tripping up the stairs to join Julianna.

It was just like Great-Aunt Elizabeth to leave without telling her the lengths she was to go to in helping Miss Marley choose a new wardrobe, Julianna thought in vexation as the ladies settled into Julianna's new town carriage.

Not knowing the young woman's financial situation, she could not decide which of the many dressmakers she favored to direct her coachman to, and was hesitating over what to tell the driver when Miss Marley, done admiring the comfortable vehicle in which she found herself, with its deep green velvet seats and its shiny new interior, remembered a note left for Miss Cresston by the duchess, and reached into her reticule to fish it out. She handed it to Julianna with the air of a schoolgirl conscientiously doing her duty.

Julianna looked at her for a moment under puzzled brows before she broke the seal on the note and read:

Julianna,
   Can't spend the day waiting for you in your morning room while you dawdle about—I have things to do. Beth—her name is Elizabeth, named for me, you know! —has a guardian who can stand huff to whatever bills you run up for her; have them sent to me, and I'll forward them to him. See that she's decked out in the first stare of fashion; the poor thing has had quite a time and deserves it. We want her to have the opportunity to make quite a splash among the ton, *and you'll*

*know how to do that; been doing it for years, I know.
Just nothing outrageous, mind! And none of those
low-cut bodices you seem to favor!*

*Yours,
Elizabeth M.*

Low-cut bodices, indeed! Miss Cresston thought crossly.
Just because one dress happened to show my shoulders . . . She
thought of several more gowns with similar décolletage in
her clothes chest, and sighed.

There was a painting of Great-Aunt Elizabeth that hung at
her home in Kent, done when Elizabeth was a young bride,
and if she wanted to talk of revealing fashions—well!

As she read the noted again, Miss Cresston said "Beth"
aloud, and Miss Marley turned inquiringly from her wide-
eyed surveyal of all there was to see from the carriage
window. Julianna smiled.

"So that is your name! When my great-aunt referred to
you as 'Beth' in her note, I realized that is the first time I've
known you by other than Miss Marley. Perhaps, if you don't
mind, I will call you Beth—"

"Oh, yes!" Miss Marley nodded eagerly, her brown curls
falling forward to frame her face in her enthusiasm. "I wish
you would. It would be ever so much more comfortable, for
I don't really have any friends in London—except for
Godmama, and . . ." She looked suddenly self-conscious
and flushed a little, and Julianna, ears perked, leaned
forward.

"And?" she questioned, suddenly remembering Miss
Marley's hastily covered reference to "someone else" not
long ago in the morning room.

Miss Marley colored further, faltering that it was just—
one other person—that she knew. . . .

Julianna patted her hand and told her that she hadn't
meant to press her; Miss Marley stuttered in great confusion
that it wasn't that she wished to keep secrets from Miss
Cresston, who was being so good; it was just that she'd
been instructed most particularly not to mention her—one
other—person.

She looked about to cry for fear of offending her companion, and with great forebearance Julianna, her curiosity whetted, patted her hand again, changing the subject to say: "If I am to call you 'Beth,' you must surely call me 'Julianna.'"

Miss Marley brightened instantly. "Oh!" she said, "I would like that! But are you sure—that is, I don't wish to put myself forward or to encroach—and I don't want you to feel obligated . . . I know you must have many friends in London, and you certainly don't need me imposing upon you . . ."

About to turn the remark aside with a laughing rejoinder that it was Great-Aunt Elizabeth, not Miss Marley, who believed in imposing, Julianna stopped at sight of the earnestness in the girl's eyes. For the first time she could remember, Julianna felt rather old.

It was not a feeling she particularly liked.

Certainly, she thought, she had many London acquaintances with whom she could spend an agreeable hour or evening, flirting or bantering or passing on the latest *on-dits;* but friends? Not since Miss Worthington had married last September and moved with her new husband to the Cotswolds had Julianna really known a young woman in whom she felt she could confide, or with whom she could exchange doubts and feelings and thoughts.

Oh, yes, she talked with Jonathan—when he wasn't proposing marriage to her, or off on one of his many gaming adventures; and she had easy and pleasant conversations with Lord Wafton. Theirs was a friendship of long standing.

But gentlemen friends were not the same. There were certain topics on which a woman could not depend on them to enter into her feelings, or to understand.

And now, here was his absurd child, looking at her in admiration and speaking to her of her many "friends."

Aloud Julianna said easily, "Well, I don't think a person can have too many friends, do you?"

Miss Marley agreed, but shyly; it was apparent the fear of being an imposition to this woman she was rapidly turning into an idol weighed heavily.

Julianna continued, "And as for bother—my dear Beth, I don't know when I have so expected to enjoy myself as I do on our excursion today!"

To her surprise, she realized as soon as she said it that it was true. For some reason—and despite her great-aunt's high-handed methods of foisting Miss Marley on her—in the past half hour Julianna had come to like this shy young creature who smiled at her so confidingly and spoke of the comfort of having a friend in town.

Perhaps Miss Marley would be a diversion to relieve the *ennui* Miss Cresston had been trying her best to surpress as the season progressed; perhaps it would be amusing to launch such a gentle little mouse into society, and to help her acquire some needed town bronze. Perhaps it would be nice to have a new friend.

At any rate, Julianna decided, thoughtfully watching the innocent face across from her, it would certainly be enjoyable to spend some of the money of this mysterious guardian Miss Marley was not supposed to mention—and to figure out the mystery behind that person!

Miss Cresston quickly gave her coachman the name of the most expensive dressmaking establishment she favored, as well as the office to start. As the carriage pulled away from her doorstep, she settled back into her carriage seat to be amused by Miss Marley's apparent enjoyment of every sight they'd see between Miss Cresston's home and the entrancingly exclusive shop of the vastly superior Madame Ledeux, dressmaker to the crème de la crème of the *ton*.

❧ *Chapter 5* ❧

It had been a quiet day at Madame Ledeux's, and that lady's eyes brightened perceptibly at sight of one of her favorite patronesses coming through the door. Miss Cresston could always be depended upon to choose a gown that, when worn, would send several female members of the *ton* to Madame Ledeux's the next day in search of a dress that would give them that certain cachet that belonged to Julianna.

And Madame Ledeux, good businesswoman that she was, could be depended upon to sell them something just as expensive as—or perhaps more expensive than—the gown worn by Miss Cresston. Sometimes it would be in the same color, at other times in the same style, but at all times Madame Ledeux would tell her so enchanting and so beautiful clients volubly and with the many Gallic interspersements that always seemed to reassure the English that the gown made them appear—how could she say?—*très charmante.* . . .

And if it was the vision of money pouring into her coffers that was most charming to Madame Ledeux, rather than the sight of these proud women in her gowns, she had the good sense not to let it show, just as she always managed to keep to herself that it was Miss Cresston who brought a certain style to her gowns, rather than the gowns that brought the style to Miss Cresston.

Thus she was considerably disappointed to hear that Miss Cresston was not shopping for herself today, but cheered up immediately upon hearing that the young friend with her favorite client, whom she had at first assumed to be Miss Cresston's maid, was in need of a whole new wardrobe, and that Miss Cresston considered Madame Ledeux the very person to provide a great deal of it.

Madame Ledeux fell in with this challenging—and extremely expensive—plan with a will, critically surveying Miss Marley in a way that made that young lady quite uncomfortable. Madame's sharp "turn!" made Miss Marley start and blush, but she obligingly did as she was told, looking timidly over her shoulder to see if Madame's reaction to her backside was any different from that to her front. The way Madame Ledeux was shaking her head and frowning as she made rapid little "tsk, tsk, tsk" sounds between her teeth made the unsure Miss Marley want to sink, and she thought that she might have backed quickly out of the shop had it not been for the sustaining presence of Miss Cresston, who caught her eye just at the height of her confusion and gave a slight—almost imperceptible—wink.

Then, having judged the time allowed Madame Ledeux for her artistic expressions sufficient, Miss Cresston briskly said, "Well?" and Madame cast off the role of critic and took on the role of conjurer. A quick clap of her hands brought two assistants running; a few mysterious words in French sent them off again, and soon both reappeared with a dozen issues of *La Belle Assemblée*, which the ladies pored over for the better part of an hour, gazing at ball gowns and morning half-dresses and walking costumes and carriage dresses. Madame Ledeux was quick to suggest appropriate fabrics and hues for Miss Marley, and her assistants staggered under the weight of bolts of silk and satin and velvet and *gros de Naples* and sarsenet and *crèpe lisse* that would set the young lady above other damsels at the balls and assemblies. Miss Marley's eyes grew rounder and rounder as she visualized how she might look, garbed in these creations.

Miss Cresston several times asked her kindly what she preferred, but Miss Marley, who had always before believed she had very distinct tastes in clothing, found herself so overwhelmed that she could only gulp and whisper, "I like blue" or "Whatever you think, Miss Cress—I mean, Julianna," in a way that made Madame Ledeux regard her more critically still, but which made Miss Cresston only smile and continue to make decisions.

By the time they left Madame Ledeux's shop the young Elizabeth had ordered several high-waisted gowns, some of sprigged muslin, others of crape, with small puffed sleeves and several flounces around the hem; demure gowns as befitted a young lady just making her come-out. In addition, she would soon own a fine blue jaconet muslin for the assemblies at Almack's, and a lovely white sarsenet which Miss Cresston told her would set her apart at the ball her godmama planned to give to help launch her into the *ton*. That dress, which would be trimmed with silver net drapery, had quite won Beth's heart, and she was even able to believe that in it she would not appear to be quite the dowd she now knew herself to be—a sad thought that had been growing upon her ever since her arrival in London, and which had peaked under the expressive eyes of Madame Ledeux.

The dresses would be delivered within the week, Madame promised, a statement that made her assistants exchange glances of great despair, for they knew who would spend day and night sewing to keep that promise. With the gowns would come a forest green velvet pelisse trimmed with ermine—a shockingly dear garment, thought Miss Cresston with satisfaction, hoping it would discomfit both her great-aunt and the mysterious guardian. A black velvet mantle and several fine Norwich shawls that were almost as expensive as they were beautiful were already packed in boxes and ready to be carried out to Miss Cresston's carriage.

Miss Marley was lost in a blissful fog when she and Miss Cresston at last took their leave of Madame Ledeux, and Beth would have gone home without hesitation to dream about the dresses that soon would be hers. Julianna, however, her shopping instincts aroused, ordered her coachman to take them next to her favorite hat shop, where Miss Marley's cup overflowed as one exquisite creation after another was set upon her head for Miss Cresston's approval.

Their only disagreement—and it was a minor one—came when a particularly dashing hat, done up in deep scarlet velvet with a tall crown and a peak over the eyes, very much like a shako, and a clever plume of black and white ostrich feathers curling over the left side, was placed on Miss Marley's head, and Julianna shook her head "no."

"Oh, but Julianna!" Miss Marley cried. "I like it so—"

Julianna, who also liked it excessively, and who had one just like it in her closet, shook her head regretfully. "My dear, I can just hear my great-aunt if I were to allow you to choose that hat! Believe me—my refusal is worth my life! Later—when you're older—perhaps. But not now, during your first season. I'm sorry."

Miss Marley stared wistfully at the hat as the shop's owner set it back on the shelf, and sighed. "It is very hard to be young," she said.

Unconsciously Miss Cresston and the shop's proprietress, both watching her face, sighed in agreement.

After such successful shopping, it seemed only natural that the young ladies, perfectly in sympathy with each other, should return to Miss Cresston's home for a late nuncheon. They were joined at their meal by Julianna's smiling mother, who inquired kindly how Miss Marley had enjoyed her foray into the world of London fashion. Beth, for once carried far beyond her natural shyness, talked on and on of all she had seen and felt and done, and of Julianna's incredible kindness.

Basking in this adoration—for her great-aunt's "It won't hurt you to bestir yourself for someone else for a change" still rankled—Julianna's mind drifted, only to be brought back as Beth, her eyes shining, said, "And to think that today I should be having such a pleasant time, with so many new clothes, when only last year—"

Suddenly the youngest member of the trio heard her own words and caught herself up guiltily, subsiding with a blush, as both Julianna and Mrs. Cresston looked inquiringly at her.

"Only last year . . . ?" Julianna prompted.

Beth shook her head, biting her lip as she did so, a shadow falling across her eyes that made Julianna even more determined to get to the bottom of the puzzle.

"It's—nothing," Miss Marley murmured unhappily, not looking at either lady directly. "I'm sorry I've been prattling on forever, boring you . . ."

Mrs. Cresston intervened to say that they were not bored—quite the contrary; they were delighted that Miss Marley was enjoying herself so much, and that they could be a small part of her enjoyment.

"Oh, but I owe *all* my enjoyment to you!" Miss Marley said quickly, raising those ridiculously expressive eyes eagerly to both ladies' faces. "You have been so kind . . . Godmama and my—that is, someone else—said you would be. . . . But I was afraid—with Godmama practically ordering you to take me about—"

The child looked so unhappy that Julianna, who felt that

the "practically" could have been left out of Miss Marley's
last sentence, found herself saying that it was no such thing;
they were pleased to know Beth because Beth was a pleasure to know. Her mother looked at her in amazement,
remembering Julianna's long and pithy comments on Great-
Aunt Elizabeth's high-handed ploys to involve herself and
her protégée in Julianna's already busy life, but Mrs.
Cresston kept silent. Perhaps Elizabeth knew what she was
doing, after all.

At any rate, Julianna's statement restored Miss Marley,
making it possible for her to finish her meal with tolerable
composure and to face with equinimity the fashionable
coiffeur Miss Cresston had summoned to give Beth's hair a
cut more in keeping with her new dresses. Seated in front of
the large full-length mirror in Miss Cresston's dressing
room, however, Miss Marley's courage deserted her at the
first snip of the scissors, and she closed her eyes tightly,
unwilling to open them until the artiste busily working away
above and behind her said, "Finished!" with a kind of
flourish that made her cautiously peek first with one eye and
then with the other before opening both eyes wide to gaze at
the elfin face staring back at her.

Gone were the heavy chestnut braids that had seemed at
times to overpower her small head; left behind were soft
wisps of curls that came forward to frame her face, accentu-
ating her large brown eyes and contributing to an air of
fragility that Mrs. Cresston thought shrewdly any number of
gentlemen would find not displeasing.

A twist of longer curls was cleverly wrought just to the
right side of her head, and even Julianna's awe-inspiring
maid, Jane, condescended to say—albeit with a sniff—that
Miss looked "quite taking," modest praise that made Beth
color as if she'd been paid the highest encomium.

Miss Marley's eyes returned to the mirror, and she
smiled. "It really is me!" she breathed.

Julianna laughed. "Of course it is you, you ridiculous
child! And unless I very much miss my guess, it is a you
that is going to be turning a few heads about London before
very long!"

The thought was meant to please, but it seemed to startle Beth considerably. She had never turned heads, or planned to. To cover their young guest's confusion, Mrs. Cresston began to talk easily to her about how she might place a flower or a comb or even some curling feathers in her hair for parties and the like. Soon Miss Marley was engrossed in this new topic, leaving Julianna to watch her with a slight pucker between her brows.

Miss Cresston had thought that her part in Miss Marley's come-out would be successfully completed when her protégée was correctly gowned and ready for her first ball. Now, however, she perceived that the young lady had no real idea of how to go on in society, and Julianna shuddered at the thought of such an innocent as Miss Marley trying to cope unaided with some of the more forbidding ladies or the hardened rakes who haunted the London scene.

For instance—her thoughts turned suddenly to the stranger she had herself encountered in the park that morning. What if such a lamb as Miss Marley had met him—alone?

Sternly she banished from her mind the realization that Miss Marley would not have been riding in the park alone, and thus never would have found herself in that position; that was beside the point.

The point was...

Her eyes returned to the naive young face before her, and she sighed. The point was, she was going to be more embroiled in Miss Marley's come-out than she had at first believed, and the dashing Miss Cresston, an acknowledged leader of fashionable London, adept in any social situation, suddenly felt a twinge of self-doubt as she realized she knew very little—and cared to know less—about the role of chaperon.

❧ Chapter 6 ❧

It was late afternoon—almost evening—when Miss Cresston's carriage set Miss Marley down in front of her godmama's house. Julianna, who had accompanied her young guest back to Great-Aunt Elizabeth's, demurred when asked if she wouldn't come in to allow the dowager duchess to thank her for all her kindness to Miss Marley—something Julianna very much doubted the duchess would do since Julianna had never heard her thank anyone for anything.

To explain her reluctance, Julianna mentioned another engagement that evening. Miss Marley's face fell, but she hastily entreated her friend to please forgive her for taking up so much of Julianna's time. Miss Cresston relented and said that she would stop for a moment.

Instructing her coachman to walk the horses for ten minutes, Julianna followed the young Elizabeth into the duchess's imposing town house, speaking kindly to the elderly butler who opened the door for them.

Findley, who had been with the dowager duchess for years, and who was almost as top-lofty as his mistress, unbent sufficiently to tell her that he was quite pleased to see her again. Then he considerably surprised her by thawing even further to tell Miss Marley—with something that looked suspiciously like a grandfatherly smile—that the duchess was awaiting her return in the library. With a guest.

The way he said "With a guest" was significant, and Miss Marley brightened and caught hold of Julianna's hand, leading her down the hall. The sight of the dark, heavy, ornately carved furniture lowered Miss Cresston's spirits considerably, as did the coming encounter with her great-aunt. After the briefest knock on a heavy door Beth entered, pulling Julianna behind her, and her face lit up at sight of the gentleman sitting beside her godmama, a glass of burgundy in his hand.

The sight of the gentleman in her great-aunt's library had quite another effect on Julianna, who did not smile. In fact, she stood in the middle of the room as if stuffed. Miss Marley hurried happily forward to greet the visitor, who rose at once.

Julianna's eyes widened; her mouth froze in a soundless "Oh!" If she had not been so shocked, she might have noticed how the man's normally harsh features softened at sight of Miss Marley, and the gentleness with which he took the small hands so eagerly held out to him. He placed a kiss on first one and then the other before turning to smile with ironic amusement at Miss Cresston.

That smile released her from her spellbound state, and Julianna voiced one word: "*You!*" Shock overcame good manners as she stared at the stranger she'd met that morning in the park. The man bowed.

The dowager duchess, watching them critically, poked the gentleman with the ebony cane that sat by the side of her chair and said crossly that she'd understood he did not know her great-niece. The gentleman said softly that they had not been introduced.

"Well, she seems to know you," the dowager duchess said shrewdly, glancing from one to the other. She scented a mystery here, and it did not please her.

In a very dissatisfied tone she continued, "Well, this is my great-niece, Julianna Cresston. Julianna, this is Marleton—the Earl of Marleton, if you can't place him. He has been out of the country."

The Earl of Marleton . . .

Julianna tried to remember what she should know about him, but could not; it seemed to her it was a scandalous story—something, meeting the amused gleam in his eye, she had no difficulty believing—but what was it . . . ?

With an effort she pulled herself together and gave him just the sketchiest of polite nods. It was befitting a guest in her great-aunt's home, but showed to a nicety that she was only being civil.

The earl grinned.

Miss Marley, worried, moved to stand by Julianna as she regaled her godmama and the earl with an account of all they'd done that day. The earl, watching her with a warmness in his eyes that made Julianna frown at him—and that made his grin widen, when he noticed it and divined its meaning (an action that only added to Miss Cresston's disgust and consternation)—said, "Your new hair style becomes you, child. You are looking very well."

The mild praise made Miss Marley blush becomingly, and Julianna thought crossly that it was just like her great-aunt to know this rude, overbearing person whose attentions to her goddaughter could only complicate the plans she had laid to make Miss Cresston the girl's chaperon. Here was just such a person as Miss Cresston most wanted Beth to avoid—at least until she was up to snuff—and what must her great-aunt do but invite him into her house, and drink burgundy with him. Come to think of it, the duchess should not be drinking burgundy when ratafia would do.

Honestly! It put Julianna all out of patience. . . .

And now it was making her late. . . .

With dignity Miss Cresston rose from the chair into which Miss Marley had pressed her only moments earlier, and said that she must go; Lord Wafton was escorting her and her mother to the theater that night, and she did not want to be late.

Her great-aunt, with that lack of tact her family so deplored when it was directed at them, sat up straight and looked her over critically. "Wafton, huh? Been dangling after you any number of years, hasn't he? You going to marry him?"

The question seemed to startle Miss Marley, who turned inquiring eyes toward Julianna. Aware that the earl also was watching her with amusement and a great deal of interest, Julianna's eyes sparked fire. *Drat Great-Aunt Elizabeth!* she thought irritably as she said, as coolly as she could, that Lord Wafton was one of her dearest friends, no more.

The duchess snorted. "You'd be wise to make him more, Miss, for he's a good man, if a bit too dull for my taste. But you want to be careful you don't get yourself past the point that no one is asking you—''

"Really, Aunt Elizabeth!" This was more than Julianna was willing to tolerate, even in the most outspoken of her relatives. "I do not think this is the time, the place, or"—she stared pointedly at the earl, who raised his wine glass toward her in acknowledgment—"the company! And Lord Wafton is *not* dull; not that it is any business of yours—''

What had started out to be a scathing speech was, she felt, turning into incoherent ramblings, and Julianna, head high, made a dignified curtsy and withdrew, quite conscious of the snicker of amusement growing behind her. She was almost out the front door when a cry of "Julianna, wait!" made her turn, and her face softened slightly as a distressed Miss Marley came toward her.

"Oh, Julianna!" Beth said hurriedly, "I am so sorry— she doesn't mean to be so overbearing—and, indeed, Lord Wafton seems *most* gentlemanly, and not *at all* dull, and I am sure that he must admire you enormously, for who could not—''

Julianna, who thought that the duchess did, indeed, mean to be overbearing, decided not to say so in the face of Miss Marley's evident dismay. And, since she did not care to discuss the rest of her aunt's outspoken comments, she shrugged and said it was of no matter.

Then, seeing that it *did* matter to Miss Marley, she added untruthfully that it was forgotten already, and when the worried look did not go out of those soft brown eyes, she changed the subject by saying that she would see Beth tomorrow.

Miss Marley brightened. "Really?"

Smiling, Julianna assured her that they had just begun to shop; a slightly staggering statement to a young woman who had never dreamed of finding herself with all the finery purchased on this one day, but who was certainly willing to go in search of more, if her dear Miss Cresston said she should.

"I'll come by—" Julianna started, then stopped, frowning

down the hall toward the library, where a male rumble of laughter convinced her that she was still the topic of conversation. "No, why don't you have my aunt send you to my house in her carriage—shall we say at eleven o'clock?"

Miss Marley agreed and they parted, Miss Cresston thinking virtuously that she could not hold the company her great-aunt chose to keep against her great-aunt's goddaughter.

Nor, she thought, brooding darkly on the duchess's recent comments, could she hold Great-Aunt Elizabeth against the girl, either.

It was Lord Wafton who shed some light on the mysterious Earl of Marleton for Julianna when, after a delightful evening at the theater, he escorted his guests to the Piazza for a late supper.

Always a thoughtful host, he had provided such delicacies as must please Julianna and her mother, as well as Colonel Higham, an old beau of Mrs. Cresston's who was as goodhearted as he was plain, and who was, at the moment, sending her mother into gales of laughter with stories of his days serving under Wellington.

That these stories were always hilarious did not hide from Mrs. Cresston the fact that the colonel, a modest man, had been a real hero, and Julianna, listening to him, liked him the better for his modesty and his desire to make her mother laugh, rather than "oooh" and "ahhh" over his courage.

She had met enough of the latter kind of man and had long ago had her fill of them. . . .

Seeing her mother so happily engaged, Julianna turned to Lord Wafton at her right. "You're very quiet tonight," she chided him with a smile, and an answering smile lit his own eyes.

"I was thinking," he excused himself.

When she asked what he was thinking about, she was more than a little surprised to hear him reply, "I was thinking that your young friend, Miss Marley, might have liked to join us tonight for the theater. She told me last night that she has never been."

Actually, Miss Marley had told him that she had never

attended a "real, grown-up theater performance," although she had been in charge of the costumes for amateur histrionics at school. Remembering the confiding way in which she'd said it made him smile again.

Julianna, who over the years had grown used to Lord Wafton's uncomplicated and comfortable company and to the knowledge that she could depend on him to squire her wherever she might like to go, raised an inquiring eyebrow and asked if he was another of the peers of the realm from whom she would soon be shielding her protégée?

She was teasing, for he had told her times out of mind that he enjoyed the bachelor life, and had no plans to ever exchange it for matrimony. A moment later she was considerably startled when he flushed and looked extremely self-conscious, muttering "No, no—that is—taking little thing; seems to need some looking after—" A thought struck him in the midst of his stuttering, and he glared at her. "What do you mean—*another*?"

Julianna, who had never before experienced Lord Wafton's glare, heard her great-aunt's words echoing through her mind—"You want to be careful you don't get to the point where no one is asking you!"

This is ridiculous, she told herself; she and Edmund had decided years earlier that they would not suit; it was just that . . . just that . . .

While she had always wished him happy—and still did, devoutly!—it had never occurred to her that his happiness might mean his defection from the rank of chief cicisbeo, which she had bestowed upon him to protect her from the more persistent of her admirers. Crossly she wondered why that had never occurred to her before; she had always believed she thought things through so well.

"Julianna?" he questioned, and with an effort she smiled at him, and said it was nothing, just that when she'd returned Miss Marley to the dowager duchess that afternoon, her great-aunt had had the Earl of Marleton with her, a man Julianna considered rude and arrogant and someone she could not believe would be a good influence on such a young innocent as Beth.

"Marleton?" Lord Wafton repeated the name thoughtfully, his head cocked to one side, his gray eyes narrowed slightly. "Marleton? That would have to be Richard . . . I didn't know he was back."

Colonel Higham turned inquiringly toward them, having heard only part of their conversation. "What's that you say? Marleton? In London? Good man in a fight, Marleton; pity about the other . . ."

Recollecting his company, he returned to his conversation with Mrs. Cresston, leaving Julianna to eye her companion questioningly.

"Pity about—?" she said at last as Edmund showed no disposition to continue their conversation, sitting back in his chair, one hand stroking his chin, the other softly tapping his quizzing glass against his knee.

Lord Wafton came to with a start, his brow clearing as he looked at her. Immediately he begged pardon for wool gathering.

"What other, Edmund?" she demanded as he reached forward to offer her a plate of sweets, then put them back as she declined the treats with an impatient hand.

"Oh, well." Lord Wafton polished his quizzing glass gently against his coat, gazing down at it to avoid her eyes. "It was family trouble . . . No more than many families have experienced. . . ."

He seemed disinclined to continue, and Julianna sighed impatiently. "I do wish you'd stop putting me off," she scolded, reaching out to touch his arm. "You know that when I want to know something I'm going to find it out, and you could save us both time and trouble by simply telling me and being done with it!"

From past experience he knew that was true, and smiled bemusedly at her. Although he was ten years her senior he could not recall a time since they had met that she could not charm whatever she wanted out of him. Resignedly he shook his head.

"All right," he said, "but there's not really that much to tell. I first met Richard when I was at Harrow; he's several years older than I, but he was always good to the younger

boys. He was the second of two sons. His father, the fourth
earl, was a stiff-backed old martinet who didn't much care
for the wild oats sown by his youngest, and cast him off
when Richard steered his boat into dun territory."

"Why, that's terrible!" The exclamation from her mother
made Julianna turn to find that she and the colonel were
listening intently to Edmund's story, and Julianna flushed.
She had hoped to make her inquiries about the earl without
others knowing of her interest.

"Was he very much in debt?" Julianna asked.

Edmund shrugged. "I don't know. Far enough, apparent-
ly. Not so far that his father couldn't have comfortably
pulled him out again, I'm sure; not so far as other sons have
gone. I don't suppose the old man would have been quite so
angry if it hadn't been for the woman—"

"Woman?" Julianna echoed, but before Edmund could
go on the word called up another reminiscence from the
colonel.

"Always has had an eye for the ladies," Colonel Higham
said enthusiastically, his face alight with admiration. "You
should have seen the high-flyer he had in keeping in Vienna—"
Belatedly he remembered his company, and coughed in
embarrassment. "Well, no—that is—maybe you shouldn't
have . . ."

An amused Mrs. Cresston patted his back and offered him
his wine glass; Julianna, who found nothing amusing in
such disreputable behavior as that being described by Colonel
Higham, turned back to Lord Wafton for the rest of the
story.

"What woman?" she demanded.

Unexpectedly Mrs. Cresston took up the tale. "Arabella
Robinson," she said reminiscently, considerably surprising
the others in the room. "I had almost forgotten that story . . ."

She smiled at her daughter. "Arabella was the most
exquisite creature, my love—and as scatterbrained as she
was beautiful, poor thing. Your story puts me in mind of it,
Edmund; she was older than the present earl, if I remember,
and engaged to his brother . . ." She looked to Lord Wafton
for confirmation, and he nodded.

"Seems Richard was in love with her, too, and she knew it; she fancied herself in love with him, in return. Richard was a much more romantic figure than his brother Charles—always had been. It annoyed Charles no end. Anyway, although Richard hadn't spoken of his love to her—too much honor, I'd say, but I don't suppose Charles saw it that way—she told his brother that she wanted to end their engagement to marry Richard.

"There was no love lost between the brothers, and I'm sure Charles had no trouble convincing his father that Richard should be sent away—"

"Pressed, he was," interrupted Colonel Higham suddenly, startling them all. "Or as good as."

As the ladies turned wide eyes toward him he blushed and excused himself, saying he shouldn't have said that; it was just that it was the truth; Richard's father and brother had the young man knocked over the head and put aboard a ship bound for India, with a note the captain was to give him when he came to telling him he was on his own, and they'd suggest he not return to England to embarrass them again. "And him no more than nineteen at the time!" The colonel sighed gustily. "Well! You can imagine what that did to a proud young man like Richard. . . ." Realizing that everyone was looking at him aghast, the colonel explained sheepishly that he had once broached a bottle—or several—with the present earl before he attained the title, and the story had come out when Richard was in his cups. "Don't imagine it's something he'd want to get around," the colonel finished apologetically. "Beg you'll forget I ever said it."

Three heads nodded in agreement even as Mrs. Cresston, her easy sympathy aroused, said, "I don't know how he survived!"

"Survived by his wits!" the colonel exclaimed, thumping the table in his enthusiasm. "He's got plenty of wits about him, has Richard!"

"I understand it took them several years to find him, after his brother died, to tell him that the title is now his," Lord Wafton put in thoughtfully. "I imagine he has just returned to London after hearing of it; last I heard they were still looking for him. . . ."

"But what happened to Arabella?" Julianna asked, her forehead wrinkling as she tried to picture the cynical man she'd met in the park as a passionate, proud youth of nineteen.

Well, proud she had no quarrel with . . .

"Oh, she wed Charles," Mrs. Cresston assured her daughter. "The earldom is a rich one, and Arabella's father was a man who loved money more than a girl child any day. She died about a year later, in childbirth. I wonder what ever became of the baby. . . ."

She turned inquiring eyes to Lord Wafton and Colonel Higham, but neither of them was aware that a child had been born to Arabella and Charles.

Lord Wafton, who remembered the fifth earl as a cold, disagreeable, pompous man, said that he did not believe he had ever heard the fifth earl speak of any offspring, and perhaps the child had died with its mother.

But then, he added thoughtfully, since the earl, like his father before him, had eschewed most of polite society—or been avoided by it—it was not likely that one would have heard about the earl's family.

Edmund himself, although he had liked Richard, had not cared for his brother Charles, and did not believe he had spoken to him more than half a dozen times in the last ten years of the man's life.

"He spent most of his time in the country, as I recall," Lord Wafton said, losing interest in the subject of the now departed earl. "Which was good for us all!"

"And now he's in the ground, which is good for Richard!" said the irrepressible colonel, thinking aloud. The shocked faces of the ladies made him again flush and beg pardon.

๛ *Chapter 7* ๛

The next day, and all of the days that followed it, passed in a welter of activity for Miss Marley, and for one who was used to living quietly in reduced circumstances—as she had been before her godmama brought her to town—it was like a lovely dream from which she hoped she would never waken.

True to her word, Julianna made sure her young charge continued to patronize the best of London's dressmaking establishments. Miss Cresston watched in amusement as her protégée grew more confident and bloomed under Julianna's careful tutelage, even going so far as to express a decided preference for a gold Berlin silk, trimmed with silk floss, as opposed to the pale pink Julianna's Aunt Sephrinia, who was shopping with Julianna and Beth that day, favored for young ladies.

The anxious way Miss Marley looked toward Julianna as the final arbiter made it clear that she was not totally sure of her decision, but the smile of relief and pride that followed Julianna's ruling on behalf of her choice showed that she had come a long way in her own estimation.

Julianna, listening with what patience she could muster to her aunt's protest that pastels were most becoming to young ladies just entering society, countered that most young ladies were not blessed with Miss Marley's coloring, and so could not wear gold as happily as Beth did.

"Your great-aunt won't like it," was Aunt Sephrinia's parting shot as she was left at her doorstep later that morning. Julianna, outwardly shrugging, inwardly thought she might be right, and was surprised, therefore, when the gold gown elicited no more than a long stare and a "most unusual" from her elderly relative before the duchess asked her goddaughter to go in search of embroidery scissors, which the old lady said she had put down somewhere.

Since it was a well-known fact that the dowager duchess detested embroidery and had not touched a stitch in years, both her companions stared at her in surprise. Miss Marley, however, being much too well bred to question the request—as well as much too kind natured and much, *much* too grateful to her godmama to consider for a moment not honoring even the most outrageous of the dowager duchess's whims—dutifully rose and went in search of the scissors.

Once the door was shut behind her, Elizabeth leaned forward to say confidentially that she had wanted to talk with Julianna in private.

"I thought so," Julianna said, amusement crinkling her fine eyes, which in the room's light were the color of warm jade, "for if ever I heard such a whisker—wanting your embroidery scissors indeed!"

"Well!" The old lady shrugged. "I didn't exactly say I wanted them—just said I can't remember where I put them down. That's true. Must have done so years ago. Haven't seen them since."

The duchess dismissed the topic of embroidery scissors with an imperious hand as she repeated that she wanted to talk with her great-niece. A thought came to Julianna suddenly, and she slanted her great-aunt a sideways glance before allowing her eyelids to half-fall and hide her expressive eyes.

"I'm glad, Aunt Elizabeth," Julianna said, "because I want to talk with you, too."

"You do?" The elder Elizabeth regarded her with suspicion; she was not in the habit of finding her family desirous of individual tête-à-têtes. To the contrary, most of them, aware of her sharp tongue, took care never to be alone with her if they could help it.

"Yes." Julianna smiled and put down the teacup her aunt had handed her moments earlier. "I want to ask you about Beth's guardian. Who is he—and why the mystery concerning him?"

"Eh?" Elizabeth raised her own cup of tea and drank deeply before frowning at Julianna. "I don't see that that's any concern of yours, Missy. Beth is my goddaughter, and that's all you need to know.''

She said the words with the querulousness for which she was famous, knowing that among most of her relatives, at least, it would depress all pretentious belief that the inquirer had need of information she did not choose to give. She was not pleased to see Julianna continuing to regard her calmly.

"It *is* my concern, Aunt," Julianna replied. "And I do not intend to be put off by your high tone, so you might as well tell me."

"Hmmmmph!" The dowager duchess was pleased by this exhibition of spunk, but not for the world would she show it. "In my day, we did not answer our elders with pertness, young lady. And *that* you can believe!"

Julianna smiled and said that she could not imagine a time in her great-aunt's life that she had not answered *everyone* with pertness. That pleased the duchess further, but she shook her head austerely and said that it was no use Julianna thinking she was going to get around her with sweet talk, because she wasn't.

"Then I will try straight talk," Julianna said, leaning back in her chair to regard her aunt seriously. "Why won't you tell me about Beth's guardian? And why does she look about to cry each time the subject arises? He isn't—" A sudden thought occurred to her. "Good heavens, Aunt, he's not in trade, is he?"

Her aunt's indignation that Julianna would even *think* that she—a dowager duchess, one of the *ton's highest* sticklers— would so far forget her station as even for a *moment* to consider foisting on society the child of a merchant was so real, and so vociferous, that Julianna at once begged pardon and said that she was just thinking aloud.

"Thinking?" her aunt sniffed, picking up her teacup and setting it down again with a click. "I'd like to know what you use for thinking, girl!"

Julianna bit her lip, but clung to her topic of conversation. "Then what is it?" she demanded.

"What is what?" The dowager duchess replied testily before instructing her guest to take herself off to the sideboard and bring back a glass of sherry. It seemed, the duchess said, frowning direfully, that their present conversation had turned her thoughts from tea.

Dutifully Julianna did as she was told, only renewing her request for information after she had handed her great-aunt a glass and taken her seat again.

"What is the mystery?" she demanded.

"There is no mystery," the duchess replied, glaring at her. "She's gently born—of a good family. Her guardian doesn't care to be known; likes his privacy. Nothing wrong with that. I like my privacy, too. Besides—*I* know him. You don't have to. And don't go pestering the girl to tell you who he is, because she can't. Gave her word. So did I. Enough of that."

It was *not* enough of that, not for Julianna, but she knew from past experience that if her great-aunt truly had given her word not to reveal the guardian's identity, nothing Julianna could say would sway her. She did believe that she might be able to pry the information out of Miss Marley, but she did not wish to seriously discomfit her young friend, or to force her into a position of being torn by divided loyalties.

"I shall find out, you know," she said, a distinct challenge in her eyes.

Her aunt glared at her. "It's none of your affair, Julianna. Let it be. I have enough other things for you to do. Want you to put it about that the girl is well dowered."

"Well," Julianna said reasonably, seeing an opportunity to gain the information she desired, "How can I do that, when I don't know her family—"

"You can do that," the duchess replied, "by taking my word for it. Unless"—there was a distinct challenge in her eye—"my word isn't enough for you, Julianna?"

Hastily her niece said that it was, and the duchess nodded, satisfied. Spunk she liked to see in her young relations, but enough was, after all, enough.

"Also," she continued majestically, as if there had been no brief detour in their conversation, "I want you to teach Beth to ride. You and Marleton—"

"*Marleton*?" Julianna repeated the name with every sign of loathing, and her great-aunt glared at her.

"Yes, Marleton!" The duchess frowned heavily at Julianna, daring her to interrupt again. "He's going to pick her out a horse—"

"He's going to—"

"Stop repeating everything I say!" the duchess snapped testily. "He's an excellent judge of horseflesh, and a bruising rider—"

"Then why don't you have him teach Miss Marley to ride?" Julianna demanded. "You hardly need me if he—"

"Confound it, girl, that's enough!" The duchess set her sherry glass down and leaned forward on her cane to glare at her great-niece, who had the temerity to glare back. "In case you ain't noticed, Marleton is a man—" Something in Julianna's face made it apparent that she had indeed noticed, and the duchess' eyes narrowed shrewdly.

"A very good looking man," she continued.

Julianna muttered that she supposed he was well enough...

"Ahhh!" A smug smile settled on her great-aunt's face, and Julianna regarded her with suspicion and more than a little annoyance.

"Anyway..." The duchess was smiling now, like a cat who got locked in the pantry with the cream, and to her disgust Julianna felt her cheeks grow hot. "He can't teach her to ride as a lady. Not right, anyway. You can. Beth is afraid of horses. You ain't. Marleton ain't."

"There are any number of people in London who are not afraid of horses," Julianna pointed out with some asperity. "We do not need Lord Marleton. I will get Jonathan—"

"Now that's a good idea," the duchess said unexpectedly. "Get that young rapscallion out of the gaming hells, and onto horseback. He's more Beth's age..."

Julianna, who was two years younger than the viscount, felt it incumbent to point that out to her aged relative. The duchess regarded her with disgust. "Of course you are, girl! I know that! But you're talking chronological age, and I'm not. You've always been older than Jonathan. Always. Taking him is a good idea. You can make up a foursome—"

Julianna had no desire to make up a foursome, and said so. Her great-aunt yawned. When Miss Cresston vowed she would not ride out with such a person as the earl, the duchess gazed at the ceiling; when Julianna said her aunt had no right to ask it of her, the duchess found a great deal to study in the heavily patterned carpet that covered the floor.

Frustrated, Julianna demanded to know why her aunt was making her job of chaperoning Miss Marley so much more difficult by allowing a hardened rake to haunt her home— even going out of her way to encourage her young god-daughter to spend time with him.

The sentence seemed to attract the duchess's attention at last. "Hardened rake?" she repeated in surprise. "Wherever did you hear . . . ?"

Miss Cresston said that she had heard stories of women— most notably, a high-flyer in Vienna.

The duchess dismissed the high-flyer with a wave of her hand. "He's a man, my dear," she told her great-niece in a kindly voice that made Miss Cresston wish to do violence.

"I hardly think that an acceptable excuse, Aunt."

Her aunt chuckled. "It's the only excuse men need, Julianna."

Miss Cresston shook her head. "I do not think him a fit companion for Miss Marley. She seems to regard him with some favor, and he looks at her in a way that . . . well . . ."

It occurred to Julianna that if the earl were to look at her in just such a way it would not be as bothersome to her as it was when his eyes fell with such evident favor on Miss Marley; hastily she told herself that was because she— Julianna—would know how to deal with him. She pushed the thought away as her great-aunt chuckled.

"Marleton isn't going to hurt the chit," the duchess said, her eyes alight at a private joke. "He has a fondness for her. Might even say he's a—friend of the family."

The thought made her chuckle again, a dried, crackling sound that only increased Julianna's indignation.

"I don't suppose you'll laugh when you see that innocent ensnared by his—his—" Not sure what it was of his that would ensnare Miss Marley, Julianna stopped crossly.

"My dear, I'd be more like to faint away!" the duchess told her in amusement, then straightened, her eyes sparkling.

"You find him capable of—er, ensnarement—do you, Julianna?"

"No, I do not!" Julianna said, more crossly still. She was angry that at this precise moment she should recall a glimpse of how his eyes had teased her at their last meeting. "At least, not for a woman who is up to snuff! But Beth does not have my experience—"

"She's young, all right," the duchess agreed, in a way that made Miss Cresston want to shout "I'm only twenty-three—hardly past praying for!"

She was kept from that, however, by the reappearance of the subject of their conversation, who came into the room saying politely that she had looked all over for her godmama's embroidery scissors, but had been unable to find them.

The duchess said that it was quite all right; she didn't believe she cared to embroider anyway.

Julianna murmured that she wished her great-aunt wasn't in such a mood for weaving, either, and a surprised Miss Marley said she did not know the duchess wove. She was more surprised when Julianna, frowning at her great-aunt from under her well-arched eyebrows, said that she was unfortunately speaking about weaving webs of deceit.

Miss Cresston's brow did not lighten when the dowager duchess laughed.

❧ *Chapter 8* ❧

Julianna's pessimistically expressed hope that her great-aunt would forget about her latest start to have Miss Marley learn to ride proved to be just that; ten days later, as Julianna was enjoying her morning canter in the park, she encountered the Earl of Marleton, who halted her progress by the simple expedient of pulling his horse sideways across the path and holding him there as she came toward them.

Julianna had, perforce, to rein up, and as she did so she gazed unconsciously over her shoulder to see if she had, without thinking, outdistanced Thomas to the point that she would be facing Marleton again without escort. Relieved to find the groom only thirty yards behind her, she turned back to the dark earl, and nodded.

"Good morning, Lord Marleton," she said coolly, fine green eyes meeting ironic brown and reading something there that made her realize how warm the morning had grown.

"Miss Cresston," the earl acknowledged, swaying easily in the saddle as his horse, disgusted at being used as a blockade, sidled and danced in an effort to make his opinion of this occupation known.

"You are blocking the path, sir," Miss Cresston continued in the same cool tone, seeking an opportunity to provide him with a well-deserved setdown as Thomas drew nearer.

"Yes," he said calmly.

Her jaw tightened, and she glared at him. "Is there a reason, my lord?"

"Yes," he said, nodding at Thomas as the groom stopped just beyond Julianna. "I wish to speak with you, Miss Cresston. Be so good as to walk with me a ways."

He swung easily out of the saddle as he spoke and walked toward her, holding up his hands to help her down. Reading the refusal in her face, he said softly, "Little coward" in a voice that carried to her ears alone, and smiled at the light of battle that immediately sparked in her eyes. Ignoring his offered help she slid hastily off her own horse, handing the reins to Thomas and telling him she would be only a moment.

The emphasis on "moment" was for the earl's instruction, not Thomas's, but Marleton seemed supremely unaware of it as he took her arm and started her down a path beaming with early crocus. Seething, Miss Cresston removed her arm from his grip as soon as they turned a corner in the path that took them out of Thomas's interested gaze.

"Be so good, my lord, as to tell me your errand so that I may ride on," Miss Cresston said as she stood facing the earl in the weak morning sun. "My day is—"

Whatever her day was remained unsaid, for the earl, after breaking a branch from a nearby bush and switching it absently against his leg, looked up abruptly and interrupted. "You have not bought Elizabeth a riding habit."

"Miss Marley," she said stiffly, "does not care to ride."

"Nonsense!" The earl dismissed Elizabeth's desire to ride or not to ride with a switch of his branch. "She has never had the chance to do so, that is all! Once she has overcome her initial nervousness—"

"But she does not wish to overcome her nervousness!" Julianna objected.

The earl's eyes narrowed. "Have you asked her, Miss Cresston?"

"Yes!" Julianna responded. "I mean, no—yes—that is..."

"That is?" he repeated silkily, as she came to a stop.

Miss Cresston drew herself up stiffly. "When she first arrived, Miss Marley confided to me that she is afraid of horses, and does not care to ride. I have not pressed her to do so."

She thought that would put him in his place, but was disappointed to find it did no such thing. It made her wonder crossly if the earl ever knew his place, which made her want to teach it to him more than ever.

"But I wish her to learn to ride," the earl said calmly, "and I have chosen a beautiful little mare for her to learn on."

"You wish—" Julianna gasped, staring at him. "You have chosen—as if what *you* wish matters!" Suspicion sprang into her eyes, and she studied him carefully. "Why do you suppose your wishes would govern Miss Marley, my lord?" she demanded.

He shrugged. "Perhaps you misunderstand me, Miss Cresston. I only wish Miss Marley to learn to ride because your great-aunt wishes it. As she has, I believe, told you."

"Ha!" Julianna said, watching him through narrowed

eyes. "As if Great-Aunt Elizabeth could make you do anything you don't want to do! I wonder—"

"No, no, Miss Cresston," the earl interrupted, tossing away the branch he held and starting her walking again. "You underestimate the duchess. A veritable dragon. Of course she terrifies me—"

"Ha!" Miss Cresston repeated, glaring up at him. "And you underestimate me, my lord, if you believe I am to be taken in by such a faradiddle! You, terrified of my aunt, indeed! I doubt that the devil himself would frighten you—"

Too late she heard the unladylike words and colored, daring to glance up only when the earl did not immediately pounce upon her indiscretion to twit her with it. She was startled to see the somber look that had come into his eyes.

"You are wrong, Miss Cresston," he said, glancing away from her to survey the wooded area beyond them. "I have been to the devil. And I was more than a little frightened."

"I'm sorry," Julianna said, unconsciously reaching out a hand to touch his arm, drawing his eyes back to her as she did so. "I shouldn't have said that."

He put one hand up to cover her fingers, resting so gently on his forearm, and his face took on a self-mocking grin. "I believe I told you once, Miss Cresston, that you will find me remarkably hard to wound."

"Oh!" Julianna snatched her fingers away and started forward again. "You are impossible—"

"Yes, Miss Cresston, I am," he agreed, catching hold of her wrist and pulling her back to a less pell-mell pace, "but I do not ask the impossible of you. Get Elizabeth fitted for a riding habit."

"But she does not wish to ride!"

"Ask her."

Julianna opened her mouth to repudiate the suggestion, found it so logical that she could not, and shut her mouth again. "All right," she agreed reluctantly. "I will. But don't think I'll force the poor child into terrifying herself to please you and Great-Aunt Elizabeth, for I won't!"

The earl nodded, satisfied. "Just ask her, Miss Cresston.

Then order something in blue. I think she looks very well in blue.''

"Ooooh!" Julianna was torn between lambasting him for his calm assumption that Miss Marley's opinion of riding would have changed because he and the duchess wished it, and wanting to kick him in the shins for paying such particular attention to which colors best became young Beth.

Since they had by now come again into Thomas's view, she contented herself with another "Oooh!" and stalked ahead of him to her horse. Looking around for a log from which she might mount, she found none, and was forced, if she wished to avoid a scene in front of the interested groom, to accept the earl's offer to toss her up into the saddle—something he did so easily that the very strength of the man irritated her, too.

"Thank you, my lord," Miss Cresston said primly as the earl stepped back to look up at her, an interesting gleam in his eyes. "Now be so good as to remove yourself—I mean, your horse—from my path, so that my groom and I may ride on."

An appreciative smile lit the earl's eyes as he heard the words "my groom and I," and he grinned. "But of course, Miss Cresston," he said with a bow, taking his horse's reins from Thomas. "My horse—and I—are entirely at your disposal."

Julianna's temper was not improved when, above the sharp canter of her horse's hooves, she heard an amused chuckle floating after her.

Julianna did not have to wait long to ask Miss Marley if her aversion to horses had undergone a dramatic change, for that young lady was awaiting her when she returned home from her encounter with the earl.

"Elizabeth," Julianna demanded as she removed her hat in her bedroom, "didn't you tell me once that you are afraid of horses?"

"Oh, yes!" Elizabeth breathed, picking up Julianna's hat

to place it this way and that on her own small head. "They terrify me."

"Aha!" Julianna nodded in satisfaction as she slipped out of her habit and stood ready for the dress her abigail was preparing to throw over her head. "That's what I thought! And so I shall tell that busybody—both busybodies—when I see him—I mean, them!"

Elizabeth gazed at her inquiringly. Julianna smiled as she slipped onto the stool in front of her dressing table so that her maid could arrange her hair. "I met the Earl of Marleton in the park today, and he had the temerity to suggest that you would like to learn to ride. Can you imagine?"

"Oh!" Elizabeth sat upright suddenly, her feet not touching the floor as she perched on the bed, "I forgot! That is—I would like to learn to ride, Julianna. If you please."

"*What?*" Now it was Julianna's turn to sit upright, to the dismay of her maid, who adjured her to quit pulling about. "Don't be silly, child! If horses terrify you—"

"Oh! Well! I mean—perhaps not all horses . . . Richard has picked out the prettiest little mare for me. And besides . . ." She smiled naively. "He says I shall look all the crack in my new riding habit."

Julianna did not hear about the mare, and she did not hear about the riding habit. One word stuck screamingly in her mind. "*Richard?*" she repeated, half starting up and seriously discomfiting the maid, who had almost finished with her hair.

"Oh, dear!" Looking extremely conscious, Elizabeth tried to rectify her mistake. "I mean the Earl of Marleton, you know!"

"Yes," Julianna assured her, "I do know. And I also know that you shouldn't be calling him Richard. And so do you!"

"But it is his name—" Miss Marley protested.

Julianna glanced at the mirror, told Jane that her hair looked fine, and sent the long-suffering—and audibly sniffing—woman from the room.

"My dear Miss Marley—Beth—" Julianna began, feeling as close to distracted as she had ever come. "You cannot understand—you cannot know—a man of the earl's reputation—it will not do to be on such intimate terms with such a—such a—''

Then the very meek and very biddable Miss Marley completely surprised her mentor as she rose from the bed and stood before Miss Cresston with eyes shining to say that she considered the Earl of Marleton the best, kindest, most wonderful man in the whole world, and she dared anyone—even her beloved Julianna—to say anything else against him in her presence.

Julianna goggled at her. ''You do?''

Breathing quickly, Miss Marley assured her that she did.

''I see.'' Julianna took a deep breath, and rose too. The situation was clearly out of hand, and it behooved her to do something about it. But what?

''I see,'' she said again. ''Then perhaps we should say no more about it.'' She reached for a shawl and led the way out of her room, pausing only at the top of the stairs to suggest—with some reluctance—that Miss Marley should, to avoid raising the eyebrows—and whetting the curiosity—of the *ton*, refrain from calling the earl by anything but his title in public.

She was relieved by Elizabeth's instant acquiesence, but made more uneasy by the reasoning behind it. ''Oh, yes,'' Miss Marley said tranquilly. ''Richard wouldn't like it.''

Chapter 9

Miss Cresston's uneasiness over Miss Marley's intimate acquaintance with the Earl of Marleton did not decrease in the next few days, and was fanned to new heights three days later when Elizabeth's riding habit was delivered. She and Jonathan were then summoned to accompany the earl and Miss

Marley on that young lady's first venture into London traffic on horseback.

With some foreboding Julianna arrived at her great-aunt's home, accompanied by an abstracted Jonathan. The earl arrived from the other direction, leading a gray mare that Miss Cresston would not have minded having in her own stables, as Beth opened the front door and came tripping down the steps, smiling up at the earl in a way that made Julianna want to do him violence. Beth was well on her way to making friends with the little horse he'd bought her when Julianna and Jonathan drew rein and stopped a few feet from them.

"Oh, Julianna, isn't she beautiful?" Miss Marley breathed, looking up in delight. "I don't think I could ever be afraid of this little lady! I'm sure we're going to be great friends, aren't we, Ri—I mean, my lord?"

Jonathan did not seem to hear the slip but Julianna did, and she frowned disapprovingly at the earl. Glancing at her, he stared in puzzlement, then, as he understood her meaning, he grinned broadly and agreed that Beth and the mare would get along famously. He put a light hand on the girl's shoulder as he leaned forward to stroke the white blaze on the little horse's head.

Regarding that movement with disfavor, Julianna dismounted and came forward to place herself between the earl and her protégée as she, too, stroked the mare. "What is her name?" she asked Beth, ignoring Marleton.

Miss Marley looked inquiringly toward the earl.

"She is to be called whatever you wish, my pet," he replied, enjoying the daggers darting at him from Miss Cresston's fine eyes.

Jonathan, coming forward, called out carelessly, "What's that you say? Her name is 'Pet'? Strange name for a horse, don't you think?"

But Elizabeth, much taken by it, smiled shyly at the earl and said firmly that "My Pet" was one of the nicest names she'd ever heard.

"For a horse, perhaps," Miss Cresston muttered. "But not for a person. People are not pets."

Jonathan stared at her in amazement. "What person are you talking about, Ju?"

Looking at the grinning earl, Julianna replied crossly that she was not referring to any person in particular, it was just an observation; she had always been opposed to people referring to other people as pets, although it often seemed that those with a less well-defined sense of social correctness used the term . . .

Noting the bemused look on her cousin's face, the astonishment on Miss Marley's, and the open laughter on the earl's, Julianna ended her explanation and abruptly suggested they be on their way.

Jonathan, feeling some explanation due for her remarkable behavior, said in an aside to the earl that Julianna could not help hearing—and which caused her to audibly grind her teeth—that his cousin had often ridden without a hat in the blazing sun when she was younger, and he personally thought *that* accounted for it. . . .

Despite Miss Marley's courageous protestations that she was not intimidated by her pretty little mount, even the unperceptive Jonathan could see that she was decidedly nervous as they set off for Green Park, the earl having decided that Hyde Park would be busier than they liked. Miss Cresston found that, much as she would like to, she could not disagree with him.

Because he was a goodhearted young man, as well as a capable—if neck-or-nothing—horseman, Jonathan soon ranged himself alongside the anxious Miss Marley, pointing out brilliant bursts of color in the park and telling her stories of his own first attempts at riding which soon had her giggling and relaxing visibly under his friendly banter.

The earl, after satisfying himself that Jonathan could handle any situation that might arise if Miss Marley suddenly lost control of her mount, dropped back to accompany Julianna, who was a little distance behind and seemed content to ride as if she were not with their party.

"You are to be congratulated, Miss Cresston," the earl said, his eyes on the young couple before them as they rode sedately along. "Your taste is always exquisite. Miss Marley's habit is most becoming."

Wishing again that he would not so closely concern himself with Miss Marley's appearance, Julianna said stiffly that his congratulations must go to the young lady; she, herself, had thought Elizabeth would have done much better with a riding habit of green.

"I see." His evident amusement made Julianna bite her lip and wish the sentence left unsaid. She had indeed tried to persuade Elizabeth to choose a green habit, but her young friend had held out for blue, even going so far as to say the green simply would not *do*.

"You seem to see a great many things, my lord," Miss Cresston said suddenly, turning to him with the light of battle in her eyes. "You see how Miss Marley looks, you see how to charm her onto horseback—where she is obviously uneasy—" It was unfortunate that at that moment Miss Marley giggled delightedly at something Jonathan said, causing the earl to give his sardonic grin. Miss Cresston frowned at him. "Some people giggle when they are nervous, you know—"

The earl smiled, and stroked his stallion's neck.

"And another thing," Miss Cresston said, determined to get herself on solid ground again. "It will not do for you to be encouraging Miss Marley to call you 'Richard'—"

"I don't," the earl interrupted in such a calm tone that Julianna glared at him.

"Don't deny it, my lord!" she cried. "I've heard her—"

He turned smiling eyes toward her. "I am not denying that Elizabeth calls me 'Richard.' I am saying that I do not encourage it. Sometimes she forgets."

"*What?*" Julianna raised her voice, saw both Jonathan and Elizabeth glance back inquiring toward her, and lowered it again. "You don't deny—and then—you call her Elizabeth—"

"That is her name," the earl said in that same calm tone that made Miss Cresston wish to slap him.

"And have you been given leave to use it?" she challenged.

It was the calm voice again. "I have."

"Oh!" Angrily Julianna wondered where her great-aunt was in all this, and decided bitterly that she probably encouraged it—if only to make her great-niece's life more complicated. That thought was confirmed when the earl said a moment later that the duchess knew of and approved of his relationship with Miss Marley.

"I see." Julianna's lips were compressed, and her eyes sparkled with barely suppressed wrath. "Well, let me tell you, my lord, that you may have pulled the wool over my great-aunt's eyes—although how you accomplished it is beyond me, for if ever an old lady was awake to every trick it is my aunt—although she does have that regrettable fondness for a rake—"

"A rake?" the earl repeated, one eyebrow lifted. "Miss Cresston, you wound me!"

She snorted. "I have it on good authority, my lord, that you are remarkably hard to wound!"

His sudden laughter startled her horse, and even as Miss Cresston reacted to bring the animal under control again, an iron hand shot out, grabbing the reins lest the horse should rear. Miss Cresston regarded the hand coldly.

"I do not need your assistance with my horse, my lord," she said.

His hand returned to rest easily on his thigh. "No? Then perhaps I could offer some assistance with your life, Miss Cresston."

"My—my—" Her eyes opened wide, and she stared at him.

He smiled. "You will find your life a great deal easier if you are not forever crossing swords with me, Miss Cresston. I have never been bested in a duel."

Julianna started to sputter, but he ignored her.

"I am telling you this in the hope that it will assist you, and that you will cease wasting your energy in fighting with me, when you might put it to better use elsewhere."

"Of all the—" Julianna fixed him with her most baleful glare. "You arrogant—what makes you think—as if I would listen to—"

She pulled herself haughtily erect, and told him that she wouldn't take his advice on which way the wind was blowing, and wouldn't want his assistance in cleaning out a stable.

"But Miss Cresston," he replied, fanning her temper, "what a charming picture!"

"You—" Two high spots of color burned in her cheeks, but she met his eyes steadily as she told him that before she would allow him to make the innocent Miss Marley the object of his gallantry, and the talk of the town, she would, herself, meet him on the park's green, early morning, pistol in hand.

It was the worst threat she could think of, and she expected him to—she expected him to—come to think of it, she did not know what she expected him to do, but whatever it was, his next move was not that.

"Miss Cresston," he replied, his tone solemn, his eyes alight as he made her an elaborate bow. "It will be my pleasure."

He was not surprised when she applied her heels to her horse's sides and rode on to join her cousin and Miss Marley.

❧ Chapter 10 ❧

Julianna's efforts to shield her young friend from the dangerous earl's attention could not be called an unqualified success, for as she morosely told her mother one morning over breakfast, the whole town seemed to have embraced the dratted fellow, and he was to be found at nearly every dinner party, musicale, and ball to which she took her young charge.

"Yes," Mrs. Cresston agreed tranquilly, "it is good to

see Marleton welcomed back into society after his long years away from it.''

"Mother!" Julianna protested indignantly. "I do not believe you've heard a word I've been saying! Here I am, trying to protect Elizabeth from Marleton's advances, and you say—''

"I say, don't be such a goose, Julianna!" Her mother laughed, regarding her fondly. "The Earl of Marleton is too much of a gentleman to take advantage of such an innocent as Elizabeth Marley."

"Too much of a gentleman?" Julianna stared at her in amazement. "Too much of a—well! He is never too much of a gentleman to me!''

"No," her mother agreed in that same tranquil voice. She had watched with interest the earl's verbal battles with her daughter. "You are another case entirely."

About to launch into a catalog of the earl's vices, Julianna stared at her mother. "What do you mean by that, Mother?"

Mrs. Cresston smiled. "Only that you are not Elizabeth Marley."

"No, I'm not," Julianna agreed, her thoughts again diverted and her eyes kindling. "And I won't be taken in, even if the rest of the *ton* ignores the earl's ragtag manners, finds his sayings amusing, and is full of praise for his horsemanship and his adventures and his . . . his . . ." Realizing too late that she was about to mention things that should not have reached her ears, Julianna stopped.

"Actually, I have always found him extremely gracious," Mrs. Cresston said musingly. "Why just last night, when we were dancing—''

"And why shouldn't he be gracious to you?" her daughter interrupted pugnaciously. "It will be a fine day when a Cresston is not on par with a Marleton—whoever a Marleton may be! Although to use the word 'gracious' in the same sentence as 'the Earl of Marleton'—'' The last part of her mother's statement penetrated her mind, and she stared at her in surprise. "Last night—" she repeated, "when you were—*dancing*?"

"Yes, Julianna," her mother said, a slight smile edging her lips. "I am not yet past dancing!"

"No, no, Mama, of course not!" Julianna countered hastily. "I didn't mean—it was just that—you always have so many partners, I can't imagine how the Earl of Marleton ever managed to get near you, much less get on your dance card—"

"He did it by trickery." Mrs. Cresston smiled at the memory, unconsciously twirling one of the soft blond curls that fell over her right shoulder. "Convinced poor Julius I must be parched for a glass of champagne, then whisked me onto the floor the minute the poor man's back was turned. You should have seen Julius's face." She looked down at her teacup and remarked, almost inconsequentially, that the earl was a beautiful dancer.

"Well!" Julianna was not amused by the earl's antics. "Of all the impertinence! I hope you gave him a sharp setdown—"

"But, my dear," Mrs. Cresston protested, opening her deep green eyes in surprise. "Julius is quite one of my oldest friends. I could not!"

"Not Sir Julius!" Julianna waved that elderly swain away impatiently. "The earl. Marleton."

Mrs. Cresston protested again. "But, Julianna, darling—I just told you—he is really the most beautiful dancing partner—"

"Mother!" Julianna regarded her in horror. "Don't tell me you, too, have fallen victim to his wiles!"

Mrs. Cresston smiled as she assured her daughter that it was no such thing; she had enjoyed an agreeable dance and an agreeable conversation with an agreeable partner.

Julianna tried to recall any conversation she had had with the earl that could be termed agreeable. "What did you talk about?" she asked.

Her mother smiled. "The latest *on-dit*. Life in the country. Life abroad. You."

"*Me*?" For some reason the last topic of conversation was the one most interesting to Julianna, and she picked up a napkin to fan her cheeks as the breakfast room suddenly grew warmer.

"Yes." Her mother's face was filled with reminiscence as she recalled the pleasant evening. "He said you were a remarkable rider, and asked if you had always been so fearless and headstrong."

"Fearless and—*headstrong*?" Indignant at the last word, and for some reason disappointed in the first, Julianna did not ask herself what adjectives she would have preferred the earl to use in describing her—although "exquisite" and "entrancing" and "intelligent" and "witty" sprang readily to mind. "Well!" she said warmly, "I hope you gave him a proper answer!"

"Oh, I did, dear," her mother assured her. "I said, 'yes.'"

"Yes? Why—*Mother!*" Julianna felt as if she had been let down, and stared at her mother in hurt surprise.

"Yes." Mrs. Cresston was not looking at her daughter as she smiled at an image the younger woman could not see. "I told him about the time you were six, and decided you were going to ride your pony to London to see your grandmama, despite our direct orders that you were to go immediately to your room, and how we found you ten miles from home, headed in the wrong direction but game as a pebble—"

"Mother!" Julianna cried. "You didn't!"

Her mother nodded, still smiling. "And about how you turned out the bailiff we hired after your father died and our good Jameson retired, when you found that the new man was treating the tenants badly, even though I would have left it to the lawyers to handle—"

"Mother!" Julianna repeated, faintly, and this time her mother's gaze returned to her. The look on her daughter's face made Mrs. Cresston blink in surprise.

"But, Julianna," Mrs. Cresston told her, "the earl was most impressed. . . ."

I'm sure, Julianna thought grimly.

"And he said everything he ought. I, in turn, am always impressed with gentlemen who hold my daughter in high esteem." She reached out and patted Julianna's hand fondly, and her daughter forebore to tell her that that must put the earl quite off her lists. Although why he should care to know about . . .

"Fearless" and "headstrong" drifted through her mind again, and she sighed. It really was turning out to be the most disagreeable season of her existence.

The disagreeableness of the season grew on Miss Cresston as the day progressed; a morning of shopping for new hats with her mother and Miss Marley produced nothing that could not be termed at best insipid, and at worst, shabby— even though her two companions protested loudly that she looked ravishing in the lace-edged chip bonnet, and extremely fetching in the dark blue.

When she called for her matched grays to be hitched to her phaeton so that she might take her rightful place in the afternoon parade in Hyde Park, it was to find that Gray Pride was mysteriously limping, and she would not be able to drive the team for at least a week.

And that night, at Almack's, she was forced to watch Lord Bassington—who only last month had sworn that he would wear the willow until his death if she did not accept his handsome offer of heart, home, and fortune—make a positive cake of himself over young Miss Bloomsley. Anyone could see that young lady would run to fat later in life, but she was now, Miss Cresston supposed, well enough, if you could overlook her inclination to squint. . . .

Catching herself up on that unkind thought, Julianna had the grace to blush and turn quickly away from the sight of the two just as the Earl of Marleton approached. Seeing her color before she raised her eyes to his, he looked about for the cause of her embarrassment, found none, and regarded her with a marked question in his eyes as he bowed.

"Miss Cresston," he said.

"My lord." She returned his bow, thinking that this was just what she needed to set the seal on an already miserable day.

The earl scanned the scene again. "Has someone been annoying you, Miss Cresston?"

"Annoying me?" she repeated, surprised.

He bowed again. "I thought that your heightened color might be due to some annoyance. Or perhaps," he said, smiling down at her, "it is my presence that makes you blush so."

"Your pres—" Her mouth opened and shut with a snap. "Of all the arrogant, conceited—yes, Lord Marleton, someone is annoying me. You, sir. You annoy me excessively."

His smile enlarged to a grin. "Come now, Miss Cresston," he encouraged. "This is just what you need! I like you much better when you are bristling with rage, than seeming oppressed by some lowness of thought—"

Miss Cresston gave him to understand that it did not matter to her in the least how he liked her, and was rewarded for her incivility by a laugh.

"And another thing, my lord," she said, eyeing him smolderingly. "I would appreciate it if you would, in future, refrain from forcing my mother to talk about me—"

"But you mistake, Miss Cresston," he interrupted, taking her hand to move her out of the way of another couple attempting to pass as the band struck up a waltz. "Your mother requires no urging to talk of you. Come. Dance with me."

"I will not!" Julianna tried to snatch her hand back, but could not free her fingers from his firm grasp without making a scene. "And let go of my hand!"

"But Miss Cresston," he protested, "if you do not waltz with me, I shall have to seek out another partner, for I am very fond of the waltz. Perhaps," he mused, as he released her fingers and she began to move coldly away, "I shall ask Miss Marley."

Julianna stopped and half-turned toward him. "Miss Marley does not waltz. She has not yet received permission from a patroness."

"Ahhh." The earl rubbed his chin, contemplating the problem. "I suppose I could find a patroness and induce her to grant permission. Or—" He eyed Miss Cresston consider-

ingly from one corner of his eye, still rubbing his chin.
"Or, I could see if Miss Marley would forgo the conventions and dance with me without approval."

"You would not!" Julianna cried, turning back to face
him fully.

He smiled at her.

"*She* would not!" she continued.

His smile grew. "Would you care to wager, Miss Cresston?"

Torn between the desire to walk swiftly away, and the
desire to protect her young friend, since she had the nagging
suspicion that Miss Marley might do any unwise thing the
earl asked, Julianna hesitated, and in that moment was lost.

"Come, Miss Cresston," the earl said, favoring her with
his most attractive smile. "Let us cry friends for one dance.
Waltz with me."

"Well . . ." Still Julianna hesitated, as she looked toward
the figures whirling happily around the crowded floor. "If
you will promise not to be disagreeable—"

"I promise," the earl told her, taking her hand and
sweeping her out onto the floor, his arm firmly circling her
waist in a way that seemed to contribute greatly to the
overheating of the room.

To her surprise, the earl kept his promise so well that
Julianna found him an agreeable and entertaining partner,
and for some reason she did not object when the band struck
up a second waltz, and he swept her out into the whirling
couples again.

Trust her mother to be right—the earl was a beautiful
dancer.

❧ *Chapter 11* ❧

Julianna left Almack's that night tolerably pleased with the Earl of Marleton, who, she decided, could be a sensible and empathetic companion when he was not bent on censoring her behavior or questioning her decisions or raising her ire over some problematic behavior or decision or action of his own. She fell asleep that night thinking that they might be on the way to an excellent understanding—something she would have said was impossible a day earlier—and that thought made her smile. It was a belief she nurtured right up until her next encounter with the earl. And this time it was not Miss Marley, but Julianna's cousin Jonathan who was the cause of their disagreement.

In her zeal to steer Miss Marley safely through her first season, Julianna had rather lost sight of her original goal to rescue her cousin Jonathan from his threatening pecuniary embarrassments. She found that she was extremely busy with the first duty, for despite the fact that Miss Marley was a well-behaved young lady who would never willingly breach the canons of strict society, she was also such a kind-hearted young woman that she shrank from giving the heavy setdowns some of her more daring young—and old—swains so richly deserved. Also, her sometimes artless observations of society had to be amended quickly before those who heard them could make her the subject of the latest *on-dit*. This kept Julianna so occupied that she had little time to work on her second objective.

When she met her cousin at different balls and events, she seldom had time for more than limited conversation. And although she had, on several occasions, straightly questioned him about his finances—even going so far as to ask him if he was badly dipped—Jonathan took care to return only the most noncommittal answers, shrugging off her last question with, "No worse than half the young bucks on the town."

The problem was, as Julianna knew, that most of those young bucks had fathers who still held the purse strings, and who could tow them out of the River Tick, if they chanced too far down it, while Jonathan had no such resource. When she tried to point that out to him he heaved an impatient shoulder and with an irritated, "Let be, Ju!" disappeared from her side, and was not seen again the entire evening. Hostesses indignant to find he had left the party before leading their daughters out to dance were quick to complain to his cousin.

Julianna had tried to smooth over his lapse of manners at one party by laughingly telling the wrathful Mrs. Smedley that her daughter's toes were safer with Jonathan gone. She then enlisted her own next partner, her good friend Lord Wafton, as a suitable substitute for the downcast Miss Smedley. Julianna could not help noticing, even as she relinquished him to Miss Smedley, that he had twice led Miss Marley out that evening, while this was the first time he had approached her.

"I will expect a reward for this service," Lord Wafton murmured in Julianna's ear before turning a smiling countenance to the twittery Miss Smedley. That young lady simpered up at him in a way that made Julianna sympathize with Jonathan's defection. Not, she thought, that she sympathized much, as she was forced to take a seat along the ballroom floor and watch what should have been her waltz with Lord Wafton—also a beautiful dancer, although perhaps not quite as good as Marleton—bungled badly by Miss Smedley's two left feet.

When Lord Wafton had deposited Miss Smedley back in her mother's care after the dance he descended on Julianna, who had been joined by Elizabeth, smiled down at them and said, meaningfully, "a very big reward." He then limped off to the refreshment room to fortify himself with several glasses of very good champagne. Fortunately, Mr. Smedley had had the foresight to realize that his wonderfully stocked wine cellars would go far to reconcile the gentlemen at the party.

"What did Lord Wafton mean?" Elizabeth asked, turning big brown eyes toward Julianna after his lordship limped away, favoring the foot Miss Smedley had trod on at least nine times.

"That I owe him five pounds of his favorite snuff," Julianna said glumly. "Or that the next time he asks to buy Conqueror out of my stables, he expects me to sell. Drat that Jonathan, anyway!"

Miss Marley again fixed her inquiring eyes on Julianna's face, and in a few brief words Julianna explained that it was because of her cousin that she now stood in Lord Wafton's debt, and that it was just like Jonathan—she had had his best interests at heart, but if he wanted to gamble his home and honor away she supposed it was nothing to her. . . .

Julianna had worked herself up into a fine rage when Beth interrupted abruptly with, "Oh! So that is why—" She stopped suddenly, and appeared conscience-stricken as Julianna inquired why *what*?

"But it cannot be . . ." Elizabeth said, looking distraught. "He would not—I must be mistaken!"

"Mistaken about what, my dear?" Julianna asked, fixing young Lord Butterington, who was approaching them to solicit Miss Marley's hand for a dance, with such a minatory eye that he bethought himself of another engagement and shied hurriedly away.

By now Elizabeth had had a moment to collect her thoughts, and she tried to smile, saying that as she must be mistaken there was no reason to think any more about it. Julianna, by far the stronger personality, pushed to know what had upset her friend so.

"I am being silly," Elizabeth said, folding her hands tightly in her lap and looking away, her young eyes troubled. "It is just that the first night I ever met your cousin Jonathan—at Almack's, you remember—"

Julianna nodded. She did.

"I noticed the particularly fine pin he was wearing in his

cravat. It is a beautiful thing—a sapphire in gold—do you know it?''

Julianna nodded again. She and her mother had presented it to her cousin on his twenty-first birthday.

''Yesterday, when I was riding with Richard, I noticed that he had a pin remarkably like Jonathan's. I was going to say something about it, but then I was diverted, and . . .'' She raised troubled eyes to Julianna's. ''You don't think he—won it—from Jonathan, do you? I know gentlemen like to gamble, but somehow, it would seem so—terrible—if your cousin were to lose to my . . .''

Julianna stared at Elizabeth's face, trying to comprehend what she had just heard. What she must focus on, she told herself, was Jonathan's loss. If he were indeed dipping so deep that he was pledging his possessions, his case was more desperate than she thought, and she must talk with him immediately.

Also looming large before her was the innocent confession that Miss Marley had been riding with the Earl of Marleton yesterday. It sounded as if this were a much more common occurrence than Julianna had expected. Then too, there was the way Elizabeth said it would be terrible if Julianna's cousin were to lose to Elizabeth's—Elizabeth's what?

Julianna placed one hand over the two Elizabeth was clasping and unclasping in her lap, and spoke quietly. ''Elizabeth, what is the Earl of Marleton to you?''

Elizabeth's eyes met Julianna's briefly, the big brown eyes of a startled doe, before looking quickly away. ''Why, Julianna,'' she said in her best town voice, ''whatever can you mean? He is my friend—you know that!''

Julianna knew that all confidences were at an end. Her dreams that night were not pleasant ones, filled as they were with plans for saving her cousin and Elizabeth from a monster that, when she confronted it, seemed to turn into a lamb. And she found that the hand she raised to shoo the monster away would, of its own volition, end up gently patting the shaggy beast's head. She awoke the next morn-

ing wondering if all monsters were really in search of a little
understanding.

So it was that when Miss Cresston next met the Earl of
Marleton, she held him responsible for the emotions raging
in her breast. When he approached her on horseback in the
park the day after Elizabeth's disclosures, the smile in his
eyes was met with a decided coldness on Julianna's part.
She acknowledged his greeting with a curt nod and accepted
his invitation to walk a bit with him with a, "Good! I have
been wanting to talk with you, too!"

Tossing the reins of her horse to her groom, she strode
briskly away and the earl, a decided question in his eyes,
stopped only a moment to deliver his own reins into the
interested groom's hands before striding after her.

"I take it something has occurred to vex you, Miss
Cresston," the earl began as soon as he caught up with her.
"I had hoped, after our last meeting, that we would find
ourselves on better terms—"

"Do not talk to me of our last meeting, my lord!"
Julianna said impatiently, removing one glove and jerking it
nervously from one hand to the other. "I should have
known that blackmail was only a part of your personality—"

The earl's brows snapped together as he repeated
"Blackmail?" in the silky voice that never failed to send a
shiver down his servants' backs. Miss Cresston, who was
made of sterner stuff, glared back at him.

"Yes, blackmail! Blackmail and gambling and winning
pins from young men who can't afford to lose them and
shouldn't be gambling in the first place—"

"Ahhhh." Enlightenment dawned and the earl's brow
lightened. "I believe, Miss Cresston, that you would do
well to address this lecture to your cousin. It might be more
in his line than in mine."

"Then you don't deny it?" Julianna asked, looking painfully
up into his eyes. Somehow she had hoped she was wrong.
"The pin Elizabeth saw you wearing was my cousin's?"

The earl shook his head. "No, Miss Cresston," he

corrected her. "It was mine. Won fair and square in a game of cards."

"But Jonathan can't afford to play cards at such stakes!" she cried.

He bowed. "I believe that must be your cousin's decision. Not mine."

"You did not have to play with him," she challenged, her eyes sparking.

"No." He looked down at her for a moment, then out across the landscape. "But if he did not play with me, he would certainly play with someone. Better he had a chance with an honest game, than to be fleeced by a shark."

"A shark—" Julianna repeated, and reached out one hand beseechingly to his arm. "Oh, pray—is it as bad as that?"

The earl's face was enigmatic as he looked down at her hand and then gazed searchingly into her eyes. "My dear Miss Cresston," he said gently, "you cannot hold yourself responsible for your cousin's behavior. He is a grown man, and he must be responsible for his own mistakes."

She shook her head and withdrew her hand, turning from him. "I cannot agree, my lord," she said, her voice low. "Jonathan is, despite his age, still a boy. And where one person cares for another, there can never be a shirking of responsibility."

He was silent for a moment and his voice held an odd note when he asked, "You care for him so much?"

Julianna turned back with a brave face and a small smile as she looked up at him. "We grew up together, you see."

He stared at her for a moment before asking, this time in a quiet tone she had never heard before, "Shall I give you back the pin?"

"Would you?" The words were out eagerly before she thought; when she realized what she'd said, she tried to palliate it by offering to pay him the sum Jonathan had lost. He waved the offer aside almost angrily, still staring down at her with that odd look she had never seen before.

"I will, Miss Cresston," he told her. "I will have it delivered to you this afternoon. But don't expect your cousin to thank you for it."

"Oh, thank you!" Julianna said warmly, ignoring his last statement as she caught his hand and squeezed it. "I did not think you could be so kind!" The twisted smile that statement drew made her blush and beg his pardon. "I didn't mean that—it's just that—that—"

"I know what it is, Miss Cresston," he replied, making her an ironic bow that bruised her heart. "I believe you have time and again made your opinion of me abundantly clear."

No, she wanted to say, *I don't believe I have. . . .* Instead she stared down at the ground and remarked consciously, "Well, as to that—"

"No, no," he said, and this time his voice held the old harsh note with which she was more familiar. "Let us not have civility caused by debt between us, my dear Miss Cresston. I would rather have your disdain than that."

Julianna looked curiously up into his face as they walked back to the waiting Thomas, but there was nothing she could read there; it was closed and masked against her.

As the earl helped her mount she placed a hand diffidently on his shoulder and said, looking down at him, "I believe I have made a mistake."

Thinking what she said applied to her cousin, he nodded grimly. "Yes," he said. "I believe you have."

❧ *Chapter 12* ❧

The earl was true to his word, and the pin was delivered by one of his servants to Miss Cresston that very afternoon. Since her cousin had been persuaded—much against his will—by their Great-Aunt Elizabeth to escort them to the theater that evening, and was dining with them before the performance, Julianna looked forward to returning it to him as quickly as possible. With that in mind she made a quick toilette and, dressing well before her mother was ready or her great-aunt and Miss Marley had arrived, she slipped down to the drawing room where the viscount awaited the ladies.

When she entered the room Jonathan sat stretched out before the fire, a glass of burgundy in hand, his air one of dejection, but he roused himself at once and rose, smiling down at her as she came toward him, a mischievous light in her eye.

"Looking lovely as usual, Ju," he told her, regarding her pale jonquil gown with approval. Then, surveying her face, he cocked his head knowingly. "Looks like you're up to something, too."

"Close your eyes and hold out your hand," she told him, her own hands pressed tightly behind her back. He regarded her with suspicion.

"Now, Julianna," he said. "What are you up to?"

"Close your eyes and hold out your hand," she repeated, and after a moment's hesitation he did so reluctantly, opening one eye to inquire if it was going to be something horrid.

"No, no." She laughed, adjuring him to close the eye again. "It's a wonderful surprise. Really!"

Reassured, he closed the second eye and she slipped the pin into his open palm. When he opened his eyes to look down at it he regarded first the pin and then Julianna with stupefaction.

"What—" he said, staring down in surprise. "How—" He raised his eyes to her face, and the relief in his own was quickly supplanted by a sternness she had never before seen there.

"Julianna," he asked quietly, his fingers closing around the pin as he gazed down at her, "what have you done?"

"Why—" It had not occurred to her that he would be anything but delighted to have his property returned to him. Suddenly the earl's warning that she should not be surprised if her cousin did not thank her floated through her mind. "I've—I've gotten your pin back for you. Aren't you

pleased?'' The soberness in his face made her falter. "I—
always thought—you liked it.''

"Liked it?'' Jonathan repeated, taking a hasty turn around
the room before coming to stand before her again. "Of
course I liked it. I treasured it! But I lost it, Julianna—I lost
it in play. How do you come to have—'' He stopped
suddenly, and his face grew angry. "Do you mean you've
redeemed it for me? How did you know?''

Hastily Julianna explained that it was Beth who had
noticed the Earl of Marleton now wore Jonathan's pin, and
when Julianna had taxed the earl with it—

"When you—*taxed*—him with it?'' her cousin repeated,
staring at her as if she had grown another head. The fist that
enclosed the pin went up to slap against his forehead, and the
enormity of what was being told him made him stagger back
to a chair, and fall into it. "You went to Marleton and—
what? Gave him money to redeem what he had won honestly
in play? You gave him *money*? What must he think—that
I'm hiding behind my cousin's skirts—''

The thought seemed to appall Jonathan so much that she
hurried to tell him it was no such thing; she had not gone to
the earl, but had met him in the park—

"You met him in the park—and—and—what, harangued
him about my debt to him? Paid it for me?'' Somehow, the
way Jonathan said it, that part of her explanation did not
sound better, and she hurried on. Since he seemed convinced that she had paid the earl to redeem his pledge, she
told him that it was no such thing; that when she had
explained the situation to the earl he had asked if she would
like him to return the pin, and when she had said "yes,'' he
had obligingly done so.

That explanation did not have the desired effect, either.
Instead of soothing her cousin, it worked more powerfully
than ever on him, and he lunged from his chair, his eyes
wide. She took a hasty step back and put another chair
between them.

"You explained the situation—'' he choked.

She nodded, trying to make him understand that once the
earl realized that Jonathan shouldn't have been gambling . . .

"You told him *that*?" he demanded. "You asked that he give the pin *back*?"

She had not actually requested it, she said conscientiously; the earl had offered to return it, and she had taken him up on the offer.

"I cannot believe you have done this, Julianna," he said, the color fading from his face and his voice low. "That it should come to this—"

"But, Jonathan," she pleaded, moving toward him, worried by the look in his eyes. "The earl didn't mind. I offered to pay for the pin, but he has so much money, it means nothing to him. And you . . . you . . ."

Still turned half away, he said, in that same low voice, filled with suppressed passion, "You don't understand, do you, Ju? You're right. I shouldn't have pledged the pin. I shouldn't have gambled with the earl. I don't have money. But I do have honor, Julianna—and honor decrees that when I play, I pay. This was between the earl and me. You had no right to meddle."

"But, Jonathan—"

"No right," he repeated, swinging angrily toward her, his voice rising. "No right at all. Do you hear me?"

"We all hear you, young man," said another voice from the door as Great-Aunt Elizabeth entered the room, followed closely by Mrs. Cresston and a wide-eyed Miss Marley. All three were regarding Julianna and Jonathan with great curiosity, and the cousins flushed under their inquiring gazes. "Perhaps you would like to tell us all what you are shouting about?"

Stiffly Jonathan begged pardon, and said that it was a matter between himself and his cousin.

"Julianna?" Great-Aunt Elizabeth inquired sharply.

Julianna bit her lip and raised her eyes to her cousin's face. "Yes," she corroborated, "it is between Jonathan and me. A matter of honor."

After dinner, as they waited for the carriage to be brought round, Julianna found a moment to whisper an urgent apology to the viscount. Ignoring her mother's inquiring eyes, and her aunt's sharp statement on the inadvisibility of secrets, she touched the viscount's arm.

"I am so sorry, Jonathan," she said, glancing hurriedly at the others to make sure they were not within hearing distance. "I did not realize . . ."

He shook his head and said heavily that he knew she meant it for the best. "I just hadn't realized the depths to which I'd sunk, Ju. To find a female, my own cousin, interceding on my behalf. Well! That's water under the bridge! I must return this pin as soon as possible. I don't know what I shall say to Marleton."

"I could do it," Julianna offered, only to see her cousin's lips tighten.

"No, Julianna," he said firmly. "You have done enough."

The audience reacted to the farce that evening with laughter, but neither the lovely Miss Cresston nor her tall, blond cousin seemed to enjoy it. In fact, the two sat as if they did not hear the lines that had others giggling behind their fans. With a rare tact the dowager duchess forebore to press them, and so they sat, wrapped in their own thoughts, until midway through the second act, when Miss Cresston gasped, her eyes wide.

Jonathan, seated beside her, followed her glance to find that the Earl of Marleton had entered the theater and was taking a seat in a box directly opposite them. "I shall talk to him at the intermission," Jonathan told her and, true to his word, was up and out of his seat the minute the curtain fell.

He made his way through the chattering crowd to the other side of the theater and advanced purposefully upon the tall figure of the earl, whom he found in the corridor in close conversation with his good friend, Lord Mitterington.

"Your pardon, sir," Jonathan said, when he had at last reached them. "I wonder if I might have a moment of your time?"

Looking coldly around to see who interrupted his conversation the earl saw Jonathan, and his face relaxed slightly. "If you will excuse me, Mitterington," the earl said with a bow, and moved lazily away with Jonathan following. When he had found a spot where he thought they might not be overheard, the earl turned to the younger man with a noncomittal "Well?"

Jonathan faced him bravely, his usually smiling eyes serious. "I believe I have something that belongs to you," he said. Reaching into his pocket, he pulled out the pin and held it out to the earl.

"Ahhh." Marleton stared down at it. "I told her I did not think you would appreciate her assistance."

Jonathan shook his head. "Julianna meant well, my lord. I hope you do not think—"

"That you sent her for it?" asked the earl, with sudden insight. "No. I do not. I believe Miss Cresston acted quite on her own. As, I believe, she is used to doing."

Jonathan's gaze was direct. "Miss Cresston is my cousin, my lord."

The earl bowed. "You are to be congratulated on your relations."

"She meant well," Jonathan repeated.

The earl allowed himself a half smile. "Yes. It is diffficult to be long angry at someone whose motive is *love*."

The last word seemed to come almost unwillingly from his mouth, and Jonathan regarded him in puzzlement. "We have known each other all our lives, you see. Ju is not only the best of my relatives, she is my best friend."

"Then you are also to be congratulated on your friends," the earl said with yet another bow, and the return of his formal manner.

"Yes, well . . ." Jonathan, his duty discharged, muttered uncomfortably that he should be returning to his box; the play would soon start again.

He had taken a step away when the earl recalled him.

"Bushnell," the earl said. "I hope you have not been too unkind to your cousin, for her actions on your behalf."

Jonathan nodded. "I hope not, too, my lord."

There was a pause, then "I shall keep your pin for you," the earl said. "Should you care at some time to redeem it, I will have it."

Jonathan's formal manner was suddenly gone. "Why, thank you, sir! That is very good of you!"

The earl placed a hand on his shoulder, turning him back toward the boxes and Lord Mitterington, who still stood waiting for his friend.

"Come along," Marleton said. "You're right. The farce is about to begin again."

Later that night, after Jonathan had escorted the ladies home, he asked for and was granted a few moments of conversation with Julianna.

As they sat together in the library, a fire burning brightly in the grate before them, Jonathan held a glass of Mrs. Cresston's best brandy in his hand and said gratefully that he thought they had rubbed through it pretty well, all things considered, and that he was extremely grateful that the earl had not been as cutting as he had feared.

"In fact," he said handsomely, "he was deuced decent about it, Ju. Said he realized you'd meant your actions for the best, and knew I hadn't put you up to it. Even said I could redeem my pin at some future time, if I wish. Wouldn't have had to say that, you know. And I'll tell you something else, Ju." The brandy was beginning to have a warming effect, and he smiled fondly at his cousin. "That's just what I intend to do. Going to get the pin back. Gave me a nasty turn to lose it, I can tell you."

"I'm glad, Jonathan," Julianna said, looking at him with a worried frown. "I hope you will. If you need a loan—"

"No, no," her cousin assured her. "I'm going to do what you told me I should weeks ago. Get my affairs in order. I'm going to reform my life, Julianna. Just you wait and see."

She said that she would wait, and she certainly hoped to see. The viscount laughed, told her she was a doubting puss, and poured himself a second glass of brandy.

❧ *Chapter 13* ❧

To his cousin's relief—and surprise—the young viscount remained true to his word for the next few weeks, engaging in such innocuous pastimes as taking a look-in at Jackson's, shooting at Manton's, and driving out to the country with his good friend Mr. Mumbleton to see a boxing match on which he wagered no more than five pounds, and won fifteen.

So happy was he at the outcome of that venture that he told Julianna he was sure his luck had turned at last—not, he added hastily, as he saw her face fall, that he meant to try his hand at any of the games of chance so dear to him in the past; no, it was just that he believed that winning his small wager was a sign that this reformed life he was leading was just the ticket to ensure his future success.

With that Julianna agreed fervently, and took the opportunity to further turn his thoughts from gaming by inviting him to accompany her and Miss Marley and—she said the name a bit consciously, but Jonathan was not the man to notice—the Earl of Marleton on what had become their daily ride in the park.

The young viscount agreed readily, said he'd be off to get his horse, and would return to her house at three, well in time for the fashionable promenade.

As he took his leave, Julianna nodded absently and sat for a moment, trying to determine when it had become such a natural part of her day that she and the earl—and Miss Marley, of course!—should go riding.

At first Beth had been the earl's ready excuse for accompanying them, saying that such an inexperienced and nervous rider should not venture out without an accomplished horseman to help her. When Julianna said tartly that Miss Marley was accompanied by an accomplished horsewoman, the earl turned her protest aside by remarking that he was glad of it, since two such companions made Miss Marley that much safer.

With that Julianna could not disagree, because she knew how often companions could become separated by a carriage or another horseman in the park, and should Beth's animal pick that momemt to bolt . . . No, she could not put her young friend to such risk merely for the enjoyment of setting down the high-handed earl, so she had, with grudging grace, agreed to his company. Surprisingly, she found it was not bad company—that is, she told herself consciously, when the man didn't seem intent on raising her temper with one of his outrageous remarks.

Truth to tell, the earl seldom was outrageous on their daily rides; in fact, he conversed so like a sensible man that she was quite in charity with him these days, except for his occasional lapses from grace when he called Elizabeth by her given name, or paid her too particular an attention for Miss Cresston's taste.

Julianna had been surprised—and, to her embarrassment, her surprise had been evident enough to raise one of the earl's mobile eyebrows—to learn that the earl shared many of her own interests, including her concern for the orphans and child laborers in London. Her amazement increased when told he had even spoken to the question one day in Parliament.

"I wish I could have heard you!" she had remarked wistfully.

The earl grinned.

"I did not move mountains, I'm afraid, Miss Cresston," he apologized. "In fact, I have a pretty good notion that half the lords in attendance slept through my words, and the other half thought of nothing but their dinners."

"But at least you tried," Julianna said, leaning forward to place her hand on his as it rested carelessly on his saddle. "So few are doing even that!"

The earl looked down curiously at her warm hand, but did not comment as a nervous shying by Miss Cresston's mare moved them apart. Marleton, who now knew better than to offer aid where none was needed, watched as she brought the horse under control again, and turned his attention to Miss Marley, who had been listening without comment to their conversation.

"Well, Beth," he said, smiling down into what Julianna could only despairingly describe as the young woman's adoring eyes, "what do you think? Are you interested in this question?"

To Julianna's surprise Miss Marley seemed to grow taller, and her voice took on a quality much older than her age. "Yes," Elizabeth said, "I think it is the duty of every gentlewoman and gentleman in this country, and in all other countries, to care kindly for our children and to not cast them off simply because they are—orphans."

Her voice seemed to catch on the last word, and Julianna, watching her curiously, was further confused when the earl dropped a comforting hand over Miss Marley's and gave the much smaller hand a squeeze before starting to converse in a commonplace tone on the sad crush experienced last night at the Seftons' ball.

Taking her cue, Julianna joined him in an artful, if wicked, dissection of those members of the *haut ton* who had been in attendance that soon had Miss Marley laughing. She exclaimed in protest that they should not—no, they shouldn't—she was sure that Mr. Simperington did not really mean to affect that stilting walk (which he did, believing it added to his consequence), and said charitably that perhaps Miss Botherbee was afraid to leave her jewels at home unguarded, and that was why she always appeared—as the earl said—as if someone had just spilled the entire contents of her jewelry box over her.

Thus it was with the expectation of a pleasant ride in pleasant company that Miss Cresston descended the stairs that afternoon to find Miss Marley and the Earl of Marleton already awaiting her, and her cousin Jonathan just riding up the street as the three stepped out the front door.

"I've invited my cousin Jonathan to ride with us today," she said, and was surprised by the look of annoyance that passed over the earl's face before he schooled himself to his usual languid manner. Miss Marley enthusiastically en-

dorsed Jonathan as a member of their party, for she liked the
young viscount as much for himself as for the fact that he was
Julianna's cousin. But Julianna wore a puzzled frown as
they rode away, Miss Marley and the viscount in front, she
and the earl following.

At length, when they had reached the park, the earl
chanced to remark on her protracted silence and puzzled
face, and she turned her full attention toward him.

"I was wondering, my lord," she said directly, her fine
eyes fixed on his face, "why you did not care to have my
cousin join us for this ride?"

The earl glanced toward the young couple chatting happily in front of them, so deep in their own conversation that
they paid no attention to what anyone else said. He tried to
turn her question aside with the light answer that perhaps he
liked having two of the most beautiful women in London to
himself, but Julianna would not let it be.

"No," she said, "that cannot be it, because when Lord
Wafton joined us two days ago, you were perfectly happy to
include him in our company."

"Yes, but Lord Wafton is not a dangerous young blade
with more flash than sense."

Too late the earl saw her fire up on her cousin's behalf, and
tried to turn the coming argument. "That is, I do not believe
the viscount to be the best of companions for such a young and
impressionable lady as my..." Again he saw the question in her
eyes, this time painful, and caught himself up to finish, after
only a fraction of a pause; "my young friend."

"My cousin," Julianna said, the words coming tight
between her teeth as she sat, backbone rigid, eyes sparking,
"is a gentleman. And let me tell you, sir, that I believe him
a much more fitting companion for your—your friend, as
you put it—than a hardened rake who no doubt eats young
girls for breakfast!"

The anger that had flashed into the earl's eyes at the word
"rake" changed to amusement at her last sentence. "But
my dear Miss Cresston," he purred in a voice that made her
long to strike him, "what very odd eating habits you seem
to believe rakes possess!"

"Don't toy with me, my lord," she said. Her anger communicated itself to her horse and made the mare side-step nervously. "I am not a child just out—"

"Ah, no," he said, rubbing his chin as he surveyed her thoughtfully, his eyes lingering appreciatively on her face and form in such a way that seemed to make the day grow hotter. "In fact, I have been meaning to drop a hint about that. Just a friendly warning, you understand, for when a woman is on her last prayers—"

"I am *not* on my last prayers!" Miss Cresston shouted in a voice loud enough to draw the eyes of Miss Marley and her cousin toward her, as well as those of several passersby.

So chagrined was she at being made the center of attention that Miss Cresston clamped her lips together and stared straight ahead, ignoring the earl's barely concealed laughter as he told her in a soft voice that reached no ears other than her own that he hadn't meant to upset her; he had just wanted her to understand that he quite understood her feelings at having reached a ripe old age where one was wont to . . .

What one was wont to do was not to hear as she retorted, "My age is not ripe! And if it will ease your—your—your *mind*—"

"My *odious* mind—" suggested the earl.

"Your *odious* mind," agreed Miss Cresston, glaring at him, "you might like to know that Jonathan is being no more than kind to Miss Marley. He is a very kind-hearted young man, you know. And"—she added the clincher, glaring triumphantly at him—"you need not worry about his contracting a romantic interest for Miss Marley, for he has proposed to me—*not* Miss Marley—so many times that I have quite lost count."

"Why you think that would make me feel any better I don't kno—" the earl began, then stopped and started again. "You're right," he agreed, as if suddenly struck by the thought. "That *is* kind of him."

The earl's voice was serious, his eyes alight, but his companion did not notice. Instead, Julianna ground her teeth, touched her heels to her horse's sides and rode smartly ahead to join her cousin and young Beth.

* * *

The viscount, sublimely unaware that the earl's distant manner toward him bespoke any more than a cold, autocratic nature, professed himself so pleased at the end of the day's ride that he invited himself to join them the next day, too. Since his suggestion was heartily endorsed by Miss Marley, the earl, meeting Julianna's challenging look, could only nod and set a time when they would all meet again at Miss Cresston's. Rain postponed that date for them, and the next, and the next; Julianna, while fretting at the grayness and wetness of the days, was secretly relieved not to find herself caught, as she knew she would be, between her cousin and the earl when their rides resumed. She was even more relieved when, at the end of a week in which the sun had not shone once, a dissatisfied Jonathan visited her to say that if the weather meant to remain so plaguey damp, he thought he'd take a bolt down to Bushy with the praiseworthy notion of seeing what he could do to put his estate in order. That suggestion was so heartily endorsed by his cousin that he left her home feeling quite the responsible lord, intent on looking into the welfare of his tenants and his land. Head high, he sailed down the street and called for his carriage to drive through the night—for it soon would be night, as his valet so thoughtfully pointed out to him—to his ancestral home.

❧ Chapter 14 ❧

When Julianna, in company with her mother, her great-aunt, and Miss Marley, encountered the Earl of Marleton at an intimate musicale at the home of Lord and Lady Ribbington the night following Jonathan's departure from London, it was with a certain amount of self-consciousness.

Their last conversation, three nights earlier at Almack's where Great-Aunt Elizabeth had dragooned Jonathan into taking the ladies, had been both tantalizing and puzzling.

Julianna had not expected to see the earl at Almack's for, like many of his compatriots, he eschewed the simple pleasures of the Marriage Mart whenever possible. She had settled into a comfortable conversation with Lord Wafton when a tap on her shoulder made her turn and start as she gazed up into the Earl of Marleton's eyes.

"Pray, dance with me, Miss Cresston," he said in tones that were far more commanding than pleading, and she was about to say that she preferred to sit when Lord Wafton, at her left, deserted her with a nod and a smile at the earl.

"Oh, very well," Julianna replied sulkily as she thought of saying she had a previous commitment, thought better of it, and read in his eyes an accurate following of her thinking.

"Most kind," he murmured as she placed a hand on his shoulder and he put his hand at her waist before sweeping her onto the floor of circling dancers.

"I warn you, my lord," she said, looking up at him, her chin raised challengingly, "if you mean to rip up at me, I shall walk off the floor and leave you standing here. I will!"

Her threat might have been the reason his hand tightened on her waist, and she thought it was that pressure which made her breath come faster, rather than the tiny gleam in his eyes as he smiled down at her.

"Why, Miss Cresston," he said, "whatever would I rip up at you for? And let me tell you," he added as she opened her mouth to speak, "you are looking quite charming tonight."

It was true, and Julianna knew it; when she'd donned this new gown of rose silk she'd thought with satisfaction that anyone seeing her in it would be hard put to describe her as a lady on her last prayers. Yet she blushed.

"Well," she said, finding to her horror and great surprise that the very words she'd meant not to say were tripping off her tongue, "it's no use blaming me for Jonathan bringing us here tonight, for that was all Great-Aunt Elizabeth's

doing, and if you want to tell her Jonathan isn't good enough
for your—young friend—''

The earl smiled and Julianna found great satisfaction in
bringing one of her heels down upon his toes as she
murmured ''So sorry'' with her sweetest smile.

The earl, not deceived, smiled back, and told her that her
great-aunt was quite in agreement with him.

''*What?*'' His statement so startled Julianna that for a
moment she stopped dancing and stared at him, to the
imminent peril of the couple whirling behind them—her
cousin and young Beth.

''Dash it, Ju!'' exclaimed her cousin irritably, swerving to
avoid her and doing great damage to his partner's toes at the
same time. Elizabeth bore the pain bravely, even managing
to smile at Julianna and the earl as she limped by.

''Blunderer,'' the earl said critically, watching Jonathan's
far from successful attempts to lead Beth through the dance.
Then he turned his attention back to Julianna. ''And tsk, tsk,
Miss Cresston! Do you always make such scenes?''

Miss Cresston, who had made no scenes until the earl's
entrance into her life, found his accusation grossly unfair,
and told him so. He smiled and said nothing.

''And besides,'' she said, returning to their original topic,
''what do you mean, Great-Aunt Elizabeth said Jonathan is
not good enough for Beth? I happen to know she is very
fond of him.''

Smoothly the earl told her that she had misunderstood;
the dowager duchess had not said the young viscount was
not good enough for Miss Marley; she had merely agreed
that the two would not suit. And she had added that neither
had more than the friendly interest of a brother or sister
in the other.

''But I told you that!'' Miss Cresston said indignantly.

''Yes, Miss Cresston, you did.''

She stared at him uncertainly, trying to read his face.
''Well, then . . .''

''Well, then?'' he repeated.

Julianna heaved an exasperated sigh. ''If you aren't here to
rip up at me for having Jonathan accompany us, and you're

not here to keep Jonathan away from Beth, to what does Almack's owe the pleasure of your company?''

The music had ended, and he gazed at her with that same teasing smile. "Your *esteemed* company, Miss Cresston," he said. "When you wish to be particularly cutting, it is best to add 'esteemed.'" He watched her cheeks redden with satisfaction, and grinned. "Besides, dear Ju—surely you can guess."

Then, before she could even question what he meant, or point out that he'd not been given leave to use her nickname, he quickly walked her back to her mother and solicited Miss Marley's hand for the next dance.

So when Julianna met him at the musicale, she did not know what to say beyond "Good evening, Lord Marleton." Her civil voice was meant to tell him, if he cared to know, exactly where he stood in her blackbooks.

The grin on his face made it apparent he understood as he asked, equally civilly, if she was enjoying the evening.

"Oh, yes," said Miss Cresston, plying her fan as she gazed indifferently about the room. "It is prodigiously entertaining, I'm sure."

"Perhaps," said the earl, "but not as entertaining, nor as good, as your performance!"

Julianna raised startled eyes toward his face, read understanding there, and smiled in spite of herself. "It is rather terrible, isn't it?" she said, lowering her voice to make sure her words were not heard amidst the chatter.

"More than 'rather,'" agreed the earl.

Julianna eyed him speculatively as she again wondered aloud why he might be there.

He shook his head. "Poor judgment, Miss Cresston," he said mournfully. "Poor judgment in walking down Bond Street yesterday just as Chuffy Ribbington was driving up it. Poor judgment in being born into a family related—albeit remotely, thank goodness!—to the Ribbingtons. Old Chuff asked me so eagerly if I was coming that what could I do but say yes?''

"Gammon!" said Miss Cresston, watching him carefully. "As if you would care about Chuffy Ribbington's feelings!"

The earl smiled. "Now there you are quite out, Miss Cresston," he said. "Chuffy was kind to me when no other member of my family even remotely cared if I lived or died. I do care about his feelings a great deal."

About to apologize, Julianna read the smile lurking at the back of his eyes, and refrained. "But that doesn't mean you couldn't have thought of a previous engagement he would have accepted," she said.

"As your cousin did, no doubt," he said smoothly, not answering her question as he led her into other conversational ground.

"My cousin," Julianna said, waving her fan to signify the supreme indifference she felt for the topic—and the earl's interest in it— "has gone out of town."

"Oh?" The earl was all polite interest, and the fan began to wave a bit more briskly. "Your doing, Miss Cresston?"

"Certainly not!" she said, shutting the fan with a snap as she glared up at him. "He has gone to Bushy. To look after matters on the estate."

"Ahhh." The earl rubbed his chin. "Viscount Bushnell as the benevolent landlord. A new role, *enfin*!"

"No," Julianna said crossly, "it is not a new role! Jonathan cares very much about Bushy! It's just that sometimes he forgets—" The light in the earl's eyes made her bite off her words as she added, "He is very young, after all."

"Yes, he is," the earl agreed.

She looked at him curiously. "Why do you prefer to think the worst of my cousin?" she asked.

"My dear Miss Cresston," he said, his voice a drawl, "the truth is, I do not prefer to think of him at all." Then, to ward off her retort, he directed her attention to her mother, who was trying to attract Julianna's notice. The earl bowed as Miss Cresston took an icy leave of him to answer her mother's summons.

"Oh, dear," Mrs. Cresston said as her daughter reached

her side and she saw Julianna's stormy eyes. "You've been quarreling with the earl again."

"Nonsense, Mama! You know I am not of a quarrelsome nature!" Miss Marley looked at her questioningly. Great-Aunt Elizabeth had the bad manners to snort, and Julianna turned a shoulder to her as she asked what she might do for her mother.

"Well, it's not for me, dear," her mother said. "But your Great-Aunt Elizabeth has developed a crushing head-ache, and Colonel Higham has kindly offered to see us all home. Our carriage won't return until after the musicale is over, and Elizabeth—"

"—Wants to go now!" proclaimed Julianna's great-aunt, with more fact than tact. Julianna stared at her and thought she looked remarkably well for a lady who felt unwell. Which she said.

Great-Aunt Elizabeth glared at her. "A lot you know, Miss! Just because I am too well-bred to swoon in a room full of people . . ."

Julianna permitted herself a skeptical smile and Great-Aunt Elizabeth's glare grew as Mrs. Cresston adjured her daughter to gather their cloaks and give their regrets to their hostess and meet them all at the door. Then she and Miss Marley turned their attention to solicitously helping the dowager duchess from her chair and moving her slowly toward the entrance while the colonel hurried ahead of them to have his carriage brought round.

Julianna found Lady Ribbington in conversation with the Earl of Marleton and, biting her lip, approached to make her family's excuses. Lady Ribbington, a vague, near-sighted woman, heard Julianna's explanation patiently and sighed.

"So sad," she replied. "There's a regular epidemic of headaches tonight—each one more severe than the last, too!" Julianna, meeting the earl's eyes at that moment, had all she could do to choke back the laughter she saw mirrored there, and was nearly undone by his sympathetic, "Just so."

Lady Ribbington, however, took his comment as a second

of her own statement, and turned toward him, struck by his perspicacity.

"You've noticed it, too, have you, Richard?" she said. "There seems to be a great deal of sickness in London these days. And it always seems to peak at the time of our little musicales." The thought made her shake her head at the vagaries of nature, and she moved away, contemplating the ill health of her guests.

"My great-aunt—" Miss Cresston began.

"Will recover," the earl supplied, smiling down at her. Julianna smiled back. "Yes. Will recover."

The dowager duchess's malady was of an amazingly short duration. Once in Colonel Higham's carriage and on her way home to a good glass of sherry and the latest bloodcurdling tale that had caught her eye at Hookham's Library, Great-Aunt Elizabeth made a remarkable recovery. She had the entire party in stitches as she described the lengths to which she'd been driven to escape the last musicale she had honored with her presence twelve—no, perhaps fifteen—years ago.

"I don't know what possessed me," the old lady remarked, shaking her head in disbelief at her own gullibility. "Not even for Marleton would I do such a thing again."

Julianna's ears pricked up at the last statement. "Lord Marleton asked you to go to the Ribbington musicale?" she asked. "Whatever for?"

Her great-aunt, after a look that on a lesser being might have been described as guilty, said stiffly that Julianna had misunderstood. She forestalled any further questions by saying querously that all this talking had made her headache worse, and she intended to say no more until she arrived home.

Then, regardless of the burning questions Julianna wished to put to her, the dowager duchess leaned back against the comfortable cushions and closed her eyes, feigning sleep. She did not open them again until the colonel, cheerfully chattering to entertain the ladies, said that he would be driving down to Bath the next day to visit his ailing aunt.

Aunt Elizabeth, with a quick glance at Mrs. Cresston, whose face was hidden in the darkness, asked how long he planned to stay there.

"Don't know," the colonel answered glumly. "Can't say. Don't really care to go, but she's sick, you know. I'm the only relative she has. Says she'd like me nearby. Says she has a desire to see my ugly face. Don't know why, but there it is."

"Yours is *not* an ugly face," Mrs. Cresston interposed, startling her daughter with the warmth of her tone. "You have a great deal of character in your face. And—" She stopped, suddenly aware of her audience.

"Do I, now?" The much gratified colonel considered her words. "Well, by Jove!" He slapped his knee, much struck, and relapsed into this new and heretofore unheard of vision of himself.

"Cousin Mathilde has been unwell," Great-Aunt Elizabeth said thoughtfully, "and she lives in Bath. I have been thinking that you and I should journey there for a day or two and see how she does, Jessymn."

Julianna, thinking to protect her mother from such a boring trip, protested that Cousin Mathilde actually *doted* on being unwell.

She was considerably startled a moment later to hear her mother ignore her and agree with the duchess that a visit to Cousin Mathilde was long overdue.

"Is it, now?" Colonel Higham said eagerly. "Does that mean that I'll have the pleasure of seeing your lovely face in Bath?—I mean—oh, dear!" He lapsed into bashful silence.

Mrs. Cresston replied tranquilly that it just might mean that, indeed.

❧ *Chapter 15* ❧

An astonished Miss Cresston arrived at the breakfast table the next morning to find her great-aunt already there.

"Good morning, Aunt." Julianna helped herself from the dishes on the sideboard and took her place at the table, offering to refill the ladies' cups for them. Her mother thanked her absently but declined.

Great-Aunt Elizabeth ignored the suggestion. "I was just telling your mother," she said, fixing Julianna with a minatory eye, "that I received word from Cousin Mathilde that she desires our presence in Bath as soon as possible. Certainly within the week."

"Isn't that a coincidence," Julianna said, "when just last night you were talking with Colonel Higham about going to Bath."

The words were to tease her great-aunt, and Julianna was considerably surprised when her mother blushed.

Elizabeth glared at Julianna. "Coincidences do happen, Miss! I'll have you know—"

"But I cannot go!" Mrs. Cresston interrupted.

The dowager duchess's response was a pugnacious, "why not?"

"Well." Mrs. Cresston waved her hand helplessly. "I have so much to do here. Who would look after Julianna?"

"Look after herself," Great-Aunt Elizabeth said. "Has for some time now. Wants to go anywhere, her Aunt Sephrinia can chaperon her. Or a dozen others. Wouldn't do her any harm to stay quietly at home for a few days. She's forever racketing about town."

Julianna opened her mouth to speak, encountered her

great-aunt's frosty stare, and thought better of it. Picking up a piece of toast, she looked thoughtfully at her mother.

"And you, Elizabeth!" Mrs. Cresston continued, "you have obligations here! What about Miss Marley?"

"Take her with us," the dowager duchess said promptly. "Daresay she'll enjoy it. She's an obliging little thing. Won't complain."

"Oh, no!" Mrs. Cresston was torn between amusement and vexation. "Elizabeth, how could you! To be sure, she won't complain, but—*enjoy* a visit to Cousin Mathilde? Besides, the child is so looking forward to the Hearthingdons' masquerade next week. She told me it's her first, and she has a new domino." Mrs. Cresston sighed. "No, it's not to be thought of."

A look at the dowager duchess's face convinced Julianna it was indeed to be thought of, and she met her great-aunt's eyes with interest as the old lady frowned at her.

"Of course!" Elizabeth said suddenly, sitting upright. The plumes of her hat waved alarmingly and little bits of feather floated into the butter. "That's it!"

"It?" Mrs. Cresston was regarding her questioningly, and Elizabeth beamed.

"Julianna can chaperon young Beth. They'll stay here, together. Your servants will look after them."

"But Julianna isn't a chaperon!" Mrs. Cresston protested. "And besides, it would be rather—I don't know—irregular, don't you think?"

The dowager duchess waved "irregular" aside and concentrated on the statement that Julianna was not a chaperon. "Why not?" she asked. "She's old enough. Why, if she were married like most of the gels her age—"

Really, thought Julianna, putting down the toast in distaste, *this constant harping on my age is the outside of enough.* She rasied weary eyes to her great-aunt's sharp ones, and said that she would be happy to have Miss Marley come and stay with her *if* her mother *really* wished to visit Cousin Mathilde.

"Of course she does!" Great-Aunt Elizabeth averred.

Mrs. Cresston looked at her daughter, blushed, and said that if Cousin Mathilde needed them . . .

Sensing her victory, Great-Aunt Elizabeth decreed that they would set out for Bath on Monday next, and rose to take her leave, stopping at the door to instruct Miss Cresston to have a care of her goddaughter while she was gone. Julianna was still searching for a suitable rejoinder when the door closed.

On Monday morning Julianna, with Beth at her side, waved good-bye to her mother and the dowager duchess, who were traveling, she thought wryly, as if they were setting off on a trip around the world, instead of the relatively short distance to Bath. In addition to the four outriders her great-aunt considered necessary to protect them from highwaymen, they were accompanied by two more coaches. One carried Great-Aunt Elizabeth's major domo and dresser, Mrs. Cresston's dresser, and a parrot the dowager duchess had received from an admirer last week. She had hit upon the happy notion of presenting the parrot to Cousin Mathilde, since she herself couldn't stand the bird. The last carriage transported their luggage and assorted items of furniture and bedding Great-Aunt Elizabeth never set out without. She was firmly convinced that her chairs were more comfortable than anyone else's and only her own pillows could be guaranteed free from lice. . . .

"What is this?" said a voice in Miss Cresston's right ear just as the carriages started forward. "The Royal Family setting off, perhaps?"

Julianna turned and smiled at the Earl of Marleton.

"Richard!" exclaimed Miss Marley. "You said you'd come!"

"I am a man of my word, poppet," he said lightly. "You must always remember that."

"But I know it already!" Miss Marley cried. "And I am so glad you are here, for Julianna and I were feeling quite bereft."

Miss Cresston said that she was not feeling bereft at all, and Beth stared at her in surprise.

"Weren't you, Julianna?" she asked cautiously. "I was sure you would be, and asked Rich—I mean, Lord Marleton— if he wouldn't come by and escort us riding. . . ."

Miss Cresston said there was no reason to bother the earl; her groom could accompany them.

The earl, noting her downcast eyes, said that it was no bother; in fact, he had been looking forward to it. Just as he was looking forward to escorting the ladies to the Hearthing-dons' masquerade.

"You?" Julianna blinked at him in surprise. "Oh no! That is, my Aunt Sephrinia—"

"Is not invited," the earl finished for her. "The dowager duchess discovered that, and asked me to serve as your cavalier, since she herself would not be here to accompany you."

"She did?" Miss Cresston echoed. "She said nothing to me about that."

"The dowager duchess," the earl replied in a smooth voice that made her stare suspiciously at him, "is not used to apprising members of her family of her actions. Nor," he added thoughtfully, "is she likely to become used to it, after all these years."

"But that's wonderful!" Miss Marley interrupted. "Now we can all be comfortable, with you to protect us, for I have heard that some people do—at masquerades, you know—go a bit beyond what is pleasing . . ."

"Yes," the earl agreed, his words calm, his eyes alight as they met Miss Cresston's, "that is true, Miss Marley. I know just what you mean."

"From experience," Julianna interjected.

"But of course." He bowed. "From experience—watching others!"

Miss Marley clapped her hands and said it would be great fun. Julianna, eyeing the earl, hoped that her mother would come back soon.

It was not her mother who walked through the library door that afternoon, but another relative, one Julianna was almost as glad to see.

"Jonathan!" she cried, springing up and coming forward to take his hands delightedly. "I did not expect to see you back in London for an age!"

Grinning, the viscount told her he hadn't been able to stay away. In truth, his bailiff's efforts to make him cognizant of the needs and requirements of his estate had so terrified him that he had bolted back to the city to see if he could raise the ready the man said was so necessary for repairs. It seemed easier to win money than to do as his bailiff suggested and hold his expenses down for several years to put back into Bushy what he had until recently been so busy taking out of it.

Remembering Julianna's views on his gambling, he didn't tell her this. Instead, he spoke of engagements made before he left that he felt he couldn't in good conscience ignore. It sounded so noble he half believed it himself, and with his cousin beaming up at him, he felt that he was becoming quite the responsible adult his family had for the last several years adjured him to be.

"One of them wouldn't happen to be the Hearthingdons' masquerade, would it?" Julianna asked hopefully, for ever since the earl announced his intention of taking them there, she had been seeking a way to add to their party to prevent any tête-à-têtes between her young charge and the earl. Not that she believed he would go beyond the line, she told herself, but if he were to do so, she didn't want it to be with such an innocent as Beth. Julianna, of course, would know just what to do, but . . .

Telling herself severely that it did not do to follow that line of thought, Julianna decided that she would ask Lord Wafton to accompany them, too, and set herself to winning Jonathan's compliance.

Since she had, from childhood, been able to bring him around to anything she really wanted him to do, that was not hard. When he left a few minutes later, he had promised that he would escort her and Miss Marley to the masquerade seven days hence, and would call upon her on the morrow to take her and her young guest riding.

Satisfied, she had one of the footmen carry a note to Lord Wafton, inviting him to join her party for the masquerade. That night she encountered him at the theater, where she and Miss Marley were with Aunt Sephrinia, and received his affirmation. When Julianna told Beth about the additions to their party, the young lady was delighted, saying that that would only increase their fun.

"Yes," agreed Miss Cresston, thinking of the dark earl's face when he heard the news. "It will."

❧ *Chapter 16* ❧

It was a shame that after all Miss Cresston's work to increase their party for the Hearthingdon masquerade, neither she nor Miss Marley would be in town to attend. Circumstance has a way of taking a hand in even the best laid plans, and turning them to naught.

In Julianna's case, circumstance was over six feet tall, and looked exactly like her cousin Jonathan.

When he failed to appear the following morning to accompany her and Miss Marley on their ride, she was annoyed, and accepted the offers of Lord Marleton and Lord Wafton—who just happened to arrive at the same time—to ride out with them. The earl seemed preoccupied and she several times surprised him staring at her with a small frown between his eyes, as if he were struggling with some knotty problem. Her annoyance with her cousin increased, but she was not worried. She knew Jonathan's tendency to forget those engagements he was not especially enthusiastic about, and she half-expected, upon their return, to find a note expressing his regret and promising to see her later.

When no such note awaited her, Julianna shrugged and decided to rake him down severely that evening at the Huntleys' ball, which he had mentioned yesterday he would be attending. She then turned her attention to young Beth's wardrobe (and, now that she thought of it, her own), and the ladies decided that an expedition to Madame Ledeux's was in order, followed by a trip to the milliner's where Miss Marley had earlier that week seen the most ravishing chip straw.

Returning home with several bandboxes, and heartily pleased with the expenditure of their time and funds, the ladies barely had time to eat and dress before leaving fashionably late for the Huntleys' with Aunt Sephrinia. There Julianna looked in vain for her cousin. A small feeling of foreboding over his continued absence grew as the evening progressed. She could not put her finger on it, precisely, although several times during the evening she believed several of the gentlemen of her acquaintance were looking at her as if trying to gauge whether or not she was aware of something.

After a waltz with Lord Wafton Julianna arrived at her aunt's side just as Lord Marleton returned Miss Marley to her chaperon. The earl seemed determined to pass her with no more than a polite bow, but Julianna held out a hand to detain him. She was oblivious to the look of sympathy that passed from Lord Wafton to the earl before Wafton led Miss Marley onto the floor.

"Lord Marleton," Julianna began, uncomfortably conscious that the gentlemen she had believed were regarding her strangely during the evening once again were doing so. Despite her best efforts her cheeks grew hot. "I was wondering . . ." She applied her fan to her hot cheeks. "That is—perhaps—have you seen my cousin this evening?"

The earl shook his head, his eyes hooded. "No, Miss Cresston, I have not. But it is highly unlikely that I would."

She considered the last half of his speech, found it incomprehensible, and smiled up at him deprecatingly. "You will say it is foolish of me, I'm sure, but I have the oddest sensation that something has happened to him. You see, he was to go riding with us this morning, and he said he'd be here tonight, and the fact that he isn't—well, probably he has taken himself out of town to see a boxing match or to buy a horse or something like that. . . ."

She was chattering, she knew, waiting for him to reassure her, but the earl merely bowed again.

"It is not for me to say where your cousin might be, Miss Cresston," he told her, his voice and face grave.

She had the feeling that he knew more than he was telling

her, and touched his arm. Suddenly aware that more and more attention was focusing on them, her hand dropped, and she met his gaze uncertainly. "We seem to be attracting a great deal of attention, my lord," she said.

He ignored the others. "Every story, Miss Cresston," he said, "has two sides. I hope you will remember that."

"What?" She was startled as he moved away, murmuring that he had already kept his dance partner waiting.

She stood, bewildered by his last remark, one hand pressed to her cheek, until his, "Miss Cresston—" made her turn, and regard him enquiringly.

"Yes?" she said when he seemed unaware of how to continue. She was even more bewildered when he hesitated, shrugged, and sighed.

"Good evening, Miss Cresston," he said, his eyes somber. He left her standing alone until Mr. Marsden, one of the kinder gentlemen of her acquaintance, quickly detached himself from a small group of people standing staring nearby, and invited her to dance.

The feeling that something untoward had occurred continued to trouble Miss Cresston. When she asked Lord Wafton if he had seen her cousin that day, he only tightened his lips and, avoiding her eyes, said that Jonathan was a resty young pup with more style than sense, and she wasn't to blame— well, anyone else—for his misfortunes. This so seriously alarmed Julianna that she pleaded a headache that would have done even Great-Aunt Elizabeth proud and persuaded her Aunt Sephrinia to take them away.

When the door had been shut upon her aunt and she'd heard that lady's carriage drive away, Julianna considerably startled the solicitous Beth by straightening from her wilted position and declaring in anything but fainting tones, "Thank goodness! I didn't think she'd ever leave!"

Miss Marley blinked at her in amazement. "But, Julianna," she asked, "are you feeling—better?"

Julianna assured her that she was indeed, and further surprised her guest by announcing her intention of going out again, this time to her cousin's lodgings in Ryder Street.

"But, Julianna," Beth protested, "it is late!"

Julianna spared an indifferent glance at the clock before agreeing that it was. As she pulled the rope to bring Broughton, she suggested that Beth might like to go to bed.

Beth, it appeared, would not.

"Julianna," the young lady said seriously, "you cannot go out at this time of night—alone—to Ryder Street. Not to a young man's lodgings!"

"It is only Jonathan's! My cousin's," Julianna protested.

Miss Marley shook her head firmly. "It simply," she said, folding her lips in a way that put Julianna forcibly in mind of Great-Aunt Elizabeth, "is not done."

About to argue, Julianna realized the justification of her remark, and sighed. "I know," she said, "but I believe Jonathan is in trouble, and I cannot let a want of resolution or a concern for what others will say keep me from him when I believe he may have need of me. Can I?"

Put to her that way, Miss Marley shook her head hesitantly, her kind heart touched. No, of course Julianna could not. But still . . . she could not go alone.

Just then Broughton entered the room, and Julianna gave the order that her carriage was to brought round at once.

"At once?" the butler repeated, astonished.

Julianna regarded him. "Yes, Broughton," she said. "At once."

He shook his head as if that might clear his ears for him. "Are you—going out, Miss?" he asked cautiously, sure that his mistress would expect him to stop her daughter from this rash unchaperoned behavior, and wondering how she would expect him to do that, with Miss Julianna looking so determined.

Julianna lifted her chin. "I am," she said, hoping that her high tone would persuade him to do as she bade.

Broughton's voice cracked. "A-lone, Miss?"

Before Julianna could answer, Miss Marley spoke in her usual quiet voice. "No, Broughton. I am going with her."

"*You*, Miss?" The butler goggled at her, as did Julianna.

"Yes," Miss Marley said calmly. "So do hurry, please. We wish to be on our way immediately."

"Yes, Miss," he responded automatically and bowed,

leaving the room to shake his head all the way down the hall. He would probably be turned off without a character for this night's work, he told himself gloomily, even though a small part of his mind argued that Mrs. Cresston was a fairer mistress than that, and would know that he could not have gainsaid her daughter for fear the young lady would do something even more dangerous if the carriage were not at her disposal. But it was not what he was used to, not at all. . . .

Still shaking his head, he went out to astonish the coachman as he himself had been astonished.

Meanwhile, in the library, Julianna thanked Miss Marley profusely, while at the same time making it clear to her that she could not possibly go with her on what Miss Marley herself had pointed out was such an improper errand.

To all of Julianna's arguments, Beth turned a deaf ear. "Someone has to go with you," she said, looking at her friend with her big eyes. "It would not be proper for you to go alone."

Julianna smiled. "Thank you, my dear, and I appreciate the sentiment, but I hardly think that a child of seventeen can be considered a chaperon!"

"Well . . ." Beth thought deeply. "At least I can be your companion. As if your maid went with you."

Julianna shook her head. "But my dear, it is not the same at all."

Miss Marley's lovely young face wore a decidedly mulish expression. "I am going with you," she said, and again her tone reminded Julianna of her great-aunt's. "Or you are not going."

Julianna pointed out that Beth could hardly stop her. Beth yawned. Julianna said that it was her house and Beth was a guest in it. Beth thanked her. Exasperated, Julianna told her that she was growing more and more like the dowager duchess every day. Beth beamed.

"Godmama would say that I should go with you," she insisted.

"No," Julianna corrected her, "your godmama would

say that we should both be locked in our rooms on a diet of bread and water for even contemplating such a thing."

Miss Marley eyed her speculatively. "I won't tell if you don't," she offered. "Of course, if you don't take me with you, I might just forget that I didn't mean to mention it when your mother and the duchess return. . . ."

"Then I *would* be in the soup." Julianna eyed her with exasperation and new respect before smiling and shaking her head ruefully.

"Well, don't just sit there," she said, bringing a bright smile to Miss Marley's face. "Get your cloak. It's time to go."

❧ *Chapter 17* ❧

John Coachman was stiffly disapproving as the young ladies climbed into the carriage. His "Well, I'll be!" and tendency to argue upon being given their direction clearly told Julianna what he thought of their expedition. Not for the first time did she think wistfully of owning a house where the servants had not known one all one's life, and did not feel it incumbent to express their views each time they felt one was doing something wrong. Lucky for her that, when all was said and done—and there was, in John Coachman's opinion, a great deal to say—this particular servant was a follower, not a leader, and took her direction, even if he disapproved of it.

While they were clattering through the streets she was again assailed by the realization that she should not be leading Miss Marley down this path, and tried to make some of her feelings known to her companion.

"Fudge!" said Miss Marley in such a way as to make it clear that she had no plans to turn back now.

At the door to her cousin's lodgings Miss Cresston felt even more strongly that she should not have brought her companion along. They narrowly avoided being seen by a trio of tipsy young men in search of a carriage. As the ladies stood in the darkness by Jonathan's door, they could hear the men in the street arguing with John Coachman over the use of his vehicle. Secure in the knowledge that her Yorkshire coachman, who had a keen contempt for the London dandies, could deal with these three and others like him, Miss Cresston turned her attention to the moment when the door opened so she could hurry Miss Marley and herself inside and close the door behind them without their being seen by anyone.

Once that was accomplished, however, their path was blocked by an elderly man who stared at them, mouth agape, scratching his head as he breathed "Miss Julianna!" in accents even more shocked than those of Broughton and John Coachman.

"Good evening, Bigley," Julianna said with her most attractive smile, as if her arrival at her cousin's lodgings just as the clock struck midnight were not anything exceptional. "I've come to call on my cousin Jonathan, as you can see."

Bigley scratched his head harder and shook it slowly side to side. "But you can't!" he protested.

"Can't?" Julianna repeated, growing uneasy. "Oh no! Surely you don't mean he's not here?" The thought had not before occurred to her, and she stared at Bigley who stuttered.

"It isn't that the viscount isn't here," Bigley said, "it's just that—begging your pardon—he is—ah—indisposed. . . ."

"Indisposed?" Julianna repeated, staring at the man. "Oh, he cannot be ill! Is it serious? Has the doctor been sent for?" She moved toward the stairs, but Bigley was before her, this time rubbing his chin as if that might put the appropriate words into his mouth.

"Oh, no, Miss," he assured her, shaking his head. "The master ain't ill. He's just—just—" One look at the inquiring faces before him made him desperate, and when he was desperate, he was at even more of a loss for words.

Julianna, her mind racing, found enlightenment. "He's drunk!" she exclaimed. "That's it, isn't it, Bigley? He's drunk."

"As a wheelbarrow," corroborated the viscount's servant, grateful for her understanding. "So if you ladies would like to go away, and I'll tell the master you was to see him, and he should call upon you tomorrow—"

He made as if to show them to the door but neither young lady moved, Miss Cresston making it clear that she would *not* like to go away, she did not *plan* to go away, and she was there to see her cousin, drunk or sober.

"Oh, no, Miss!" Clearly Bigley was horrified. "'Twouldn't be proper!"

"I have seen my cousin a trifle above par before," she assured him, but the old retainer shook his head, great gloom descending upon him as he did. His expression caused the ladies to eye each other uneasily.

"Not like this you haven't, Miss," Bigley said with a sigh that Miss Marley thought might well break his heart. "Truth be told, neither have I."

He meant the words as a warning, and renewed his efforts to persuade the ladies to leave, but his deep concern only increased Julianna's. She told him firmly to stand aside, because she *was* going up to see her cousin, and to have conversation with him, if she had to drop a bucket of cold water on his head to sober him up enough to do so.

Bigley said pessimistically that it might well come to that, but let them pass. He said he would be up shortly with a mug of porter for the master, and shuffled off toward the kitchen. Julianna, meeting Miss Marley's questioning eyes, was moved to explain that Bigley had always been given to exaggeration, and pinned a smile on her lips as she marched up the stairs toward her cousin's sitting room.

Once there she knocked lightly, and then harder. When her third assault on the door drew no response, she opened it cautiously and peered in. Only the now dying fire in the grate and a single candle lit the scene, but there was enough light for Miss Cresston to note that the room was in considerable disarray. The dimness was so great that for a moment she had difficulty seeing her cousin, but the sound of gentle snoring drew her attention to the sofa. She advanced on him purposefully, advising Miss Marley to make up the fire and to light any candles she might find.

As Beth complied, Julianna shook her cousin's shoulder, crying, "Jonathan! Jonathan!" At first this interrupted his snores but did not awaken him. Disgusted, she removed her hat and used the plumes to tickle his nose, saying firmly, "Wake up, you idiot! I have to talk with you!"

Whether it was her words, or the violent sneezing the application of her feathers to his nose produced, her cousin was at length roused from his brandy-induced slumber. He sat up abruptly, clutched his head and fell back upon the pillows, staring up at her with an uncomprehending gaze and a "Hu—wha—?" She stepped back, satisfied that he was now among the living.

Gradually his gaze focused on her face, and the curious face of Miss Marley, standing just behind her. "What?" he sputtered, trying to sit up, and finding the feat such an effort that he sank back again. "You, Ju? Here? I must be dreaming!" He moved an arm and pinched himself experimentally to find out if that was true, then winced as he found he was indeed awake.

"No, Jonathan, you are not dreaming," his cousin assured him.

"Oh." Manfully, the viscount tried to think. "Entertaining, am I?" He glanced down at his rumpled shirt and the cravat that had gone sadly askew as he'd made serious inroads on his cellar. "Forgot. Would have changed, you know. Bad form to entertain in a dirty shirt—"

Suddenly it occurred to him that that could not be the case, and he eyed his cousin uneasily. "Can't be entertaining," he informed her. "Bachelor establishment. Wouldn't have asked you here." It occurred to him that he had no clear memory of just what he *had* done in the last eighteen hours, and he eyed her cautiously.

"*Didn't* ask you here, did I, Ju?" he asked, once more trying to sit up. By dint of taking his time he was able to do so with only a small moan as he transferred his feet to the floor, and leaned his forearms on his knees.

"No, you ridiculous boy, you didn't ask me here!" Julianna replied, brushing his hat and gloves from a chair so that she could pull it forward to sit close in front of him, and motioning Miss Marley to do the same with another chair. "I've come to talk with you."

"Oh." The viscount digested this, his eyes closing as if in great pain when the book Miss Marley was moving from a chair to the table fell from her hands. Beth's soft spoken apology made him open his eyes again, and stare at her.

"Didn't invite Miss Marley either, did I?" he asked cautiously. He was assured that he had not.

"Didn't think so." He said the words with satisfaction. "Bacon-brained, but not as bacon-brained as that." He drew himself up and regarded them both sternly. "Shouldn't be here. Have to go. Hate to be uncordial, but there it is."

"Oh, Jonathan," Julianna said, reaching for his hand, "will you sober up? I told you—"

She was interrupted by Bigley's slow entrance, a mug of porter in his hand. "Maybe this will help, Miss," he said, handing it to his master and watching with gloomy satisfaction as the viscount sipped the contents and frowned. "Not that it's going to make what has happened any better, him being sober." And with that melancholy pronouncement he took himself out of the room, sighing gustily.

Julianna watched him go, then turned back to her cousin. "That, Jonathan, is what I want to talk with you about."

"Huh?" The viscount struggled to understand. "You mean old Bigley? That's just his way, Ju, you know that. The man always looks like a tooth-drawer."

"No, no!" Julianna shook her head in disgust. "I don't want to talk about Bigley. I want to talk about whatever it is *he* is talking about—whatever it is that's wrong."

"Wrong?" The viscount took another swig of the porter, and as he came more fully awake he remembered what the brandy had for a time driven from his head. A cloak of tragedy seemed to settle upon his shoulders, and he looked dully at his cousin. "You heard, then?"

Julianna shook her head in perplexity. "No, Jonathan, I haven't heard. That's why I'm here. I've had a sense all day that something was wrong, but—"

"You don't know?" He was gazing at her in disbelief, and she shook her head. "Oh, Julianna, I can't tell you! It's too terrible! I wish I were dead!" He dropped his head into his hands and Julianna, who had never before seen him so disturbed, was seriously frightened. She hurriedly moved to sit beside him on the sofa, and put one arm around his shaking shoulders. For a moment she thought he might be ill, then realized that he was crying.

"Jonathan, my dear," she said gently, patting his back as if he were seven. "What is it? Nothing can be as bad as all this. If you just tell me we'll put our heads together and figure out a way...."

Her words trailed off as he raised haggard eyes to her face, and shook his head slowly. "It *is* that bad, Julianna," he whispered. "It's the worst. I've lost Bushy!"

❧ *Chapter 18* ❧

"*Lost*?" For a moment Julianna could only stare at him blankly, the full magnitude of what he said not penetrating her shocked mind. Miss Marley's startled gasp made her shake herself and lean toward her cousin again.

"Lost Bushy?" Miss Cresston echoed. "But, Jonathan, how?"

"At faro." He shook his head miserably, not looking at her. "Last night."

"But, Jonathan, you said you would not gamble anymore," Julianna began.

He turned toward her, anguished. "Don't you think I know that, Ju? I never meant to! But then, after I went

down to Bushy, and my bailiff told me of all that needed to
be done, I thought, if I could just manage one big win . . ."
His words drifted hopelessly away, and he stared unseeing at
the floor.

Julianna regarded him in horror. "I cannot believe that
you would wager Bushy," she began.

"Oh, no," he said wearily. "Not even *I* would do that.
But after I'd lost so heavily, I realized I have no other way
to pay than to sell Bushy and settle my debts. It is a matter
of honor, Julianna. You must understand that!"

"Honor?" she repeated, her eyes flashing. "How honorable is it for one man to take from another what has been in
his family for centuries? How honorable is it to fleece a boy
who—"

"I am not a boy, Julianna," her cousin said quietly, "and
I knew when I played that I ran the risk. It is no one's
responsibility but my own. I—" His voice cracked, and he
stared at the floor again. "I am the one to blame."

They sat in silence for several moments, the ladies
looking helplessly at one another, before Julianna ventured
another question. "Jonathan," she said quietly, "how much
have you lost?"

He bit his lip and looked away. "Seven thousand pounds."

She took a deep breath; it was a great deal. "I could lend
you—"

He turned on her almost savagely. "No," he shouted,
wincing at the pain the effort cost him. "No, you can't. I
may be beggarly, but not as beggarly as that. I will settle my
own debts!"

"Perhaps the gentleman you owe the money to would
wait," ventured Miss Marley. Julianna seconded the idea,
and both ladies gazed expectantly toward the viscount, who
groaned.

"You don't understand," he said, shaking his head. "I
can hardly ask Marleton to wait years until it is convenient
for me to pay—"

He stopped abruptly, for his words had a startling effect
on his audience. Both ladies turned white, and repeated
"Lord Marleton?" as one. Jonathan nodded.

"It was he who held the faro bank," he explained.

"Oh, no!" said Miss Marley.

"How could he?" countered Miss Cresston.

Jonathan stared at them in surprise. "What do you mean?" he asked.

"Marleton knows you are not plump in the pocket," Miss Cresston said, staring beyond him as if he weren't there. "How could he—oh, how *could* he let you play?"

"Come now, Julianna," the viscount said, clearly irritated. "How could he stop me? He could hardly forbid me the table."

"But he should have!" Julianna cried. "He knew—"

Jonathan cut her short. "It would have been unforgivable for him to do so. Besides"—he shrugged wearily—"I'd as lief lose to Marleton as to anyone."

"Oh, no," Miss Cresston said sadly. "If it had been anyone but—"

Jonathan was staring at her, clearly puzzled.

She pulled herself together to smile, albeit tremulously, at him. "Now, Jonathan," she said, "you must tell me everything that happened, and then we will put our heads together to see what can be done."

Jonathan did not believe anything could be done, but his head hurt dreadfully, and he knew that if he were to voice his belief his cousin would argue strenuously with him. Since strenuous argument was the thing he most disliked, he obligingly told them his tale. There was a horse named Faro running in a race the previous day, and Jonathan had backed it with a modest bet to win. The horse did. In fact, the mare paid off so handsomely that Jonathan *knew* that faro was to be his salvation, and he had taken his winnings that night to the popular club where the Earl of Marleton just happened to be the patron holding the bank when the viscount walked in. He had placed his first bet, and lost, but—

Julianna gaped at him. "You lost?"

He nodded.

"But . . ." she groped for words. "If you lost, why didn't you leave? Why throw good money after bad?"

Seriously, he informed her that a good gambler always

knows the luck is going to change, if he just stays the course. The ladies forebore to point out that staying the course had cost him seven thousand pounds, and he continued.

"It wasn't long before I was punting on tick," he said. Noticing Miss Marley's white and confused face, he kindly explained that it meant he'd been exchanging IOUs for the privilege of continuing. "I kept thinking that one good win . . . but then, Marleton had been like a caged panther ever since I came in, and at three A.M. he said he was closing the bank for the night, despite everyone's disgust at calling it such an early evening."

Miss Marley blinked and Julianna stared hard at him before saying, in a hollow voice, "You played until three in the morning, losing all the while?"

Her cousin nodded.

"And you would have gone *on* playing, had the earl not withdrawn?"

The viscount nodded again.

"Jonathan," she told him roundly, "you are a fool!"

Sadly he agreed, and sat silent.

With a heavy sigh she invited him to continue.

"Well," he said, "when I totaled up my vowels, I could scarcely believe it—seven thousand pounds, Ju! I wandered the streets for a long time, walked down to the river and considered throwing myself into the Thames, but . . . well . . ." He regarded her sheepishly. "You know what a good swimmer I am, Ju. I knew I couldn't even drown myself right. So I came home, intending to shoot myself, but Bigley said he couldn't find my dueling pistols, and while he was looking he brought me the bottle—no, several bottles of brandy, and—well . . ."

Julianna made a mental note to hand the old retainer a large gratuity as she sat, eyes fixed on her cousin's face. These plans to end his life frightened her, for while she believed that when he'd had time for reflection, he would be in no hurry to do so, she was afraid that in his highly overwrought state he might do himself an injury.

"Now, Jonathan," she said briskly, "this is foolish talk.

You wouldn't care to hurt your mother or me or any of your other relatives by—''

She had meant it well, but at mention of his mother, his face went white, and he stared at her in horror. "My mother," he muttered, his eyes widening. "What am I going to tell my *mother*? Oh, lord, Ju!" He once again dropped his head into his hands, his fingers causing further havoc among the already disarrayed curls there. "What am I going to *do*?"

The plaintive words vividly recalled her childhood playmate. Julianna patted his hand automatically while she cudgeled her brain for the answer to his question.

"What we must do," she said practically, "is think of a way out of this difficulty. I still think a loan. . . ." She raised her eyebrows inquiringly and the viscount, with real nobility, refrained from accepting what was becoming a most attractive offer.

"No, Julianna," he told her firmly, "I thank you, but it will not do. I have not yet sunk to taking money from the female members of my family. Unless . . ." He strove to lighten the situation with an old joke. "You wouldn't care to marry me, would you, Ju?"

A scheme forming in her head, Miss Cresston considerably startled the company by gazing at him for a long moment and then saying, in a remarkably firm voice far at odds with her inner qualms, "Yes, Jonathan. Yes, I would."

❧ *Chapter 19* ❧

Her companions' response to her acceptance of the viscount's proposal could hardly be called flattering. Both Miss Marley and Jonathan sat bolt upright. *"What?"* they cried,

making it apparent that they thought she had taken leave of
her senses.

Miss Cresston regarded them ruefully. "Thank you," she
said gently. "Jonathan—I am pleased to see that I have
made *you* so happy!"

Her cousin blushed. "Delighted, of course!" he said
hastily. "That is—never thought—that is—" He stared
doubtfully at her. "Feeling quite the thing, are you, Ju?"

"But, Julianna," Miss Marley all but wailed, interrupting
the viscount, "you cannot marry Jonathan! You are to
marry . . ." She met Miss Cresston's eyes, hesitated, and
lamely ended, "Someone else."

Miss Cresston's voice grew gentler still. "No, no,
Elizabeth!" she protested. "You quite overwhelm me with
your felicitations."

Miss Marley blushed. "Of course I wish you happy,
Julianna," she said. "It is just that . . ." She stared at the
viscount questioningly, and then returned her gaze to her
friend. "I mean—*Jonathan*!"

The viscount opened his mouth to agree, thought better of
it, and turned toward her suspiciously. "What do you
mean—*Jonathan*?"

For once Miss Marley was flustered out of her good
manners. "I mean," she told him forthrightly, "that you are
hardly the husband I would wish for my dear Miss Cresston.
She could do much, much better than you!"

Honesty forbade argument. He nodded. "She's right,
you know, Ju." He sat for a moment, regarding his cousin.
"Ju?" he repeated. "Ju?"

He had to call her name several times more, for Julianna
was not attending. Instead, her mind was rapidly working
out a plan whereby she could remove her cousin from London
long enough to give him time to realize that rash acts in-
volving such things as late night drownings in the River
Thames or personal accidents with dueling pistols would be as
ill-advised as they were unseemly, and that he must overcome
his tedious scruples and let her loan him the seven thousand
pounds, at a reasonable rate of interest. To that end she

had agreed to marry him, not for a moment meaning to go through with it. When he had had a few days to think . . .

She blinked and gazed complacently at her companions. "Jonathan," she said, "I will need your escort as my fiancé tomorrow. It is incumbent that I leave London for Northumberland."

Had the situation not been so desperate, Miss Cresston would have laughed at the bemused faces before her. Silence greeted her pronouncement and two pairs of eyes stared blankly at her until at last Jonathan spoke.

"Go to—Northumberland, Ju?" the viscount said. "Dashed out-of-the-way place to go! Why?"

She had foreseen the question and forestalled it by replying that just that day she'd received a notice from the bailiff of her Northumberland estate concerning a problem he felt she should look into immediately.

"You did?" Miss Marley questioned, surprised.

Julianna said that she had forgotten to mention it in the press of the day's activities.

Jonathan was watching her suspiciously. "A journey to Northumberland is hardly something one forgets, Ju," he said. "What are you really up to?"

Julianna clung to her story tenaciously, adding with downcast eyes that if he did not care to escort her . . .

No, no; ever chivalrous, Jonathan said that he would of course go, since she couldn't go alone, except that . . .

Miss Cresston eyed him expectantly.

"Well, dash it, Ju, people will think we're eloping, if we just ride north like that!"

Julianna, who had not thought of that, and who wanted it to be the last thing people thought, was almost at a standstill. Seeing his advantage, the viscount pressed on.

"Besides that," he said, watching her, "what about Miss Marley? What's she to do? Can't leave her in your house all alone, your mother and Great-Aunt Elizabeth having nipped off to Bath. Although why anyone would want to go to Bath—tasted the waters there myself once, you know, Ju. It's enough to make you sick if you aren't already!"

Miss Marley giggled at his indignant face, and Julianna looked at her thoughtfully.

"I am sorry, Beth," she said, "but I do believe Jonathan is right." The viscount sat back, glad she'd seen reason. Her last words made him move forward again. "You must come to Northumberland with us."

"Dash it, Ju!" Jonathan said, rising to take a quick walk around the room, despite his pounding head. "The girl don't want to go to Northumberland. Nobody wants to go to Northumberland who doesn't have to! Tell you what— we'll pop over to Bath, see your mother and Great-Aunt Elizabeth—"

"But, Jonathan," Julianna reminded him sweetly, "you do not like Bath."

"Like it a dashed sight better than Northumberland," he told her frankly. "Think of Miss Marley."

Miss Marley said she would accompany her dear Miss Cresston anywhere. The beleaguered viscount glared at her. "You'll miss that masquerade you've set your heart on," he reminded her.

Miss Cresston squirmed guiltily. "Oh, dear," she said, "I'm afraid he is right, for I doubt we will return in time for the Hearthingdons' ball, Beth. If you like, I will see if you may stay with Aunt Sephrinia. Except that would mean telling her I am going out of town with Jonathan, and then the cat *would* be out of the bag."

Miss Marley said there was no reason to involve the Lady Sephrinia; she had no intention of being left behind.

"Mad, both of you," Jonathan pronounced gloomily, sinking once more down upon the sofa.

Julianna raised pious eyes skyward. "*We* are not the ones who trusted our luck to a stupid horse, taking the name 'Faro' to be a sign . . ."

"But the nag won," the viscount protested weakly.

His cousin glared at him. "Did you?"

The question was so unanswerable that he shrugged an impatient shoulder and asked her what time she wished to leave on the morrow. Since it already *was* the morrow, Miss Cresston hesitated, saying they would need to pack and

Jonathan would need time to set his affairs in order, visit the earl to tell him that the viscount was called out of town for several days, but his money was shortly forthcoming; to hire a post chaise—

"A post chaise?" Jonathan questioned. "Why should I hire a post chaise when you have a perfectly good carriage?"

"Because," she explained patiently, "if my mother were to return while we're gone, I would not so want to inconvenience her by having taken the carriage away. And you had best hire a driver too, unless you wish to drive us yourself."

It did occur to Jonathan, as it obviously had not to his cousin, that if people were to hear that they had driven north in a hired post chaise they would *certainly* think an elopement in progress, but since he and Julianna were to be married anyway . . .

Married! He dropped his head into his hands and again he groaned. Misunderstanding, Miss Cresston said kindly that they had kept him long enough and would be off. A considerably more sober Jonathan accompanied them down the stairs and out to where John Coachman sat glaring balefully at him. Although the coachman didn't know it, he could think no more harshly of the viscount than the viscount now thought of himself.

Miss Cresston would have preferred to leave early in the morning, but that was not to be. Jonathan's good Bigley had a terrible time rousing his noble employer at dawn as he'd been instructed to do, and once the viscount was awake, he showed no disposition to arise, merely lying in his bed staring at the curtains for some time before asking quite cautiously, "I say, Bigley, was my cousin Julianna here last night?"

Bigley, in the middle of laying out the viscount's raiment for the day, turned and nodded. "Yes, sir. She was."

Jonathan nodded glumly. "Thought so."

There was another silence. Bigley readied his master's shaving gear as the viscount turned his bleary eyes to watch him.

"I say, Bigley—" he began again. "Did I commit myself

to accompanying my cousin to—to—" He seemed to find it difficult to say the place.

Bigley obligingly supplied it for him. "To Northumberland, my lord," the servant said with a slight smile. "Miss Julianna certainly said you did."

"Hmmmm." The viscount sat wearily up on one elbow, and shook his head slowly, wincing at the pain that small movement caused. "And did I—Bigley, do you happen to know—did I—propose—to my cousin Julianna, last night?"

That, Bigley said primly, he could not say; however, if it were indeed so, and if the lady had been so obliging as to accept his lordship, might he offer his warmest congratulations. . . .

His lordship nodded drearily as he climbed out of bed, and accepted the congratulations with the same enthusiasm he might have shown for a walk to the guillotine.

"I make you a vow, Bigley," the viscount said, yielding himself up to his manservant's tender ministrations and closing his eyes against the sun, which streamed heartlessly through his windows, "I will never touch brandy again."

"Very good, sir," said Bigley, too polite to add he would believe it when he saw it. He then set himself to the not inconsiderable task of readying the young viscount to face the day.

So it was that the viscount arrived at Julianna's home in Grosvenor Square just a little past one in the afternoon, having spent the better part of the morning in hiring a post chaise and getting his affairs in order. To that end he had visited the Earl of Marleton, only to find that his lordship was not at home. Jonathan then asked the earl's butler if he might leave a note for his master, and the butler furnished him with paper and pen and invited him to be seated at his lordship's writing table, to compose his note.

Jonathan, for whom writing had always been a struggle, inscribed a few lines which he read and frowned over, trying to think of something better. After a few moments he gave up, sanded the sheet, folded it, and handed it to the butler with a request that it be given to the earl the moment he returned. Nodding loftily, the butler showed the viscount out and set the note on the hall table.

Feeling he had discharged his duty, the viscount returned home to collect his bags. Bigley, who had expected to accompany his master, was considerably shocked to learn that he was not to go along, and his sensibilities were wounded when Jonathan pointed out that he could hardly afford to hire one post chaise, and he'd be dashed if he was going to hire two to carry along his valet or Miss Cresston's maid.

That thought so galvanized him that he set off for Grosvenor Square immediately, where he was considerably relieved to find that Miss Cresston had no intention of taking either her own or Miss Marley's maid, since she desired to keep the purpose of the trip a secret.

Jane Robson, who had been Miss Cresston's maid since that young lady first emerged from the schoolroom, could not believe that she was to be left behind, and had a great deal to say about her mistress's queer start and this perceived necessity of going off without her.

"Come now, Jane," Julianna coaxed as Jane reluctantly packed her bags, "surely you don't think I can't dress myself without you!"

Jane did harbor that belief but was much too polite to say so, so she merely folded her lips together and sniffed. "I'm sure it's not for me to say, Miss," she began, ignoring Julianna's gentle agreement that it was not. "But what your mother will say when she finds out . . ."

Julianna did not at that moment want to think about what her mother might say about this latest plan, and bethought herself of something that needed doing in the book room, merely directing Jane to have the footman carry the trunk and valise downstairs as soon as she finished packing.

The truth was, Julianna was suffering second thoughts. While her motives were pure, and she was sure her mother would agree with her that Jonathan must be helped out of this serious trouble into which he had pitchforked himself, she was not so sure that Mrs. Cresston wouldn't be a bit appalled to learn that she had left town—with only her cousin and young Beth—for an indefinite stay. Julianna did not know how long it would take her to talk Jonathan out of his ridiculous idea of selling Bushy. She was also pretty certain that if Mrs. Cresston returned to London while she was gone, she would have no real idea why her daughter had left for the estate in Northumberland.

She decided to write her mother a note, but when she sat at the writing table she found, as Jonathan had done at the Earl of Marleton's, that words did not come as easily as she'd hoped. Finally she wrote:

> "Dearest Mother,
> Jonathan has gotten himself into a terrible coil, and I am determined to get him out of it. That requires going north for a bit, but we shall return directly and Make All Known to you. Miss Marley goes with us—she is a Dear Girl, as you know, and Jonathan thinks her quite the Best of the young ladies of his acquaintance. So perhaps it will not be so Terrible after all."

Scratching her signature at the bottom, she prayed devoutly that Cousin Mathilde in Bath would not pick this, of all times, to effect a miraculous recovery, and went out to see if Miss Marley had also finished her packing. With any luck at all, she thought optimistically, she would be back before her mother even knew she was gone. What she did not stop to consider was that luck and her cousin were, at the moment, quite out.

❧ Chapter 20 ❧

Julianna breathed a sigh of relief when the post chaise pulled away from her town house and the disapproving faces of her maid and butler disappeared from view. She and Beth had the coach to themselves; Jonathan had elected to ride his horse, saying he did not care to be cooped up in a stuffy carriage with two females. His cousin thoughtfully forebore to point out that one of those females was his fiancée.

As the carriage made its way through London, she leaned back against the cushions and gazed unseeing out the window. The events of the last few days passed through her mind, and several times the Earl of Marleton's face—for once devoid of the mocking expression she was used to seeing—rose before her eyes.

At Almack's, the last time she had seen him, he had said to her, "There are two sides to every story, Miss Cresston. Please remember that."

She could not imagine what other story could be told about taking a foolish young man's home away from him, but if the earl wished to try to explain it...

Resolutely she shook herself. "There can be no explanation," she said firmly.

"I beg your pardon?"

Startled, Julianna turned to find Miss Marley's eyes on her. She felt her color rise. "Oh, I was just thinking that—that there can be no explanation for this badly sprung chaise they've sent us off in!"

The statement was true; as they'd left the city and reached open spaces, the horses had quickened their pace, and the poor condition of the carriage caused the ladies to be jostled by each bump in the road.

"I've never so much missed my own carriage as now, I can assure you!" Julianna said.

Miss Marley agreed that one's own carriage must, of course, be so much more comfortable, in a weak voice that made Julianna stare closely at her. In the time since they'd left London, Beth's complexion had taken on a chalklike color that was growing more pronounced by the minute.

"My dear Beth!" Julianna cried. "Whatever is the matter?"

Beth pressed her handkerchief to her lips, and tried bravely to smile. "I fear—that the carriage movement

is—is . . ." It was apparent what the motion was doing, and
a startled Julianna put her head out the window and sharply
commanded the driver to pull up.

Considerably mystified but obedient, he did so.

Jonathan, who had ridden ahead of the coach to get out of
its dust, came galloping back and demanded to know what
they meant by stopping just as Julianna solicitiously helped
her friend down. Julianna glared at him and Beth murmured
disjointedly, "So sorry—so silly of me—don't mean to be
such a bother . . ."

Julianna replied soothingly to each utterance and suggested
that perhaps if they strolled around a bit, Miss Marley might
feel better.

"Oh, yes," Beth said gratefully, leaning slightly on her
companion as they started a slow walk around the carriage.
"That always helps. Thank you!"

Jonathan, who by this time had assimilated the fact that
Miss Marley did not look to be in very good point, dismounted
to help. The three of them walked around the carriage
several times.

"It seems," Julianna said, sending her cousin a stern
message with her eyes, "that the movement of the carriage
has made Miss Marley ill."

Jonathan stared at her in stunned surprise. *"What?"* he
demanded. One thought rose uppermost in his mind. "But—
but—we're going all the way to *Northumberland!"*

The justice of his dismay was not lost on Julianna, who
had been so concerned for her young friend's present
discomfort that she had not thought of the coming conse-
quences of the malady. She bit her lip as they made several
more trips around the carriage, each time picking up the
pace. Julianna and Jonathan were lost in thought as Miss
Marley, supported between them, tried several times to get
their attention.

"You know what I think?" Jonathan said suddenly, as
they started around the carriage for the ninth time.

"No, no," Julianna interrupted. "What *I* think is—"

"Please!" The desperate note in Elizabeth's voice made
them both look down at her in surprise as she gave a mighty

tug and freed her arms. "What *I* think—no, what I *know*— is that if you do not wish me to be unwell immediately, we had better walk the other way around this blasted carriage!"

"Oh." Both Miss Cresston and the viscount stopped abruptly. "Of course."

"I do believe, Julianna," Jonathan said, patting Elizabeth's shoulder kindly as he explained for his cousin's benefit, "that we made Miss Marley dizzy."

"You," his cousin returned tartly, "have that effect on people."

Jonathan puzzled over that while Miss Marley slowly regained her color, and Julianna pondered what they were now to do.

Meanwhile, as Jonathan escorted two ladies around and around a post chaise on the king's road, the Earl of Marleton approached the young viscount's lodgings with every appearance of a man about to have a tooth drawn. After several hours at his club and a spot of boxing at Jackson's, he had convinced himself that a private talk with Bushnell was, if not wanted, certainly needed.

The earl had spent considerable time seeking a solution to the problem he believed the viscount presented him with, for while he did not want or need the young man's money, he had won it in fair play and there was the matter of honor to contend with. A sticky thing, honor, and the viscount was a proud young man. That was apparent in the way he'd carried himself out of the room that night after his loss, when those who knew his circumstances—of which, the earl hoped, there were mercifully few—also knew that he would much rather have been swallowed up by the floor and forgotten.

It was a new turn for the earl, this awareness of and sensitivity to another's situation. There had been many nights in his past when he had won larger amounts from young men in straits even more dire than the viscount's, and thought nothing of it. But none of those young men displayed a pair of fine green eyes so remarkably like . . .

No, he told himself firmly, that was not the tack to take.

The viscount had been kind to Miss Marley; he appreciated that. The fact that he was a favorite of Miss Cresston's might also weigh with the earl, who did not wish to be on bad terms with Miss Cresston, but . . . .

He raised one hand to knock on the viscount's door, but before he could the door opened and a servant with a basket over his arm emerged. Bigley stared at the earl in some surprise, but upon hearing the gentleman's polite request that his master be informed that the Earl of Marleton wished a few moments of his time, answered civilly that the viscount was away.

Marleton, frowning deeply, asked when the viscount might return.

"That I cannot say, my lord," Bigley answered.

"I see." The earl eyed him questioningly. "Odd, he'd go off like that, when he had promised to call on me tomorrow."

"As to that, I cannot say, either, my lord," Bigley replied, "although I do believe my master visited your home this morning."

"Oh, he did, did he?" The earl eyed Bigley with misgivings; it was apparent he knew more than he was saying. "And to what end, pray?"

Bigley bowed slightly. "I would imagine, my lord, that he wished to speak with you."

"Ahhh." The earl, realizing he should have seen that coming, rubbed his chin and smiled slightly. "And what about, I wonder?"

Bigley bowed again. "As to that, my lord—"

"You really cannot say." The earl finished the sentence for him, and Bigley nodded.

Baffled, the earl returned to his house to learn what his servants could tell him about the viscount's visit. His estimable butler was away, but a footman pointed out the note on the hall table. The earl took it into the library and poured himself a glass of sherry before breaking the seal and sinking down into his favorite leather chair to read:

My Lord,
I beg to inform you that I have had to leave London

*unexpectedly to oblige my betrothed. I had hoped to
find you at home to assure you that I will soon meet
my obligation to you. I regret that I cannot meet you
tomorrow as planned, but be assured that the debt will
be paid the day after I return to London. I cannot at this
time say when that will be, for we journey north, but I
have hopes that our trip will not be protracted. Regret-
ting any inconvenience this might cost you, I remain
your servant,*

> *Bushnell*

The earl read the note, then read it again, thinking idly
that he had not known Bushnell was engaged; in fact, he
would not have considered the young chub to be all that
interested in marriage. The only women Marleton could
remember seeing him with more than once were Miss
Cresston and Elizab—

The earl set his glass down with a thump, and frowned
heavily at the letter. Suddenly the viscount's affairs interested him mightily. Shouting for his footman, he ordered that
his horse be saddled and brought round in fifteen minutes,
then went purposefully up the stairs to change.

The outcome of the earl's visit to Miss Cresston's home
was not happy. Neither Miss Marley nor Miss Cresston was
at home, Broughton told the earl loftily, and when Marleton
inquired where they had gone and when they might return,
the reply was one he was growing quite tired of.

"Really, my lord," Broughton replied, his upper lip
lengthening, "I cannot say."

"Are you telling me that your mistress has gone out of
town and you don't know when to expect her again?" the
earl demanded.

Broughton remarked austerely that it was not for him to
expect Miss Cresston; the earl pounced on his answer.

"Ah," Marleton said, "so you admit that she has gone
out of town?"

Broughton neither admitted nor denied; he simply folded
his lips together and stared woodenly ahead. He would have

shut the door except for the earl's forethought in placing his foot across the doorsill.

"Well, then," Marleton asked, "can you tell me if Miss Cresston and Miss Marley are together?"

Broughton thought, and decided that he could.

"And Miss Cresston's cousin—Viscount Bushnell—is with them?" the earl continued. Broughton allowed that he believed that was true.

"I received a note from the viscount that he was journeying north," Marleton said, watching the butler closely. Broughton inclined his head as if politely interested, and said that he really could not say. Silently the earl swore; aloud he said, "If you're ever turned off by the Cresston ladies, come see me. I like a man who can keep his tongue between his teeth."

Broughton bowed and asked that the earl remove his foot from the door. The earl countered that he would like to step in for a moment to leave a note for Miss Cresston and Miss Marley. Broughton hesitated. The earl was a frequent visitor to the house, and Mrs. Cresston and Miss Marley—as well as Cresston's Great-Aunt Elizabeth, of whom Broughton stood in considerable awe—seemed to look on him with favor, but Miss Julianna . . .

Still . . .

With a shrug Broughton decided that allowing the earl to leave a note could not be construed as dereliction of duty, and majestically he held the door open to allow Marleton to enter. "If you would be so good as to follow me, my lord," he said with a stately bow. After ushering the earl into the library and seeing that he had pen, paper and ink, he withdrew with a promise to send in a glass of the ladies' best wine. The earl thanked him but said no, he would only be a moment, and Broughton wasn't to bother.

The earl had settled down and written two lines when the note Miss Cresston had penned to her mother and placed on the mantelpiece caught his eye. Not bothered that it was not addressed to him, he broke the wafer and scanned the contents quickly, his face growing more grim with each word.

"*So perhaps it will not be so Terrible after all,*" he read, then reread it. "*Miss Marley goes with us—she is a Dear Girl . . . Jonathan thinks her quite the Best of the young ladies of his acquaintance.*"

Suddenly he saw Bushnell's note before his eyes. "*I had to leave London unexpectedly . . . my betrothed . . .*"

The earl swore softly. Suddenly it was so clear to him; the viscount was carrying Beth to Gretna Green to relieve his financial difficulties. Everyone knew she brought a considerable dowry with her; Marleton had circulated that rumor himself, at the dowager duchess's request. The trip north. "*Quite the best of his acquaintances.*" Elizabeth liked Bushnell; the earl could picture her laughing with the young viscount as they rode, or danced together. He couldn't believe she'd elope, however, so maybe she didn't know; maybe the viscount hadn't told her the real reason for the trip . . .

Only briefly did he wonder what Miss Cresston's role in the elopement was; engaged couples rushing to Scotland to be married over the anvil seldom carried a third person along for company. So, if she were along—it must be her fault. Her idea.

Her idea! That managing, headstrong, irritating . . . out to save her cousin, regardless of the cost to others! Beth probably thought she was only accompanying the other two!

The earl ground his teeth and thought of the many words he would have to say to Miss Cresston as soon as he caught up with the trio. He could hardly wait.

❧ Chapter 21 ❧

Miss Marley was persuaded to reenter the post chaise after Julianna promised that they would proceed at a much more decorous pace and would stop frequently so that Elizabeth could take short walks to regain her equilibrium. To the viscount's expostulations that it would take them *ages* to get to Northumberland at that rate Miss Cresston turned a deaf ear, and his grumblings were cut short only when Miss Marley raised melting eyes to his and said that she would *try* not to be so very sick.

A good-hearted young man, he patted her awkwardly on the shoulder and said that it did not matter; they would see more of the country that way, and he was a beast to make her unhappy, which hadn't been his meaning at all.

"Oh, I know," Miss Marley said, favoring him with her sweet smile. "I don't believe you would ever willingly hurt anyone, would you?"

With that she stepped into the carriage, followed immediately by Julianna, who was working hard to suppress a grin at the suddenly arrested look on her cousin's face. Not for a long time—perhaps never—had a young lady given him such a heroic picture of himself, and she could tell that it pleased him. A considerably mollified Jonathan mounted his horse and gave the coachman the direction to start—but at a much slower pace, mind!

The coachman, who thought disparagingly of the pace, but who realized he was being well paid to maintain it, shrugged philosophically and settled himself more comfortably on the seat, where he was soon half-asleep.

Inside the carriage, Julianna eyed her companion with both sympathy and vexation. "My dear Beth," she asked finally, unable to refrain, "why didn't you tell me that long rides in a carriage make you so ill?"

"I hoped it wouldn't be so bad," Miss Marley said softly. "I thought perhaps I had outgrown the illness. You're not to worry about me. I'll just fix my mind on being well . . ."

The words were uttered bravely, but it was apparent that Miss Marley's mind would not be able to conquer this matter, and Julianna sighed.

"You know, my dear, if you had told me, I would have made other plans for you. Not for the world would I wish you to be ill all the way to Northumberland. You must know that!''

"Yes, I do," Elizabeth said, fixing her earnest gaze on Julianna's face, and disarming her completely with her next words, "but I thought it my duty to come with you, Julianna, as your companion and—chaperon! I know you think I'm too young, but you've done so much for me, I couldn't let you go off in this ill-advised way with only Jonathan. Not for the world would I have you go alone! After all''—and here she shook her head wisely—''Jonathan is not very *wise*, you know. And if you were to fall into any scrapes, he is not the best person to get you out of them, I think.''

Torn between her friend's touching gratitude and concern, and the conviction that she did not like her plans described as "ill-advised," Julianna compromised by agreeing that Jonathan was not very wise. She forebore to point out that a young damsel of seventeen summers might also fall into that category, and hoped devoutly that there would be no scrapes from which she would need to rescue not only herself, but her two would-be protectors, as well.

Such was not to be the case.

Their slow pace kept them on the road much later than Julianna would have liked, for she had hoped that two hours earlier they'd all be settled into a very good inn she'd once heard Lord Wafton recommend. Darkness had fallen around them an hour before, and from time to time she could see Jonathan's form by the light of the half-moon as he rode beside the chaise. She was just wishing that she'd thought of bringing her own horse, when a loud crack rent the air, followed immediately by another as the sound of pounding hooves approached the carriage.

Jonathan's quick cry, and a shout from the coachman, roused from his abstracted contemplation of the landscape by the sight of three masked and heavily armed men galloping down on him, made Julianna and her companion exchange startled glances.

"Highwaymen!" Miss Marley gasped, her face pale in the shaft of light that filtered in the chaise's windows.

"Oh, surely not!" Miss Cresston replied, only to be proved wrong when Jonathan raced close to the carriage window, firing one pistol at the approaching men and thrusting a second pistol through the window into Julianna's hands.

"Don't fire if you don't have to," he told her hurriedly, keeping one eye on the riders, "but just in case—"

He veered off to come to blows with a man now hard upon him, cudgel in hand. Julianna, watching aghast from the carriage which had stopped, saw Jonathan fighting grimly to ward off the man's assault. All at once one of the rogue's companions approached from the side and fired at the viscount. Jonathan went down; at the same moment Julianna's pistol sounded, and the thief who had shot her cousin sagged heavily in his saddle.

"I'm hit!" cried the injured man.

His companion, holding the cudgel, looked in panic toward the chaise and called to the third highwayman: "Slope off, slope off—there's another cove in the carriage and he's shot old Jem!"

It took no further encouragement for the two to turn and ride hurriedly away. "Old Jem" alternately shouted pleas that they wait for him, and called down curses upon their heads because they did not do so.

Meanwhile, the "cove" in the carriage scrambled out of the vehicle and stood, shaking slightly as she stared at her injured cousin, who lay unmoving on the ground. "Here," she said, thrusting the pistol into Miss Marley's hands. Beth laid the gun gingerly on the coach seat and got out to stand beside Julianna, her eyes large.

"Is he—is he—" Miss Marley whispered, but could not bring herself to complete the sentence.

"Of course not!" Julianna answered sharply. "He's just—just—"

"Ah." The coachman above them sighed heavily. "A brave young man, he was. So sad to see him cut down in the very bloom of youth."

"Stop that!" Julianna ordered, glaring at him. "He's not—not—"

The coachman eyed the viscount in gloomy satisfaction. "Looks it," he offered.

"Well, he's not! Now climb down and give me a hand!" Julianna stepped forward to kneel beside her cousin, and as she turned him gently she was greatly relieved to hear him groan.

"Well, I'll be gormed!" exclaimed the coachman from his perch, then flushed at Julianna's irate expression. "Beggin' your pardon, Miss. I thought for sure the young gentleman had stuck his spoon in the wall."

"*Will* you stop jawing and climb down here and give me a hand?" Julianna demanded.

There was a fierceness in her tone that made him think it best to do so—and quickly.

"He's bleeding quite badly," Julianna said. "If I could only see—" She looked up and ordered the coachman to bring the lattern from the chaise; obligingly he did so, and knelt beside her so that he, too, might examine Jonathan's wound.

"Ahh," he said, his head shaking slowly, "it's bad." The thought seemed to afford him satisfaction, and Julianna glared at him.

"I don't believe the bullet struck any vital organ," she said, her fingers exploring the site of blood, "but it seems to be lodged in his shoulder, and he's losing so much blood—"

"Like as not, he'll die," her Job's Comforter announced.

"He will not!" Julianna snapped the words and told Miss Marley to hurry back to the carriage and find something for a bandage to bind up her cousin's shoulder. At that moment Jonathan opened his eyes, and stared blearily up at her.

"Ju?" he muttered, as if his sight deceived him.

"Yes," she returned, patting his hand comfortingly. "Don't try to talk."

"Eh?" Jonathan thought deeply. "Why not?"

"Because you're wounded," she replied, waiting for Elizabeth's return. "You should conserve your strength."

"Oh." The viscount thought again. "Dashed glad to hear it—thought I was quite cast away . . ." The full import of her words hit him, and he tried to sit up, only to fall heavily back into her lap. *"Wounded?"* Memory returned. "Oh yes—highwaymen—shot me, did they?"

He appeared not so much disturbed as interested, and Miss Cresston restrained a strong impulse to slap him.

"Oh, yes, my lord," Miss Marley told him. She had returned with a petticoat, which Julianna hurriedly tore into strips. "And Miss Cresston shot the one who shot you, and they all rode off, but you must lie very still now, for you're bleeding dreadfully."

The viscount looked down at his soiled shirt and jacket, and agreed. "Lord, yes," he said. "Bleeding like a stuck pig!" His interested gaze returned to his cousin's face. "Shot him, did you?" he said with satisfaction. "Glad to hear it!" He looked again at Miss Marley for approval. "It was I who taught her to shoot, you know!"

"And a very good thing it was, my lord," Miss Marley agreed warmly. She reached out to hold the thick pad Miss Cresston had just finished putting in place so a strip of fabric could be wrapped around it to hold it securely.

"I'm proud of you, Ju," the viscount said, gazing at her.

"Oh, devil take pride!" Miss Cresston replied, exasperated. *"Will* you hold still and be quiet?"

Both Miss Marley and the viscount stared at her with some astonishment, but it was the viscount who replied. "Why, Ju," he said, grinning weakly, "I think you're worried about me. Never fear, my dear—I'll do!"

Before she could respond, he fainted away again. Above him Julianna said grimly, "You can wager you will do, Jonathan, Viscount Bushnell, because I'll see to it! You're not getting out of scaring me to death this easily!"

And with those words which, the coachman later related to his bosom-bows over a tankard of heavy wet, fair had him gormed, she, the coachman, and Miss Marley carried the unconscious peer to the carriage. A moment later Miss Cresston stuck her head out the coach window to order the coachman to "spring 'em!"

❧ *Chapter 22* ❧

The Earl of Marleton arrived at the Black Swan within an hour and a half of Miss Cresston's party. It was not the sort of establishment the earl normally frequented, and he would not have thought of looking for the runaways there had he not seen a post chaise lodged at an angle in the ditch hard by the short lane leading into the establishment.

Marleton's eyes were hard as he strode into the inn shouting "Innkeeper! House!"

His already exacerbated temper had not been improved when no ostler appeared to take his horse, and he'd had to leave the animal tied to a post in front of the inn. Now it did not help that it was several minutes before the landlord came in answer to his call, so distracted that he could hardly tell if he were on his head or his heels, and only able to answer the earl's questions haphazardly.

Yes, his lordship was right, there had been an accident, right outside his establishment. But if that wasn't bad enough, there'd been another, more serious accident—well, no accident it was, and what was the world coming to when highwaymen could attack coaches carrying innocent ladies—

"Highwaymen?" the earl interrupted sharply, his eyes narrowing.

Yes, that they were, the innkeeper corroborated, or that's what the coachman said, if you could believe him, who was even now in the taproom taking something for his nerves—although if you asked the innkeeper, which he realized his lordship hadn't, but still, if he had, it was the lady who needed something for her nerves—not that she'd asked for

or taken anything, not a jot, when there she stood, all
covered in blood—

"*Blood?*" repeated his lordship, more sharply still. The
landlord nodded in satisfaction. Never before had he had
such an attentive audience.

"Aye, blood." He recalled the scene with relish. "There
was blood everywhere. And the young lady who had to be
carried up to my best bedchamber was white as a sheet and
all unconscious—"

"Young lady?" This time the earl's sharp tone was
accompanied by a heavy hand on the landlord's shoulder,
and the innkeeper gaped at him in surprise. "Where? *Where
is she?*"

"Upstairs, my lord—" the landlord began, but got no
further. His audience had left him and was taking the stairs
two at a time in search of Miss Marley. When he reached
the top of the stairs the earl suffered a slight check, for there
were two doors there. After a moment's hesitation he
opened the one to the right and walked into a low-pitched
room lit by a fire in the fireplace and several candles that
cast a wavering glow over the victim in the quilt-covered
bed—and Miss Cresston.

She turned expectantly at his entrance, but the welcoming
light in her eyes was replaced by one of blank astonishment
as she stared up at him. "You!" she gasped.

"Yes, Miss Cresston," the earl agreed as he walked
farther into the room, seeming to shrink its size by his
presence. "It is I." He approached the bed and stared down
at its occupant for several moments, before turning to
Julianna with a dangerously affable tone. "And I am looking
for Miss Marley."

"For Elizabeth?" Julianna continued to stare at him
blankly. "She's in the other—" A quick thought struck her,
and her blank look turned to one of suspicion. "Why?"

"Because, Miss Cresston," the earl said, his never easily
controlled temper slipping its leash again, "I will not let her
be sacrificed on the altar of your cousin's improvident
behavior."

Julianna stared at him blankly again. "Sacrificed?" she repeated.

Nettled, he congratulated her on her ability as an actress. "One would almost think you hadn't planned this wild elopement to the border so that your cousin might marry an heiress," he said. "Once I thought you a young woman of principle, if not of impeccable judgment, Miss Cresston, but now—give me leave to tell you that you are a—a—"

What she was remained unuttered. Miss Marley, who had been lying on the bed in the other chamber and who had recovered enough to rouse herself to see how the viscount and Miss Cresston did, peeked into the room. At sight of the Earl of Marleton, all hesitancy left her, and she ran forward to throw her arms around his neck, all the time crying, "Uncle Richard! Uncle Richard!"

"Uncle—" Julianna repeated, dumbfounded, feeling as if the room had taken a decided list. She put one hand to her head and sank into a chair.

The earl, looking up from where he had buried his head in Miss Marley's hair, kept his niece within the circle of his arms and smiled his usual mocking smile.

"Yes, Miss Cresston," he said in that odiously soft voice Julianna was coming to hate, "*Uncle* Richard. Elizabeth is not without relatives who will do whatever possible to prevent such an improvident match. And you should know, Miss Cresston, that what is possible for me is a great deal."

By this time Elizabeth had pulled back to gaze up into her uncle's face, and was regarding him with some confusion. "But, Richard," she protested. "What do you mean? What improvident match?"

The earl looked down at her and smiled. "There, there, child, don't worry. We'll find you another, more worthy young man to whom you can give your hand and heart. You must believe me, Elizabeth, no gentleman worth having would ask you to make this flight to the border to wed—"

"What?" His niece was staring at him in such honest puzzlement that he raised his eyes to Miss Cresston's face. That lady, standing as if she were stuffed, also was staring at him in amazement.

"What's this?" his lordship asked, glancing from one to
the other. He glared at Julianna again. "You didn't tell her,
did you? You and this—this—" He indicated the unconscious Jonathan in the bed. "You lured her away without
telling her of your plans. I *knew* she would not—"

"Telling me what?" Miss Marley interrupted, letting go
of his hand to place herself between the earl and Julianna.

"I have it on good authority, my dear—from the viscount
himself—that he is about to be wed—"

"Oh, yes." Miss Marley nodded. "Jonathan and Julianna
are recently engaged."

"What?" Now it was the earl's turn to stand as if stuffed;
the enormity of his mistake struck him and he looked at
once at Julianna. "Miss Cresston—I apologize—I thought—I
thought—"

"No, my lord," Julianna answered coldly. She stepped
from behind the bed and glared at him. "You did not think.
Because if you had, you could not have imagined even for
one moment that I—or my cousin—would do such a despicable, cruel—oh!" She raised her hand as if to strike him,
then let it drop again.

As more light fell on her, the earl made a startling
discovery. "My dear girl," he said, "you're covered in
blood!"

Miss Cresston looked down at her crimson-stained traveling gown, then up again into his eyes. "Yes, my lord,"
she said, "I am. And I can only wish that it was yours!"

The earl understood perfectly the justice of her remark,
but Miss Marley could not allow it to pass. Eyeing her
friend reproachfully, she said it was too bad of Julianna,
when the earl had come to help.

That thought made her gaze trustingly up at her uncle
again. "But how did you know we were in such difficulties?" she asked.

Hastily he told her that it was a sixth sense. Provoked by
a most unladylike snort from Miss Cresston, he added that it
was also an awareness of the company his niece kept.

"Of all the—" Miss Cresston began, but was interrupted by a knock on the door, followed closely by the

entrance of a small man with a black bag and a cross expression.

"Well?" the stranger demanded. Julianna moved forward.

"Are you the doctor?" she asked.

The man held up his black bag. "Of course I'm the doctor." He eyed the blood on her gown in disgust. "And give me leave to tell you, ma'am, that if you are the patient, I can't approve of your being up and about with that loss of blood."

Hastily Julianna assured him that she was not the patient, and motioned toward her cousin's bed. The doctor stomped across the room, ignoring them all as his sharp old eyes ran quickly over Jonathan's still form. "Ahhh!" he said.

Julianna, who had formed no good opinion of him when he first mistook her for the patient, was not reassured by the "Ahhh!"

"Ahhh?" she repeated doubtfully; the doctor glared at her.

"What happened here?" he demanded, and at once two female voices filled the room. He silenced them with a testy, "I can't make anything out of both of you gibble-gabbling at me at once!"

Julianna, who had had a most trying day, and who wanted it known, in no uncertain terms, that she *never* gibble-gabbled, was further incensed when the doctor turned to the earl and said, "You, sir, you look like a sensible man." Both the doctor and the earl chose to ignore Miss Cresston's loud "Ha!" "Suppose you tell me what happened?"

But that the earl could not do, which afforded Miss Cresston considerable satisfaction as the doctor was forced to turn to her again. Briefly she told him about the highwaymen and the bullet that she believed was still lodged in her cousin's shoulder. She had, she added, for the doctor's benefit as well as for the earl's, bound Jonathan's shoulder tightly and had the coachman drive them swiftly to the inn. His speed had caused the accident now littering the nearby ditch. Then, Julianna said, she immediately ordered the ostler to ride for a physician.

If she expected some commendation or even a sign of grudging respect from the medical man, she was disappointed. "Hmmph!" he said, opening his black bag and not looking at her. "As you should have. As you should."

"Well!" Julianna said.

The earl intervened, suggesting smoothly that the ladies might like to retire while he and the doctor tended to Jonathan's wound. The doctor seconded his suggestion, but Julianna was not about to be routed by these two men who had such exaggerated ideas of their own importance.

"I," she said, drawing herself up to her full height and looking down her nose at the little doctor, "shall stay."

"Can't," the doctor interrupted. "There'll be blood. Women can't stand the sight of blood. Faint dead away. Won't have it. Won't have it at all."

Acidly Miss Cresston pointed out that she already had seen a great deal of blood that night, was covered in it, as a matter of fact, and had not done, nor would ever do, such a paltry thing as faint dead away.

"The innkeeper said the young lady had to be carried into the house—" the earl interrupted, thinking aloud.

Head hanging, Miss Marley confessed she was that young lady. The earl patted her shoulder consolingly.

"Never mind, my dear," he soothed. "Any young lady of good breeding would do the same—" His sentence ended abruptly as Miss Cresston's eyes flashed. With a shrug he opened the door to usher Miss Marley out, and gave Julianna a speaking look.

"I," she said, through gritted teeth, "am staying."

The earl shrugged again, and shut the door. "Women!" said the doctor in tones of great disgust, and proceeded to ignore her, issuing his orders to the earl as if Julianna were not there. Content to be on hand if her cousin had need of her, she resigned herself to watching from the foot of the bed.

Just before the operation started, Jonathan opened his eyes and stared painfully up at the earl's face as Marleton braced himself to hold the viscount down against the onslaught of the doctor's probe. For a moment Jonathan's gaze was uncomprehending, then he groaned. "Oh, lord," he whispered, screwing his eyes shut tight, "I've died and gone straight to the devil!"

"No, no," Marleton assured him, willing himself not to laugh, "you're not dead. And you behold me here in the guise of ministering angel."

Cautiously Jonathan opened one eye. "It *is* you, Marleton, isn't it?" he demanded.

The earl assured him it was.

"And I'm not dead?"

The earl assured him he was not.

"Good," the viscount said hazily. "I told Julianna I'd live, and if I'd died, she would have killed me."

Glancing at Julianna, the earl saw a small smile upon her features—a smile she quickly erased as she became aware of his study. Her chin came up and she looked challengingly back at him.

"Are you ready, my lord?" the doctor inquired, and at the new voice, Jonathan opened his eyes again.

"Who's that?" he demanded.

The earl told him it was the doctor, adding apologetically that he was afraid they were going to have to hurt him a bit to get the bullet out.

Jonathan's words were slurred. "It's no matter," he assured the earl, starting to slip back into unconsciousness again. "Can't feel much worse than I do now. Going to Northumberland, with Julianna. Highwaymen. Bullet. Bushy gone. Going to be married." He sighed heavily. "My luck is quite out, you know."

The earl pretended not to hear the indignant gasp at the end of the bed as, obedient to the doctor's nod, he braced himself for the involuntary protest Jonathan's body would make against the probe's search for the bullet lodged in his shoulder.

❧ *Chapter 23* ❧

Miss Cresston remained at her post at the foot of Jonathan's bed until the doctor had removed the bullet, dusted the wound with basilicum powder, and proclaimed with dour satisfaction, ''He'll do.'' Then she slipped quietly away. The earl, carefully watching the doctor's handiwork, was aware of her leaving only when the door shut softly behind her. His eyes met the doctor's; the physician shook his head. ''Women!'' he said again. Silently the earl nodded.

Later, when he had received the doctor's instructions on Jonathan's care, and the assurance that the physician would return in the morning to check on his patient, Marleton went in search of Miss Cresston, knowing that he owed her an apology, and feeling quite unable to make one she would accept. The enormity of his own folly was not lost on him. He liked admitting his mistakes as little as the next man, and was grim-faced when he tapped on Miss Marley's door. Julianna was not there, nor was she in the small private parlor of the inn, which the landlord said was the earl's for his commanding. The earl commanded, and the innkeeper promised supper for two in half an hour's time. Miss Marley already had eaten in her room while the doctor was with Jonathan.

Stepping outside, the earl allowed his eyes to become accustomed to the darkness before beginning a leisurely stroll around the grounds. He was drawn at length to the stable where a weak light shone; he entered to find Miss Cresston talking gently to a tall roan as she fed the animal carrots cajoled from the landlord's wife. Stepping forward, he surprised signs of wetness on her cheeks, and when she saw him she turned abruptly away to hide her face in the horse's neck.

146

"I was just seeing to my cousin's horse," she said, her voice muffled by her close proximity to the animal. "Jonathan would never forgive me if something happened to Charger."

"I see." The earl's tone was sympathetic as he reached into his pocket and produced a large square of snowy linen, which he handed to her.

Miss Cresston took it and blew her nose defiantly. "I am *not* crying," she told him.

"Of course not."

"I *never* cry."

"I can't imagine why you would."

Miss Cresston half-turned and eyed him suspiciously. "Are you making fun of me?" she demanded. Gravely he assured her that he was not.

She turned back to the horse. "Then what do you want?" she asked, one hand stroking the mane in front of her.

"Miss Cresston," the earl began, "I—that is—what I want to say is..." Struggling, he began again. "Miss Cresston, I believe I owe you an apology."

"Yes," Julianna said, looking at the horse, her back turned resolutely to the earl. "You do. But since I have no intention of accepting any apology you make me, you may as well spare yourself the trouble."

"But my dear, I cannot," he said, coming up behind her and putting his hands on her shoulders. She could not move forward because of the large roan; reluctantly, she turned and faced him.

"Don't call me that!" she said sharply.

The earl feigned ignorance. "Don't call you what?"

"You know!" she charged. "What you said—just now." The earl raised his eyebrows. She shook her head angrily, her eyes falling on his hands which still rested gently on her shoulders. "And take your hands off me!"

At once he stepped back and let his arms fall. Curiously, Miss Cresston found that his action did not afford her the pleasure she had expected, and she frowned at him.

"You, sir, are a scoundrel!" she told him.

His eyebrow raised further in surprise. "Just because I

called you 'my dear,' Miss Cresston?'' he said. ''Perhaps it
makes me a bit forward, but not—''

''No, no, no!'' she said, stung by his patronizing tone
and the small smile that hovered on his lips as if he realized,
as well as she, that her nerves were now suffering a reaction
to the evening's events. To cover the helplessness she
felt she tore at him with her words. ''Because you stole my
cousin's money!''

''Stole?'' The smile vanished abruptly as the earl took a
hasty step forward. ''If Bushnell told you I stole his money—''

''Oh, no,'' Julianna said bitterly. ''Jonathan says it was
all very fair, a game of *honor*, he'd as lief lose to you as to
anyone, but . . .''

''But?'' the earl repeated, his voice very quiet.

''You knew!'' Julianna cried, the hurt in her voice also
apparent in her eyes. ''You knew how he is situated, what
his circumstances are, and still you let him play!''

''Tell me, Julianna,'' he said, walking away from her and
propping a foot casually on a wooden bucket, ''what would
you have had me do?''

''What?'' She had not previously considered the question, and it stopped her for a moment. ''What do you
mean?''

''What would you have had me do?'' he repeated. ''Your
cousin came to play. Should I have sent him away, embarrassed
him in front of his friends, treated him like a little boy—''

''But he *is* a little boy—in so many ways,'' she cried.

''But he chooses to play the games of a man.'' The earl's
voice was very quiet. ''And those games carry risks and
responsibilities.''

''He's very sorry,'' Julianna offered.

''Yes.'' The earl nodded; he was gazing out into the night.
''So am I.'' He considered telling her that he had visited her
cousin's lodgings in London for the purpose of reaching
some sort of agreement, but did not. He considered telling
her that he would give the money back. He considered
telling her that he could never willingly hurt anyone who
looked at him with her eyes. Instead, he turned back to her
and asked abruptly, ''Miss Cresston, will you marry me?''

Many feelings struggled in Julianna's breast: shock, surprise, dismay, and—and—she refused to identify any more of them. This was just like the man—heedless of her terrible day and the ridiculous situation and setting in which they now found themselves, he proposed marriage as casually as if it were a stroll in the park or a ride in the country, or—or—or the purchase of a new hat! Angrily she glared at him.

"Not," she said scornfully, "if you were the last man on earth. Besides . . ." She had forgotten the final clincher until now, and lifted her chin to deliver it. "I am to marry my cousin Jonathan."

The earl nodded, too late recognizing his mistake. "Ah, yes. I forgot. The happy couple." Knowing that that shaft had gone home as both remembered Jonathan's recent tumbled words in his sickroom, Marleton smiled. "Then, Miss Cresston, would you do me the honor of joining me for supper?"

The Earl of Marleton, Julianna thought resentfully as she sat across from him at the small table in the innkeeper's private parlor, had much too clever a way of throwing her off balance. She did not know what she had expected his reaction to her refusal to marry him would be, but it certainly was not an invitation to dine.

She had almost refused him when the rumblings of her stomach informed her she was hungry; from the interior of her mind rose her mother's gentle admonition that when a woman blights a man's hopes for wedded bliss, it behooves her to let him down as easily as possible. With that noble purpose in mind, she accepted the earl's offer of supper as gracefully as she could, promising to join him as soon as she changed her gown.

A wash and a fresh gown, as well as the luxury of pinning up her hair again (for it had fallen sadly down during the day's and night's exertions) put her in a much better frame of mind, and she was actually looking forward to her supper when she came down the stairs again to be greeted by the earl. With a show of ceremony never before seen in the humble Black Swan, he ushered her into the parlor to what was an excellent, if simple, meal.

And now they sat, midway through their supper, which

both had fallen to with a will, and which Julianna had been quite enjoying until the earl remarked:

"I believe, Miss Cresston, that unless I am much mistaken, it is considered in the polite vogue to talk to your host during the meal."

Julianna choked on a large bite of chicken and gazed at him reproachfully. Resisting the urge to tell him that he was not one to instruct her in the gentle art of manners, she seemed to consider for several moments before saying, with a softness of tone that matched his own, "Ah, but you see, I am not talking to my host. Not now. Not ever."

"Oh." The earl digested that bit of information along with his bread. "Ever is a very long time, Miss Cresston."

She nodded, smiling sweetly, and said that it was almost long enough.

"And yet, for someone who is not talking to me, you can bring yourself to tell me these things," the earl mused.

Miss Cresston informed him that she was not talking to him on a social basis; they must, because of their present circumstances, communicate now, but that was not the same as polite talking.

"I see." The earl continued to chew as he sat watching her. Under his close scrutiny her own appetite lessened, and she put down the piece of chicken she had just picked up.

When staring back at him did not in any way seem to discompose the man, she asked him in the haughty tone that had been known to send more than one young buck about his business, "Was there something else, my lord?"

He chewed ruminatively for several moments before a slow smile spread across his face and there was laughter in his eyes. "I believe, Miss Cresston," he said, "that it is only fair to tell you that I cannot now, nor have I ever been able to, resist a challenge."

"You can't?" she echoed, taken aback.

His lordship's smile grew. "I can't," he corroborated. "But what I can do is pass you the potatoes!"

The rest of their meal was eaten in lofty silence, or a silence that on Miss Cresston's part would have been lofty had his lordship seemed to notice it. When they finished, Julianna rose and with a dignified curtsy said she would bid him good night; she planned to spend the hours between now and dawn by her cousin's bedside. The innkeeper's wife was with him now, but the poor woman could not be kept up all night.

The earl frowned. "Miss Cresston," he said abruptly as her hand touched the door latch, "a moment, please!"

She turned back with a haughty expression he did not appear to see as he sat staring into the fire, still frowning.

"Have you thought at all about what is to be done?" he asked.

She stared at him. "I just told you," she said, aggrieved, "I am going up to sit with Jonathan so that the innkeeper's wife can go to bed—"

The earl dismissed the innkeeper's wife as inconsequential and directed a penetrating stare at Julianna.

"No," he said, waving her reply away. "Not now. I mean tomorrow. Have you thought of what you'll do tomorrow?"

Julianna looked at him in surprise; actually, she had not. All her energy after the shooting had been bent on getting her cousin and Miss Marley to safety, fetching a doctor, making sure that Jonathan would be all right . . .

"Tomorrow?" she repeated, dully. "No—that is—" For a moment she leaned her head against the door, but now she straightened her shoulders and said valiantly, "I shall think of something, I'm sure."

The earl informed her that he already had thought of something; her noncommittal "Oh?" was uttered with such caution that it made him want to laugh. Instead, he told her smoothly that while she might not be aware of it, he had an estate, one of his smaller holdings, only ten miles from the Black Swan, and if she did not object, he proposed that she, Miss Marley, and her cousin remove there as soon as Jonathan was able to travel.

It did not come as any great surprise to him that Miss Cresston *did* object; she objected long and violently. She and her charges did not, she begged to inform him, need either his help or his charity.

He said that as Miss Marley's guardian, he could not approve of her staying in such—and here a sneering look around the room was put to devastating effect—humble surroundings; nor, he was sure, would his great friend the dowager duchess approve of his leaving her great-niece and nephew to the ministrations of those not used to waiting upon the Quality.

Julianna said that when Jonathan was able to travel, the three of them would journey on to another inn.

His lordship countered that while he was, of course, not cognizant of the contents of her reticule or the viscount's purse, he doubted that either of them had between them the funds to pay for a protracted stay in a first-class hostelry—for the doctor had made it clear that while Jonathan *would* mend, his convalescence would not be rapid.

"Then, too," the earl continued, watching Julianna out of the corner of his eye, "unless I very much miss my guess, your cousin is going to be wanting his man, and wishing to get up, and there is little to entertain him here once he *is* up—"

He let the words trail off as he watched the play of emotions on Julianna's face. On the one hand, he knew, she would like to throw his offer in his face; on the other hand, she had the responsibility of Miss Marley and the viscount to think of.

Responsibility won. Tight-jawed, and in a voice filled with everything but gratitude, Julianna thanked him stiffly for his kind offer.

"My dear Miss Cresston," he said, rising to make her a magnificent leg, "it is my pleasure to have you honor my humble home with your presence."

He was not surprised when the door closed behind her with unnecessary violence. Nor was she, on her way up the stairs, surprised to hear him laugh.

❧ *Chapter 24* ❧

Not quite an hour had passed when Miss Cresston was startled by a soft knock on the door. Since she had bade Miss Marley good night before entering her cousin's room, declining that young woman's offers to sit up with her dear Miss Cresston and the poor viscount, she did not believe it could be her young companion. And, since the landlord's wife had, with a quickly smothered yawn and a few words of good will, made clear her intentions of retiring to her bedchamber straightaway, she did not expect that good woman. The earl had long since left the inn for his nearby estate, so that left the coach driver. Perhaps he wondered what she now expected of him.

She was trying to make up her mind how to answer that question as she opened the door, and so intent was she on it that she did not for a moment register that the face staring down at her was the earl's. She stood looking up at him blankly until, with a slight start, she collected her wits and stepped quickly out into the hallway.

"Are you quite all right, Miss Cresston?" the earl asked. He had noted her look of confusion, and thought that after the events of the day it was not surprising.

"Oh, yes . . ." Julianna put a hand to her forehead, wishing the pounding that had been growing there the last hour would stop, "that is—I did not expect—I thought it would be the coachman."

"You were expecting the coachman to call?" The amusement in his voice made her lift her head and stare icily at him.

"I thought *you* had left," she said, her long look meant to put him in his place. Since it showed no visible signs of doing so, she continued rather petulantly, "And I can't imagine why you haven't. This affair is no concern of yours."

She could have bitten her tongue as soon as the word "affair" slipped out of her mouth, and her chagrin increased as he raised an eyebrow.

"Affair, Miss Cresston?" he asked, all rapt interest.

She regarded him crossly. "You know perfectly well what I mean—and you know perfectly well it isn't . . ."

He stood, listening politely, his shoulders resting negligently against the hall wall as he gazed down at her. He bore all the appearances of a man prepared to be amused, and Miss Cresston had no intention of amusing.

"I thought," she said, pulling herself up to her own elegant height, and trying for a lofty tone, "that you had gone to your estate over an hour ago."

"But I haven't."

She ignored the caveat, and continued to speak in a civil way meant to convey just how little she cared where he did or did not go. "Was there something you wanted?"

He shrugged his shoulders away from the wall and handed her several sheets of paper. As she stared down at them he said, "I have written down the doctor's instructions as they were given to me. I thought you might like to have them."

"Oh—I see." One hand went to her head again, as Miss Cresston looked from him to the papers, and back again. "You're right—I would." He enjoyed the look that passed over her face before she remarked, albeit stiffly, "It was very kind of you, I'm sure. Thank you."

She turned to enter her cousin's room, but he detained her by catching her wrist as she turned away from him. She looked pointedly down at his strong hand, and then up into his equally strong face, when her first glance did not work.

"Was there something else?" she asked, gazing pointedly at her wrist again.

"Would you like me to stay with your cousin tonight?"

The amazement she felt at his offer was evident in her face, and his own gave a small twist of self-mockery as he correctly read her opinion of his skills as a sickroom nurse. She recovered with, "It is very kind of you to offer, but my cousin is no concern of yours, and—"

"And you wish I'd go away," he finished for her, dropping her hand. Abruptly, Miss Cresston missed the warm pressure there.

"I didn't say that."

"No, and it was very civil of you." The amusement was back in his voice, and she looked up to see he was smiling. Without thinking she smiled back.

"It is kind of you to offer," she told him, "but Jonathan has not moved since I entered his room, and he is likely to remain that way throughout the night."

The earl nodded. "The doctor said he'd drugged him heavily. You're to give him another dose at"—he reached for the papers she held in her hand, and scanned them— "three A.M. The bottle is on the table beside the bed."

Julianna nodded.

"It is my guess you've never sat up with a wounded man before, my girl," he said, watching her shrewdly. "I would be glad to keep you company. Nights can get very long, you know."

Julianna, who expected this night to be very long indeed, and was not looking forward to it, sighed. It would be nice to have company, but . . .

She shook her head. "I cannot impose upon you, my lord, nor would my cousin choose to do so. Especially" —her eyes darkened—"after the low regard you showed yourself to hold him—and me—in, by coming here to—to—"

"Call him out," the earl supplied, obligingly.

Miss Cresston glared at him. "So you admit it!"

"My dear girl, I have already admitted it," he replied in a tone she did not feel was adequately—or at all—repentant. "I came here expecting to put a bullet through that young idiot, but some enterprising highwayman was before me." He paused, considering, oblivious of the storm signs gathering in her face. "Actually, your cousin may be quite lucky the bullet in his shoulder prevents me wreaking further havoc with his health, for of all the mismanaged, ridiculous starts—to set off for Northumberland, engaged to you, with Elizabeth along for company—''

"The trip to Northumberland was my idea," Julianna said through clenched teeth. "And I do not consider it either ridiculous or—or—mismanaged!"

"Ahhh." The earl nodded. "I see. You *intended* for a highwayman to shoot your cousin—''

"I most certainly did not!"

"Then I fail to see how you think you managed well!"

That was so unanswerable that Julianna could do no more than take a hasty step down the corridor. Turning to confront him again she said, "I do not believe, my lord, that your help was requested here, and it is certainly not needed. Be so good as to leave."

The earl made an elaborate leg, and turned to go. He sauntered casually to the stairs, turning back when he was almost out of sight to say, "Your wish is my command, Miss Cresston. I shall leave instructions as to my estate's location with the innkeeper; if you have any need of me tonight, you need only have him send the ostler, and I shall return immediately."

Goaded, Julianna replied that she would not have any need for him—not this night and not any night.

He smiled. "Another challenge. We shall see, dear Ju. We shall see." Then he was gone, laughing softly as he heard what sounded suspiciously like a foot stamping behind him.

Miss Cresston seated herself by the fire to read the directions the earl had so kindly written out for her. Really, she told herself grudgingly, that *had* been quite kind of him. He was such a puzzling person, one minute mocking and the next doing something that could make a woman like him very well—if she were so inclined, which, of course, no bright young woman would be.

She dragged her thoughts back from the earl to the instructions, and finished reading them by the light of a candle near her cousin's bed. She busied herself for several moments with rearranging the candle so that its beam would not fall so close to Jonathan's eyes, and that necessitated moving everything else on the table, as well. She looked doubtfully at the bottle of dark brown medicine the doctor had left, and was glad that she did not have to swallow any of its contents. Curious, she took the stopper out of the bottle and sniffed, then was more than ever pleased that it was not meant for her.

She was concerned, in fact, that Jonathan might not care to take it; and when he awoke shortly before three A.M., muttering and trying to find a comfortable place on the pillow, she held out a spoonful of it to him with some trepidation.

"What's that?" he asked, not quite awake and staring suspiciously at the spoon before his eyes wandered up to her face, and his confused look grew. "And what the—*Ju?*"

"Yes, Jonathan." She spoke soothingly and used her free hand to press him back against the pillows, since he showed every disposition to sit bolt upright in astonishment at seeing her, and she was sure that could not be good for his shoulder. "It is I. Here with your medicine."

"Medicine?" He stared at her blankly, looked down at the bed, and then up at her again in growing indignation.

"Ju, I'm in my nightclothes!" he told her.

"Yes, I know." She sat down on the bed and held the spoon out to him again. "You were shot, remember?"

"Shot?" He moved restlessly, and the pain in his shoulder confirmed it as he came more awake. "Oh. Yes. Now I remember." He paused a moment and thought. "But that doesn't explain what you're doing in my bedchamber, my girl, unless..." his eyes widened, and he stared at her in horror. "Good Lord, Ju, we ain't married yet, are we?"

She bit her lip to contain the laughter she felt bubbling up at his apparent terror at the thought, but managed to shake her head and say soothingly that no, they were not yet married. She was just serving as his nurse, and he was to take his medicine and go back to sleep.

He eyed her thoughtfully for several moments. While he could find no apparent flaw in her plan for his immediate future, his sense of propriety—lax where he himself was concerned, but considerably stricter when it applied to the ladies in his charge—was offended. "Oh, all right," he said, swallowing the medicine and immediately accusing her of trying to poison him before he returned to his original train of thought, "but it ain't seemly, you being here."

Julianna patted his hand comfortingly and watched with satisfaction as his eyes grew heavy and started to close again. A final thought drifted through the viscount's mind as consciousness was deserting him, and he dragged his lids open to regard her.

"Julianna," he said slowly, the words coming as if from far away. "I dreamed—Marleton—"

She patted his hand again. "Marleton," she said firmly, "is not a dream, Jonathan—he's a nightmare. And you needn't worry. He's gone."

Satisfied, a slight smile creased the viscount's face as he drifted off to sleep again.

❧ Chapter 25 ❧

Although her cousin did, for the most part, sleep peacefully through the night, Julianna did not allow herself to drift off in case he might awake and have need of her. With only the snapping of the fire to keep her company, she settled into her uncomfortable chair and thought about the day's events. The earl's comments were constantly in her mind, and although she resented his choice of words—"*mismanaged*" and "*ridiculous*," indeed!—her innate honesty made her admit that she could certainly understand why he might choose them.

Not for anything did Julianna plan to tell Marleton that her engagement to her cousin was for the sole purpose of lending Jonathan the money to pay his gambling debt and save Bushy. The earl already held the young viscount in low esteem, and she did not care to see Jonathan sink further. Although why she cared what Marleton thought . . .

Miss Cresston hastily diverted her thoughts from that line of reasoning; she did not at this moment, in the midst of one of the long nights the earl had spoken so knowingly of, care to inquire too closely into why she *did* concern herself with what Marleton thought. Telling herself it was because he was Beth's uncle, and she and Jonathan were both fond of Beth, and would not care to see their relationships with her constrained, she moved on to consider the knotty problem of what they were next to do. She gazed abstractedly into the fire and nibbled one fingernail as she pondered; each solution she hit upon only presented more problems, and she was still considering when Mrs. Briskly, the innkeeper's kind spouse who was as efficient as her name, popped her head in the door to ask, in a conscientious whisper that filled the room, if Miss would like a cup of tea?

Glad of the distraction, Julianna said that she would indeed, as well as some bread and butter which she'd eat in the sickroom, when Mrs. Briskly could manage it. The landlord's wife looked shocked, and said that no, miss was to come down and have a proper breakfast in the private parlor, just as soon as the other young lady was awake and ready.

"It will do you good," she said, earnestly shaking her white-capped head at Julianna. "A good breakfast will put the life right back into you, as his lordship said when he bespoke the meal and parlor for this morning—"

Julianna, who had thought longingly of the images the words "a good breakfast" conjured up, felt her aching back straighten at the landlady's last words.

"His lordship?" she questioned.

Mrs. Briskly beamed and bobbed. "Yes, miss, his lordship, that nice Earl of Marleton, who lives just seven miles over at Little Haven, where my sister is housekeeper—" Mrs. Briskly broke off, suddenly struck by the thought as she allowed that it was a small world, after all, when the earl, who was her sister Betty's new employer—her not having met him before, what with him being off so far in foreign parts—showed up plump at her inn, and she got to meet him before her sister did. . . .

Mrs. Briskly pulled herself up abruptly, confused by the

curious light in Miss Cresston's eyes, and apologized profusely for letting her tongue run on. "Anyway," she said, smiling and bobbing again, "the earl bespoke the private parlor and he says to me, he says, 'Mrs. Briskly, you see that the ladies get a good breakfast, will you?' And him all the time smiling at me just like I was somebody, instead of good George's wife. So." She paused and smiled expectantly. "I promised that I would, and I've got my daughter Betty—her that's named after my sister, who works at Little Haven, and very proud we are of her, too, for rising in the world to the position of housekeeper to an earl—anyway, *my* Betty is down in the kitchen right now, a-carving on the bacon, and as soon as you and the young lady . . ."

Smiling as she came toward the door, Julianna repeated her request for tea, bread and butter, adding kindly as she saw disappointment on Mrs. Briskly's face, "I am sure Miss Marley will partake of your breakfast when she awakens."

She was about to close the door through which the worried landlady peered when the door to the room next to Jonathan's opened and Elizabeth stepped out, looking remarkably refreshed and becomingly dressed in a green sprig muslin that fit her to perfection. Julianna could not help glancing down at the dress she herself wore, badly wrinkled by the night spent in the chair, and slightly stained where she had spilled a few drops of Jonathan's medicine on it.

"What will Miss Marley do?" Elizabeth questioned, coming toward them with a smile for both Julianna and the innkeeper's wife. Hoping for an ally, Mrs. Briskly explained the situation again, with much handwaving and entirely too many "his lordships" for Miss Cresston's taste.

When Mrs. Briskly was finished, Miss Marley surprised Julianna by saying calmly, "But of course you must sit down to breakfast in the parlor, Julianna. You have been in the sickroom all night."

"But Jonathan—" Julianna began. "He shouldn't be left alone—"

"While we are having our breakfast, I'm sure Mrs. Briskly or her good husband will sit with Jonathan," Elizabeth continued, just as calmly. Mrs. Briskly agreed at once that

that would be just the thing, she should have thought of it herself, now Miss could have no objection to eating her fine breakfast, which, although Mrs. Briskly was sure she shouldn't say it, for fear of being thought one of those bold and bragging housekeepers she, herself, detested, Mrs. Briskly *did* dare hope her breakfast would rival even those found in the finest London homes. . . .

It was apparent that her housewifely mettle was, in her opinion, so at stake that Julianna at last sighed and, worn down, said she would descend to the breakfast parlor as soon as she changed her dress.

"And I," said Elizabeth, moving forward, "will sit with Jonathan while you do so." Opening the door that Julianna had been holding half-closed, Beth moved back so that Miss Cresston might step out.

Julianna automatically did as was expected of her, only turning back to say, before she disappeared into the bedroom she shared with Beth, "I believe, my dear, that I am beginning to see a strong family resemblance between you and your so commanding uncle."

Beth smiled, and said nothing.

The ladies were at breakfast when they heard a horse galloping into the innyard; a few moments later booted feet made their way toward the private parlor, and the Earl of Marleton stood on the threshold, surveying them.

"Uncle Richard!" Elizabeth said joyfully, half-rising to greet him.

He came swiftly forward and dropped a kiss on her forehead before stepping back to survey her closely. "Well," he said, his eyes alight, "you seem to have survived yesterday without any untoward effects."

He then turned to Miss Cresston, and the quick raising of his left eyebrow made it clear that he could not say the same for her. Annoyed, Julianna bit back the protest that she had spent the night nursing her injured cousin and proceeded to ignore him.

With a grin Marleton returned his attention to his niece. Smiling as she poured him a cup of coffee, Beth said tranquilly that she was feeling quite recovered; she had enjoyed an excellent night's sleep, and upon reflection had decided that nothing half so exciting had happened to her since—and here she cast an adoring look toward the earl— her knight-in-shining-armor uncle had come and rescued her from her horrid relations.

"What?" Julianna said before she could stop herself, and Beth turned to her, eyes still shining.

"I'm glad that I am finally free to tell you, Julianna," she said, "for I have wanted to every time you've thought my uncle cruel or rude or unfeeling."

"That many times . . ." the earl murmured, and Julianna flushed.

Elizabeth continued as if she had not heard. "After my father died, I was sent to live with some distant relations of Mama's—nasty, purse-pinching people who expected me to be grateful for their charity! Ha! *Charity*—they used me as a drudge! I was nursemaid to the youngest children, and a housemaid, and—and—" Her eyes filled with tears at the memory, and the earl placed a hand on her shoulder in comfort. Automatically her fingers went up to cover his.

"It's over now," the earl said. Beth nodded.

"Then Uncle Richard came, and took me away, and the things he said to those people before leaving—oh, Julianna, I know it shouldn't have, but it made me feel so *good!*—and he took me to my Godmama, and we all decided that I should come to London."

"But why," Miss Cresston cried, her forehead wrinkling, "did you not make your connection known?"

The earl seated himself and leaned forward. "Would you want it known that you had such an uncle, my dear?"

Really, Julianna thought crossly, he was growing much too familiar with his "my dears"; before she could answer Elizabeth interrupted hotly to say it was no such thing; she would claim him in London or anywhere.

"Then why . . ." Julianna repeated.

The earl sighed. "Because, Miss Cresston, both your great-aunt and I thought Elizabeth would be much better received under her protection than under mine. We were not, at that time, certain whether polite society would care to receive me, and if they did not . . .'' He shrugged. ''I did not care to have Elizabeth's chances blighted simply because her father, her grandfather, and I had been such fools.''

''But you're *not* a fool!'' Elizabeth protested, ''and you mustn't say so, for it makes me quite angry!''

In the face of such partisanship Miss Cresston could think of nothing further to say. She met the earl's eyes, saw the amusement there, and looked away.

''The dastardly earl in the guise of a hero,'' Marleton said, reading her thoughts. ''A new role, *enfin*?''

''I don't know what you mean!'' Julianna answered crossly.

He grinned. ''That, Miss Cresston, is patently untrue. The times you have tried to save my niece from the advances of a—er, rake, I believe, was the word you used—''

''Well!'' Julianna felt herself flushing. ''You might have told me! I mean—if I had known—''

''But if you had known, Miss Cresston, I would have been deprived of a most amusing season!''

Julianna put down her cup with a clatter, and rose. ''If you will excuse me, Elizabeth,'' she said, ''I believe I must return to Jonathan now. The doctor should be coming shortly.''

She swept from the room, her grand exit spoiled only by the sound of an infuriating—and decidedly male—chuckle.

❧ *Chapter 26* ❧

The doctor arrived just as Julianna was making her way up the stairs, and they entered Jonathan's room together to find that the viscount was awake and demanding breakfast of a flustered Mrs. Briskly.

''Oh, there you are, Doctor,'' the landlady said with

obvious relief as the man of medicine made his way into the
room. "I was just telling his lordship here that I will not
bring him a plate of rare beef, and a bottle of claret, as
he's demanding, unless you say as how it's all right."

The doctor smiled sourly. "No beef for you, young sir,"
he said, preparing to open his bag. "Not today, and not
tomorrow, either. And *certainly* no claret. Thin gruel is what
you'll get. No more, no less."

"Gruel!" Real indignation brought the viscount bouncing
off his pillows, only to fall back at once as his shoulder
made it clear such actions were not to be tolerated.

"Aye," the doctor said, surveying him grimly, "that hurt,
didn't it? Now let's have no more of this nonsense. Gruel it
will be. I'm going to look at that wound, and if need be,
I'm going to cup you—"

"Oh, no you're not," Jonathan said, returning the doctor's grim stare. "Not going to cup me, I mean. You can
look at the wound, but . . ." His attention turned to Julianna
and Mrs. Briskly, standing nearby. He frowned. "Not with
ladies present."

The doctor turned from his patient to survey the room's
other occupants. "Oh, go away, do!" he said irritably.

"Now just a minute—" Julianna began.

Jonathan interrupted to say that he really would appreciate
it if she would take herself off until this curst sawbones—a
title that seemed to appeal to the doctor, who almost
smiled—had his way. "Then," he said, his eyes on the
suspicious-looking instruments the doctor was now laying
out on the table, "we must talk about what we're to do."

"You're not to do anything, my good man, for many a
day," the doctor put in. Jonathan grimaced at Julianna
behind the physician's back, rolled his eyes, and said that he
would talk with her later. Reluctantly she followed Mrs.
Briskly from the room, and set herself to pacing the hall,
pausing now and then outside Jonathan's door, behind
which she could hear muffled voices but could not make out
any words. When the doctor emerged after half an hour he
was backing from the room, saying, "I won't cup you
today, but tomorrow . . ." He let the threat sink in before

adding, "And it's to be gruel, today—don't you go badgering Mrs. Briskly after I'm gone, for she'll not be feeding you what you shouldn't have, and shouldn't ask for."

He shut the door behind him and turned to find Miss Cresston at his elbow. He harumphed. "Resty young pup," he said, looking at her from under his beetling brows.

Julianna asked what she was to do for her cousin.

"Keep him down," the doctor said. "Keep him warm. See that's he's not upset, and that he sleeps as much as he's able. I left a different bottle of medicine on the table; see that he takes it morning, noon and night."

Julianna nodded, and the doctor stomped off, only to turn at the top of the stairs to say gruffly that she looked as if a prescription of sleep could benefit her, too.

"I gave your cousin a draught of the medicine before I left him," the doctor said. "Like as not he's asleep already. You'd be wise to follow his lead."

Before she could think of a reply, he was gone, and she wearily turned the knob to Jonathan's room and stepped inside. The doctor was right; her cousin already had drifted off, his uninjured arm pillowing his head, a half-formed smile on his face. She looked toward the chair in which she'd spent the night; it looked even more uninviting in light of day. And there was nothing to do while Jonathan slept.

Unless . . . since he was asleep, there could be no harm in leaving him for the few moments it would take to go into the adjoining bedroom and find the book she'd brought to read while in Northumberland. This lowness of spirits she now felt was alien to her character, and she was determined to shake it off immediately.

With that praiseworthy notion she went to the bedchamber she shared with Beth. It took her a moment to find the book and she sat down on the bed to search for her place in it. As she was about to rise, her gaze was drawn to the inviting plumpness of the pillows. How comfortable it would be to rest her head on them for only a moment. . . .

Sighing, she slipped out of her shoes and curled her toes under the comforter that covered the foot of the bed. With a promise to herself that she would awaken long before

Jonathan could have stirred, she gave herself up to the luxury of Mrs. Briskly's best featherbed, and dropped into a sleep as deep as that of her cousin.

Julianna awoke with a start and sat up, disoriented in the darkening room. From the courtyard she heard loud meowing and realized that sound had awakened her. For a moment she could not remember where she was, and when she did, she slipped back into her shoes to go to the window to see what the noise could be.

Below her Miss Marley and the landlady's daughter, Betty, were making their way toward the stable; Betty had milk buckets in hand, while a hopeful string of cats followed her. It must be an evening ritual, Julianna decided with a smile, for Betty was talking back to the cats just as they talked to her, adjuring them to keep their tails on, there'd be milk for them soon, if they was good. . . .

Elizabeth must have felt Julianna's eyes upon her just then for she looked up suddenly and grinned in a carefree way that made Julianna smile back. A big tiger-colored cat rubbed happily against Elizabeth's legs, and she called, "This one is Tom; he's my favorite!" before turning back to the stable to watch Betty do the evening milking.

Evening, Julianna thought, the smile lingering on her lips as she watched her friend and the milkmaid disappear with their feline entourage. *I've slept most of the day away. . . .*

She straightened suddenly. "Jonathan!" she gasped, and hurried out of the room and into her cousin's bedchamber, only to be brought up short by the sight of the viscount engrossed in conversation with the earl, who sat in the hard-backed chair in which Miss Cresston had spent the night. Both men looked up at her hasty entrance, and the earl smiled.

"I have been keeping your cousin company while you slept, Miss Cresston," Marleton said, rising as she came forward.

She flushed guiltily, and her anxious eyes were on Jonathan. "Are you all right, my dear?" she asked. "I only lay down for a minute, and—"

Jonathan waved the apology away. "Lord, Ju," he said, with more honesty than tact, "it's a good thing you *did* get some sleep. You were looking quite hagged this morning—made me feel even worse than—"

The indignant look on his cousin's face, and the choking sound that Marleton hurriedly turned into an unconvincing cough, made the viscount break off. "That is—"

"And when I think of all I've done for you!" Julianna told him roundly. "Sitting up all night—worried to death—and then you have the effrontery to say I looked hagged—*well!*"

Her cousin favored her with his most placating smile. "You look a great deal better now."

"I feel a great deal better, too," she said, fussing around the bed and tucking in covers where they'd come out, "which is why I'm not going to come to cuffs with you over your last remark."

She straightened and regarded the men quizzically. "So, what have you two been talking about while I've been sleeping?"

"You," the viscount answered promptly, with the same deplorable lack of tact. The earl frowned at him and Jonathan, realizing he had been precipitate, added, "Me. Miss Marley. What we're to do." There was a glint in his cousin's eyes, and he temporized with, "Actually, I haven't been awake very long."

The earl sighed and asked Miss Cresston to sit down. She perched on the foot of her cousin's bed and the earl resumed his seat in the chair.

"Your cousin and I were just discussing the inadvisability of your remaining at this inn, Miss Cresston," he told her gravely. "We both feel—"

"You *both* feel?" Julianna repeated, eyeing her cousin closely. Jonathan, who had seen the impropriety of two well-born ladies residing unchaperoned in such a humble establishment as soon as it was pointed out to him, nodded.

"We both feel," the earl continued, "that it would be best for you and Miss Marley to remove tonight to Little Haven—the estate I mentioned I own not far from here. You may be comfortable there, and when Viscount Bushnell is able to travel, he shall join you.''

"Probably by the end of the week," Jonathan interrupted. They both looked at him. "The doctor said I could probably travel a short distance by the end of the week." Both ignored him again and his voice trailed off, muttering that it wasn't to be a long distance, mind, but a short distance would be all right.

Miss Cresston's eyes were fixed on the earl's face as she bade him continue. He said that his carriage awaited her convenience.

"Ahhh." Miss Cresston tilted her head to the left as if she were giving all he'd said her fullest consideration. "And tell me, my lord, this estate of yours—who is your hostess there?"

The earl said that he had a fine housekeeper.

"Yes." Miss Cresston nodded. "I know. Mrs. Briskly's sister. But she is not, I believe, your hostess."

"Dash it, Ju," Jonathan interrupted, "of course she's not his hostess! She's his housekeeper. He just told you that. And why it matters—"

Julianna turned limpid eyes toward her cousin. "But, Jonathan," she said, "it would not be seemly for me to allow Miss Marley to reside in a house where there is no respectable hostess."

"But surely in her uncle's house—" the earl interrupted smoothly.

Julianna bit her lip; that bit of information was still so new to her that she had not considered it. "But you are not *my* uncle," she pointed out, and flushed when the earl's *sotto voce* "Thank goodness!" made her cousin laugh.

"No," Miss Cresston said, gazing at them both severely, "I appreciate your kind offer, my lord, but I do not feel it would be fitting for us to stay in your home unchaperoned."

"Even if I were not there?" the earl suggested.

"Even if—" Miss Cresston began firmly, then goggled at him. "You were *not there*?"

He had played his ace card, and was smiling in triumph. "Surely, Miss Cresston," he said gently, "you did not think that I would abandon your cousin here to the ministrations— albeit tender ones—of strangers? I shall escort you and

Elizabeth to Little Haven, and then return here and occupy the bedchamber next to Jonathan's. That way, if he needs anything during the night, he has only to shout, and I will be here to tend him until his man arrives.''

"Yes, but . . ." Julianna felt ground slipping away from her, and tried desperately to regain it. "What if he is too ill to shout?''

"Dash it, Ju," the viscount objected, "I ain't at death's door, you know. Of course I can shout!" He proceeded to demonstrate, and was so successful that Mrs. Briskly's astonished face soon appeared around the bedchamber door.

"Was you needing something, your lordship?" she inquired.

"No, thank you, Mrs. Briskly," the earl told her, while Jonathan grinned. "His lordship was just demonstrating his lung capacity for us.''

Mrs. Briskly nodded, bewildered, and withdrew, making her way slowly down the stairs, and pausing on each step to shake her head over the strange ways of the Quality.

"There now," Jonathan said after the landlady withdrew. "What other objection can you have?''

Julianna considered telling him that her strongest objection was that she did not want to go; she did not want to be beholden to the Earl of Marleton; she did not want that—that—*man*—ordering her life; she was perfectly capable of managing her own affairs.

Instead she rose and, pacing restlessly, said, "I see no reason for Elizabeth and myself to remove from this inn when we are under your protection, Jonathan.''

"Ha!" Jonathan said. "Some protection! It isn't that I wouldn't make a push, dear girl—you must know I would—but truth is, I'm weak as a cat! Why, if those highwaymen were to ride up tonight, do you think that I could save your gewgaws from them?''

"No," Miss Cresston replied frankly, "but I think *I* could!''

About to argue, her cousin remembered her recent efforts on his own behalf and conceded the point. He then disconcerted her by grasping one of her restless hands in his good one and pulling her down onto the bed again. "The thing is,

Julianna," he said, "I'd feel a great deal better if you'd accept the earl's offer—"

"*Obliging* offer," the earl interjected, his lips prim, his eyes alight.

Miss Cresston glared at him, but Jonathan agreed that it was most obliging, and continued. "I wouldn't be worried about you then, you see. And you and Miss Marley really shouldn't be here. Think what your mother would say. Think what *my* mother would say. Think what Great-Aunt Elizabeth—" That thought seemed to so totally overwhelm him that he let go her hand and closed his eyes for a moment. "No," he said. "Let's *not* think what Great-Aunt Elizabeth would say." He opened his eyes so like her own to gaze up at her again. "Oblige me in this, Ju," he said pleadingly. "The earl says you can drive or ride over every day, if you like, to see me. Please."

She gazed at him for several moments before giving his hand one quick squeeze and releasing it.

"My lord," she said, standing and glancing enigmatically toward the earl, who watched her with an expression just as hard to read, "I shall be packed directly."

❧ *Chapter 27* ❧

Julianna had not expected to like Little Haven; in fact, she had quite decided to dislike it intensely, to find fault with everything put before her, and to behave, in general, as one of those cold, haughty women who most exasperated her in this world. That had been her plan when the Earl of Marleton handed her and Miss Marley into his carriage, and escorted them to this, one of the smaller of his country homes.

To the earl's polite inquiries she returned only frosty monosyllables during the ride, leaving the gentle art of conversation to Miss Marley, who stepped into the breach with ease. Beth conversed pleasantly with her uncle, Miss Cresston and—at times—herself, and acted for all the world as if she were in company with a delightful set of friends at Almack's, and not confined in a carriage in which the electricity threatened to discharge and explode at a chance word or deed.

When they arrived at Little Haven Miss Cresston remained wrapped in her dignity—or sulks, depending on who was describing her actions—as she swept up the shallow stone steps and into a timbered hallway that was well lit and warmed by the glow of welcoming candles. As Mrs. Briskly's sister Mrs. Brown approached, Julianna raised her chin in her best imitation of a grand dame, but she found she could not sustain the role for long; the good housekeeper was so eager to please, and so conscious of their comfort and their needs, that Julianna soon found herself thanking the woman for her kindness, and meekly agreeing to drink a glass of warm milk with Miss Marley before retiring for the night. Chancing to glance up as the happy Mrs. Brown trotted away to her housewifely duties, Miss Cresston surprised a look of unholy amusement on the earl's face, and frowned at him.

"Poor Miss Cresston," he murmured, for her ears alone, "how provoking to be undone with kindness, when one is so *determined* to be cross."

Julianna opened her mouth to retort, but he had already turned away from her, and was tapping Miss Marley lightly on the cheek as he bade her to be a good girl and see that their guest was well taken care of. Beth seemed to grow several inches in this new role of hostess, and the earl grinned. Then he cocked an eyebrow at Julianna, made a profound bow that showed to a nicety how well he understood her feelings, and was gone, the shutting of the door making the candles flicker briefly before they resumed their steady light.

"That man—" Julianna said, met Miss Marley's inquiring eyes, and clamped her teeth firmly together.

"Yes?" The feelings seething in Miss Cresston's breast were at odds with Beth's gentle voice, and for a moment

Julianna could not reply. Casting her eyes around the glow-
ing hall, she sighed.

"Has a lovely house," she substituted for her more
vehement language.

Beth nodded. "It is, isn't it?" she agreed. "I am sure
you will find the sitting room especially comfortable. Shall
we wait there for our milk?"

Julianna agreed and followed her friend down the hall.
She could not help contrasting the prosaic ending to this day
with yesterday's events, when she had shot a highwayman,
and spent the night in a straight-backed chair beside her
cousin's bed. She was not at all surprised to find that when
the good Mrs. Brown returned she was accompanied by a
footman carrying a tray containing not only warm milk, but
also a plate piled high with biscuits. Unaccountably, the sight
of that tray made Julianna laugh—a bit hysterically.

Julianna sat in the garden three days later, awaiting the
summons to luncheon. She found it hard to believe that she
and Miss Marley had been at Little Haven such a short a
time, so comfortable had it grown to her. It was, in fact,
almost like being home.

The first morning she'd risen late, only to find that Beth
was not yet up; the housekeeper, fussing over her at breakfast, confided that it was no wonder Miss Marley was done
up, what with all the excitement, and her being so delicate
and small, and not used to such goings on.

Encouraging her to ramble, Julianna wondered ruefully
why no one ever seemed to describe *her* as delicate and in
need of strong protection from the world's wicked ways.
Through her mind floated the memory of her first season
when one of her more moonstruck admirers had tried to attach
the word "delicate" to her appearance, only to be greeted
by great glee from her Cousin Jonathan.

"Delicate?" he'd howled, to her indignation and her
ciscebo's discomfort. "Lord, she's strong as a horse! She
can outlast you, and twelve like you, Hawthorne, and don't
you forget it!"

Mr. Hawthorne had not, and was soon seen paying tribute

to a much smaller and more ethereal creature. Julianna had
not then missed his defection from her ranks, but as she sat
at the breakfast table and heard herself described by the
friendly Mrs. Brown as, "not one of your ladies given to
faints and starts, I can tell; you're steady as a rock," she
decided it was all of a piece, and sighed.

At that moment the Earl of Marleton walked into the
room, and Julianna could tell by his expression that he had
heard his housekeeper's last comment. Flushing, she straightened as Mrs. Brown, with someone new to feed, exclaimed
happily, and bustled out to order the cook to whisk up an
omelette and several earl-size slices of ham.

Left alone with him, Julianna continued to munch her toast
and sip her tea. At last he spoke.

"And how are you this morning, Miss Gibraltar?"

Julianna choked and coughed, and put down her teacup hurriedly. When she could breathe again, she frowned at him.

"I am *not* a rock," she said.

The earl grinned. "Believe me, Miss Cresston, there are
much worse things to be called, or to be, for that matter."

"Well, I don't doubt you've been called them!" Julianna
retorted, her color rising at his quick laugh. "That is, I
mean—"

The earl shook his head. "You mean exactly what you
say, my dear," he told her. "It is one of the things I
particularly liked about you. Don't change it."

Miss Cresston was torn between vexation at being pushed
into rudeness when she wanted to maintain her dignity with
him, and the novel notion that there were things he particularly liked about her. She looked at him cautiously.

"Are you roasting me?" she asked. He laughed again.

"My dear Miss Cresston," he said, "I beg of you—do
not pass such expressions on to my niece. The world does
not expect to hear such words on the lips of gently bred
young ladies, I assure you!"

Julianna gave him to understand that she did not consider
him an expert on the language and deportment of young ladies,
and was not amused when he told her he had had much
time—and experience—to study such things. She frowned.

"Why," she asked him suddenly, "are you here?"

The earl raised an eyebrow in pained surprise. "I live here, Miss Cresston. Surely you have not forgotten that. Besides"—he helped himself to one of his cook's prize muffins, and slathered it liberally with butter—"it's time for breakfast."

She frowned at him. "That is not what I meant. What I meant is: why aren't you with my cousin? How could you leave him helpless and alone?"

The earl reached for another muffin, and this time covered it with jam. "My man is with your cousin," he told her disinterestedly. "I've come to escort you and Beth to visit him. By the way, where is Beth this morning?"

Julianna told him that Miss Marley had not yet awakened.

The earl nodded.

"Quite worn out, poor thing," he said.

Julianna tried not to feel that she had a great deal more reason to be worn out than Beth, and was disconcerted when she glanced up and found that the way the earl watched her made her feel that he knew exactly what she was thinking. Her temper was not at all improved when he said, in the blandest voice possible, "My dear Gibral—I mean, Miss Cresston, do, I pray you, have a muffin."

With difficulty Julianna refrained from hurling her teacup at him.

That had been the first day, and the second was much like it. Accompanied by the earl, she and Elizabeth visited Jonathan in the afternoon. Julianna was relieved to find her cousin a bit stronger each day. They planned to visit again this afternoon; the earl was expected shortly after luncheon. When she heard a carriage she was not surprised, believing that his lordship must have decided to come early and join them for the mid-day meal. She thought about rising, but did not; curious lethargy had settled over her the last few days, and she found it quite pleasant to sit alone in the garden and stare out at the neatly sculpted bushes and lawns and do her best not to think.

She did not want to think about how close Jonathan had come to death, and how she was to unravel his financial difficulties, or about how she had carried young Beth off from London, or about the rumors no doubt circulating about them right now or about the Earl of Marleton, and the way she often felt curiously off balance when he was present, and horridly flat when he was not. Most particularly, she did not want to think about what she was going to say to her friends and her family.

It turned out she did not have to think about the last for long. The familiar sound of Miss Marley's voice as she came through the tall doors that opened onto the gardens calling, "Oh, there you are, Julianna," was followed immediately by, "We have company! Isn't this grand?"

Surprised, Julianna glanced up to encounter the worried face of her mother, the outraged face of her great-aunt, and the bluff, good-natured face of Colonel Higham. She experienced many feelings in that moment. "Grand" was not among them.

"Oh—" Julianna said faintly. She rose, letting the hat she'd been holding by its ribbons fall from her lap. "Mother—"

Mrs. Cresston hurried forward to wrap her daughter in a fond embrace. "My dear," she cried, "are you all right? Such a story we received—about your engagement, and highwaymen, and being the earl's guest—"

"Story?" Julianna echoed. "But—how—"

Her great-aunt moved stiffly forward. "Julianna," she said, "I am greatly displeased. Greatly." The puce feathers on her hat shook with the vehemence of her last word, and Julianna stared at her.

"Of course you are," Julianna agreed faintly.

"Now, now—" Colonel Higham murmured. "Nothing done that can't be undone; least said, soonest mended—" His words broke off before the dowager duchess's frosty stare, and he turned toward Julianna. "Glad to see you looking so well, my dear," he told her kindly. "Told your mother you'd stand huff. Not one to fall apart over any little thing."

"No," Julianna agreed, more faintly still. "So good of you to say so. And I'm sure I'm very glad to see you, too. It's just that..." She could think of no tactful way to put it. "*What* are *you* doing here?"

At that the little colonel looked extremely self-conscious, met Julianna's mother's eyes pleadingly and glanced away, clearing his throat as he uttered disjointed statements about not wanting the ladies to travel alone, having wanted to visit this part of the country, having a partiality to the earl—

The dowager duchess cut him off. "Your mother," she told Julianna regally, "is engaged."

"Oh." Julianna thought for a moment before turning to her mother. Surprised to find that lady blushing, she cautiously inquired, "Engaged—in what, Mama?"

Mrs. Cresston was spared a reply as the dowager duchess swept into speech again. "Not engaged *in*, Julianna—engaged *to*! Your mother and Colonel Higham are engaged to marry."

"Really, Elizabeth—" Mrs. Cresston said, shaking her pretty blond head reproachfully at the unrepentent duchess, "You might have let me tell her." She patted her daughter's arm as Julianna sank down onto the bench behind her, having found her legs suddenly disposed to buckle. Julianna, her mouth slightly ajar, stared up at her mother.

"Really, Mama?" she questioned. For all her training, and her reputation for having manners that were the toast of London, it was, at the moment, all Julianna could think to say.

Her mother smiled. "Really, Julianna. Julius"—and here she held out her hand to the blushing colonel, who hurried to take it—"asked me to marry him four nights ago in Bath, and I've accepted."

Julianna looked from her beautiful mother to the plain, round-bellied little man who stood gazing so adoringly at her. "I never thought...that is..." Her eyes swept the group and she realized that sometime during the last few minutes they'd been joined by the Earl of Marleton, who stood several steps behind the dowager duchess, watching her. His face was sober; he seemed to realize the shock she'd received. He quickly grasped the colonel's hand and bowed politely to Mrs. Cresston.

"This calls for a celebration," he said, after wishing both of them happy. "I believe we have time for a glass of champagne before luncheon." Deftly he turned the newly engaged couple toward the house, making sure that the colonel escorted both his betrothed and the duchess, while Miss Marley, in her new role of hostess, walked slightly ahead of them, turning back to exclaim her happy congratulations with every other step.

The earl offered his arm to Miss Cresston and she rose, glad for the support. She was surprised to find her fingers trembling slightly on his arm, and looked up to find him watching her closely.

"He is a very good man," the earl offered.

Julianna nodded. "Of course. It's just that—I hadn't realized—so unexpected—"

The earl smiled. "Sometimes," he said, "I'm sure even Gibraltar feels she might be swept away by the waves."

Miss Cresston nodded again, and squared her shoulders. She could not remember when she had felt less like a rock.

❧ Chapter 28 ❧

"You have had a great number of surprises lately, Miss Cresston."

Julianna and the earl were on their way to visit Jonathan in the earl's curricle. Miss Marley had elected to stay at Little Haven to entertain the newly arrived guests, and Julianna's tentative suggestion that they all might like to visit the ailing viscount had been waved aside by her great-aunt, who regally decreed that they had had enough bouncing about in a carriage for one day, and would call upon the sufferer tomorrow.

"It will give him time to—anticipate," the dowager duchess said, a light in her eye that made Julianna feel very sorry for Jonathan.

While Julianna's mother and the colonel had not looked particularly tired from their travels, at the duchess's words they fell goodnaturedly in with her plans, deciding to take a leisurely stroll together in the gardens to relieve the journey's strain.

Now, as the earl spoke, his voice was for once devoid of

its usual teasing note, but Julianna, deeply wrapped in her own thoughts, did not notice. After considering her for several moments, he repeated his sentence. When her mind rejoined her body she turned toward him with a start.

"I beg your pardon," Julianna said, putting one hand up to steady her wide-brimmed hat, which was caught now and then by the stiff breeze. "I was not attending."

The earl smiled. "I said, Miss Cresston, that you have had a number of surprises—one might even say shocks—in your life lately."

"Oh." Julianna looked down. "Yes. Well. I am sure I am very happy for my mother."

He assured her that he did not doubt that, and she looked up again.

"It's just that it's so sudden—"

"No." The earl shook his head gently, and transferred the reins to his left hand so that he could drop his other large brown palm over the smaller white hands that fluttered restlessly in Julianna's lap. "My dear, it is not. Your great-aunt and I have seen it coming any time these last months."

Julianna stared at him, open-mouthed. "You have?"

He nodded. "That is why the duchess was so out-of-reason cross when the colonel got called to Bath; the romance was progressing nicely and she did not want to run the risk of having it foiled by time and distance."

Julianna's mouth opened wider. "But—" she sputtered, "if that's true—I never even noticed—"

The earl smiled. "You have had other things to think about, my dear."

One part of her mind noticed that that was his second "my dear" in the space of moments, and considered calling him to task for it; the other part told her she was not up to the fight. She sighed.

"It will be very—odd—having a stepfather in the house," Julianna said, thinking aloud. "We have been just the two of us, my mother and I, for so long—"

"But you are to be married," the earl interrupted smoothly, "so you will be setting up your own house-hold, and only visiting your mother and the colonel from time to time. Perhaps that won't seem so strange, after all.''

Somehow Julianna did not think this the moment to mention that she had no intention of marrying her cousin—not now, not ever—even if she cared to make such an explanation to the earl, which she did not.

She sighed again.

"He is not very like my father," she said, not looking at her companion as she continued to think aloud.

The earl, who had seen the portrait of Julianna's late father, which hung prominently in the Cresston family's library, agreed that the two men were not alike in appearance. "But the colonel is a good man," Marleton continued. "Kind. Loyal. Honest. And he adores your mother." He paused a moment, gazing at her downcast head. "There are worse things in this life than being adored, Julianna."

His pressure on her hands increased, and she moved them from under his to fidget with her hat strings, tying them first this way and then that, and finally removing the offending article entirely.

"You should not call me Julianna," she told the earl.

"But it is your name."

"I have not given you leave to use it."

He smiled at her—a warm, intimate smile that made the day grow quite hot, and she fanned herself liberally with her misused hat. "Give me leave," he said.

Julianna turned her head away. "You are forgetting, I think, that I am an affianced woman."

The earl's smile grew. "I know you are, my dear. It is just that you are betrothed to the wrong man. We must do something about that—soon."

Those words brought his companion's head around with a snap, and her backbone straightened. "I beg your pardon?" she said.

The earl's face was tolerant. "Come now, my dear," he said. "You don't really think anyone believes you are serious about this scheme to marry your cousin Jonathan?"

Julianna's jaw worked. "Jonathan does!"

"Yes." The earl made the mistake of laughing. "And we

can all see how delighted the thought makes him, to be sure!''

"Of all the—" Julianna glared at him. "I will have you know, my lord, that there are a goodly number of gentlemen who have sought my hand and heart over the years!"

"And so many years there have been, too," agreed the earl smoothly.

"Oh!" Miss Cresston gave an angry bounce on the seat, and as she did so, her hat billowed out in the breeze. About to pull it back to her, she gazed down at the ribbons, had an idea too powerful to resist, and let the hat go. Instantly the wind carried it away from her, to the side of the road.

"Oh!" Miss Cresston said again. "My hat! My lord—my hat!"

The earl, looking down, could see that the straw confection was no longer in her lap, and it took him only a moment to locate it near the road's hedge.

"You must fetch it for me, my lord!" Miss Cresston implored, turning toward him with her hands clasped to her breast. "My favorite hat!"

Not knowing that moments before she mentally had consigned said hat to the rubbish heap, the earl obligingly halted his horses, and gazed again at where the straw tied up with blue ribbons lay. As they watched, the breeze caught it and carried it farther away from them.

"Oh!" shrieked Miss Cresston (who had always wanted to shriek), "it's getting away! It must be rescued—at once!"

His lordship hesitated. "I fear, Miss Cresston, that since we have no groom with us, you will have to hold the horses while I go after your hat."

"Oh, yes!" Miss Cresston breathed, in happy imitation of all the sweet sillies she'd seen for years in the Marriage Mart. "Of course! But don't let it get awa—Oh! There it goes!"

The despair in her voice prompted the earl to thrust the reins into her hands and to vault down and take several running steps after the hat before caution raised its head, and he turned suddenly to stare at her.

Gone was the unhappy damsel driven to distraction over the loss of her hat. In her place sat a smiling Julianna, who held his horses in check in a most businesslike way, and who gave them the office to start even as he watched. "I believe, my lord, that I can dispense with your escort today!" she called cheerfully to him. "Perhaps it will be beneficial to you to let your legs run as fast as your tongue!"

The earl made a really praiseworthy effort to catch her, but she was driving his grays—and well up to their bits, too, he noted before she swept the next curve with style and was out of his sight—and he had no chance.

For several moments he stood in the center of the road, feeling—and, he was sure, looking—remarkably foolish; then, with a sigh, he walked after the hat, which by now had hung itself up in the hedge and was no longer in danger of blowing away. Gently the earl removed it from its thorny perch, and looked about for a place to sit. When he spied a fallen log off to his right he made for that, the hat still in his hand. After seating himself comfortably he tenderly smoothed the ribbons which had so recently encircled Miss Cresston's chin, and picked gingerly at the stock of flowers that sat perkily on the brim. Then, smiling, he gazed at the hat's crown, and cheerfully drove a fist through it.

He was still seated there, two hours later, when the sound of a vehicle bowling down the lane at a spanking rate made him look up in time to see Miss Cresston coming toward him with a style that could have won her a place in the Four Horse Club, had that august body been open to females. Her rich laugh bubbled up as she spied him seated there, and as she neared him she pulled the team up obligingly.

The earl rose, and sauntered toward the curricle.

"Your hat, my dear," he said, bowing deeply and holding it up for her inspection. Her laughter sounded again.

"Thank you, my lord," she said demurely, reaching down for the straw and tossing it onto the seat beside her.

"No, no," his lordship protested. "You must put it on, Miss Cresston. Your favorite hat, after all."

The lady shook her head; her eyes danced. "Do you

know, my lord," she said, "I have quite decided that this
hat does not do, after all. But I thank you for your efforts on
its behalf!"

The earl shook his head. "But my dear," he said. "After
all I have been through to retrieve it for you, surely, putting
it on, to please me, is the least you can do?"

Miss Cresston hesitated. "Well—" she said. "After all—
fair is fair—but—" She stopped and stared sternly down at
him. "I do this to please myself, my lord. Not to please
you!" And with those words she crammed the hat on her
head. The torn crown flapped in the breeze in an excellent
imitation of a scarecrow, and the earl burst out laughing.
Miss Cresston joined him.

"I hope, my lord, that you enjoyed a pleasant stroll?"
she asked politely when they had sobered; it was apparent
that the thought was in danger of setting her off again.

The earl said tranquilly that he had found the verdure his
town soul craved, and he thanked her for it.

"What a whisker!" Miss Cresston said as she slid over so
that he could climb into the curricle again and take the
reins. "As if you'd ever—"

He raised an eyebrow and she bit her lip, not speaking
again until he asked if she had enjoyed driving his horses.

"Oh, yes!" Julianna's enthusiasm was real. "Such sweet-
goers! Such—"

"Yes," the earl agreed pleasantly, his eyes on the road,
"they are. And if you ever dare take them again without
leave, I shall cheerfully wring your neck!"

"Well!" Miss Cresston was about to protest when a
memory of those very same words, spoken by her father
when she had taken out one of his teams without permission, echoed in her ears. She had known it was fair then,
and she knew it was fair now, so she changed her tone a bit.
"They came to no harm, my lord," she offered.

The earl nodded. "I did not expect them to."

"I enjoyed driving them immensely."

"I am glad."

"I do hope I shall be permitted to drive them again in the
future."

Her docile tone made him grin, and there was a decided sparkle in his dark eyes as they met her mischievous green ones. "We shall see, Miss Cresston," he told her. "We shall see."

Then he regarded her sternly. "But you will not do so without leave!"

❧ *Chapter 29* ❧

Julianna drove with the earl to the stables, and, after they'd left the curricle and team in the care of his head groom, strolled up to the house with him, her hand lightly on his arm as they talked of the fast passing month, and the wealth of color in the garden, and the curious fountain of an upside-down fish spouting water that Little Haven's first owner had installed.

Near that fountain they encountered Julianna's Great-Aunt Elizabeth sitting in the shade, Miss Marley on her right side, and on her left, a glass of the earl's best sherry. "So!" the duchess greeted them mellowly as they came into view. "How did you find young Jonathan this afternoon?"

"I did not find him at all—" the earl started, but Miss Cresston cut him off to say that she had found Jonathan resting quite comfortably.

"In fact," she added in a tranquil tone at odds with the mischief in her eyes as she gazed at the earl, "the doctor has told him he can join us here tomorrow."

Looking sharply from one to the other of them, the duchess ignored the news about Jonathan. "Julianna," she demanded, "what have you been up to?"

"Up to, dear Aunt?" Julianna repeated innocently.

"Yes, up to," the old lady repeated. "And *what* has happened to your hat?"

Julianna tried to hide that damaged article behind her back; she'd been swinging it by the ribbons again, and had quite forgotten its disheveled state. Her aunt repeated the question. Julianna sighed.

"Well, the truth is, Aunt," she said sadly, "my hat—my poor, defenseless hat—was attacked."

"Attacked?" repeated Miss Marley, blinking at her in surprise.

Julianna nodded, her eyes downcast.

"But—how?—who?—"

Julianna heaved another sad sigh. "By a deranged earl," she said. "In the lane between Little Haven and the Black Swan. It was not a pretty sight."

Behind her the earl choked and Julianna, spurred by the sound, told them that she would like to stay and chat, but she had to see her mother before dinner. Without another word she was off, her great-aunt and Miss Marley staring openmouthed after her. The earl started to follow, but was recalled by a loud, "You, sir!" from the dowager duchess. Obligingly he turned, and met her challenging gaze with a quizzing one of his own.

"Yes?"

"Would you care to tell us what that was all about?" the duchess asked.

The earl smiled. "No."

"Well, do so, sir, anyway!"

With a resigned shake of his head the earl told them briefly of the afternoon's events; when he had finished, the duchess was regarding him closely.

"Left you standing in the lane, did she?" the old lady asked.

He said she had.

"Took you up again when she came back?"

Again he answered affirmatively.

"You bashed her hat?"

"Yes."

"She put it on?"

"Yes."

The old lady nodded, satisfied. "Must be love," she said.

The earl grinned. "That or influenza," he told her. "The symptoms seem to run remarkably the same."

The duchess cackled as he took his leave, hastening his steps as he approached the door through which Miss Cresston had vanished. "Ah, yes," Great-Aunt Elizabeth said reminiscently, slowly waving her fan as she gazed toward the now-empty door. "Ain't love grand?"

Viscount Bushnell arrived at Little Haven in good time the next day, having been tenderly escorted there by his loving cousin, her mother, and Miss Marley, who drove him near to distraction by inquiring solicitously about his shoulder each time the carriage was jounced by a hole in the road. More than once he wished he were riding outside the vehicle with the earl and Colonel Higham.

Yet by the time the party reached the earl's estate Jonathan could not help admitting he was quite glad of it. Although he would never tell the ladies, the journey had tired him more than he expected, and his shoulder ached dreadfully despite his aunt's and cousin's best efforts to pillow it for him against the coach's movement.

His relief at arriving at Little Haven was short-lived, however, for as he was helped down from the carriage by the earl and the colonel, the front door of the gray stone house opened, and his great-aunt appeared upon the doorstep, looking, as Jonathan later told Julianna, for all the world like an avenging angel. The gentlemen escorting him toward the house had to stop, perforce, as the viscount stared at her.

"Great-Aunt Elizabeth!" Jonathan said, automatically trying, despite his weakened condition, to make her his best bow—a maneuver that would have landed him on his face had not the earl and Colonel Higham had a good hold on him.

"Jonathan," the old lady replied, staring down at him. He had the distinct impression he had been carried back in time to the day he was six, and severely chastised for ruffling the feathers of one of his great-aunt's peacocks. He looked surreptitiously at the gentlemen on either side of

him, and then down at his own long legs, and was relieved
to find that he had not actually shrunk, after all.

"How are you, Aunt?" he asked, striving to carry the
moment off.

The dowager duchess's lips folded austerely together.
"I," she said, and he almost believed her nose lengthened
as she stared down it at him, "am excessively displeased,
Jonathan."

The viscount felt his collar growing tighter. "Are you,
then?" he asked politely, glancing wildly around for help.

"Excessively," the duchess repeated.

The earl came unexpectedly to his rescue. "No doubt you
will wish to visit your nephew later, my lady," he said,
moving himself, the viscount and the colonel forward again,
"but for the moment, I believe we had best get him to his
chamber. Unless I miss my guess, he's feeling quite worn
after the carriage ride, and would like to seek his bed."

Jonathan, who had spent a good amount of time during
the journey from the Black Swan telling his female companions that he was quite tired of his bedchamber there, and did
not intend to trade it for yet another, no matter what they
said, saw the excellence of his lordship's suggestion, and
nodded gratefully.

"I *am* feeling a bit pulled," he agreed as the other
gentlemen edged him around his still frowning aunt and
toward the door held open by the earl's excellent butler.

"As well you might be," the duchess said, following
them inside, "for what you meant by getting yourself shot
at by highwaymen—"

Without thinking the viscount protested that he had not
meant to be shot at by highwaymen—in fact, were anyone
to ask, it was on his list of things he would as lief as not do
in his life.

His words trailed off under his great-aunt's minatory eye
and her pronouncement that it was all of one piece with his
other foolishness.

Not sure which foolishness she referred to, the viscount
decided, just as he opened his mouth to ask, that it would be
better not to know, and meekly put his lips together again.

"Very wise," murmured the earl as he turned the invalid and the colonel toward the staircase, and the three made their slow way up the stairs. Jonathan heaved a long-suffering sigh and said nothing.

The duchess, robbed of her intended victim, watched the three men disappear, then turned around just as her great-niece was trying to make good her own escape by slipping into the library. "Julianna, a word with you, if you please!" she called imperatively.

With a suppressed sigh Julianna turned back toward the others, met her mother's and Miss Marley's sympathetic eyes, and determinedly pinned a smile on her lips.

"Yes, Aunt?" she said. "Is it something we need to do now, because I have just thought of an errand I should do immediately—"

"No doubt," the dowager duchess said, her tone very dry, "but I believe your errand must wait while you grace the morning room with your presence. If you please." She motioned toward the waiting butler, who sprang to throw open the doors for them. The duchess followed Julianna inside, stopping only to tell Miss Marley and Mrs. Cresston, who seemed determined to accompany them, that she wished a word with Julianna in private.

Once again Miss Marley and Mrs. Cresston exchanged commiserating looks with Julianna before obediently slipping away. Julianna watched them go philosophically, and directed her full intention toward her great-aunt as the dowager duchess came into the room to seat herself in a wingbacked chair directly opposite her great-niece.

"Julianna," the dowager duchess began after several moments of silence had lengthened the distance between them, "about this idiotic notion you have to marry your idiotic cousin—"

Julianna stiffened and replied that she was very fond of her cousin Jonathan.

"Your lovable idiotic cousin," the dowager duchess corrected, willing to concede the point. She leaned forward suddenly, her old eyes worried and intense. "My dear, it will not do."

Julianna considered telling her that whom she married was none of the duchess's business; she considered telling her that she had no intention of marrying Jonathan; she considered throwing herself on the floor and drumming her heels and shouting her frustration throughout the house. She settled on an alternative. She asked, "Why?"

"Oh, don't be a ninny, Julianna!" her great-aunt snapped, the little patience she possessed exhausted in two seconds, "It's not like you love the boy." A thought occurred to her, and she regarded her great-niece anxiously. "Do you?"

"I have always been very fond of Jonathan," Julianna repeated, two spots of red color staining her cheeks, "and I am *not* a ninny!"

The duchess's face relaxed. "We are all ninnies when it comes to love, Julianna," she replied, settling back in her chair with a reminiscent smile. "Even I."

"Even—" Julianna gazed at her in surprise. "Even *you*?"

The duchess's smile grew. "Of course, even I! Why else would I have married my poor departed Ferdie?"

"Why, I never thought of that." Julianna blinked. Her great-aunt had taken her by surprise. No one in the entire family would even dare think—much less *say*—that the duchess was ever anything but in perfect control, and now, here was her aunt, herself, admitting . . .

Julianna gulped. "I guess—I always thought—I mean— you were *born* to be a duchess!"

"Well, yes." The dowager duchess accepted the statement as a matter of course. "That's true. But did you really think I married Ferdie for rank?"

Julianna, who did, maintained a respectful silence.

"Oh, my dear." The duchess laughed tolerantly. "No rank is worth the trials of marriage! At least, not to me, and not at my stage in life! No, I married Ferdie because I did not wish to be without him, and if the marriage made me a duchess, and paid off several scores to persons who had tried to come high-handed over me in the past, well . . ." She paused, and shrugged philosophically. "Some things in life are meant to be!"

Julianna smiled, and that action brought her great-aunt out of her reverie; the old lady sat up briskly and said, "But we are talking of you, not of me! My dear, what ever possessed you to be such a goosecap as to get yourself betrothed to your cousin, just when things were looking so promising with—"

She broke off suddenly, and Julianna stared suspiciously at her. "What were you saying, Aunt?"

The dowager rose and took a hasty step around the room, frowning at her niece as she did so. "I was saying that I was always used to think you the brightest of my young relations, Julianna, and I cannot conceive of what prompted you to be such a peagoose as to agree to your cousin's proposal. Lord knows he's made you any number of them over the years, and it's apparent you can do much better, and are so taken with Mar—er, someone else—that you don't know if you're on your head or your heels. . . ."

Again her words trailed off, and she met Julianna's frown with an audible sniff. "Well?" the duchess challenged. "What do you have to say for yourself?"

Julianna rose, and the duchess was disgusted to find that her slim great-niece towered above her. "I believe, dear Aunt, that you have let your imagination run away with you," Julianna said quietly as she walked toward the door. "You are correct—I do not plan to marry Jonathan; I only told him I would so that I could get him out of town long enough to persuade him to listen to reason and accept a loan from me to pay his gambling debts, rather than sell Bushy."

"I knew it!" the duchess crowed, interrupting Miss Cresston in delight. "I knew you couldn't be so foolish as to forego—"

Julianna cut her off ruthlessly. "But as to having a—a *tendre*—for—someone else—"

"A *tendre*!" the duchess chuckled. "Oh, yes, my dear, a *tendre*!"

"Oh, no, dear Aunt!" Julianna corrected her. "Oh, no! I hope I would not so make a cake of myself as to—"

"But of course you would, Julianna," her great-aunt

corrected her helpfully. "Everyone does, at some time or another! There's nothing wrong with—"

Julianna turned from the door to say, "I hope you will keep the contents of our talk private, ma'am, until I have the opportunity to speak with Jonathan. He does not yet know that I do not plan to wed him."

"Ah, yes!" The dowager duchess's eyes danced. "He's bound to be crushed, I'm sure!"

Julianna frowned. "I wish," she said tartly, "that the world would stop acting as if there were few fates worse than being married to me!"

Her aunt chuckled. "You really ought to tell your cousin soon, Julianna—put him out of his misery." She caught the look of indignation that flared in her niece's eyes and, magnanimous in victory, changed it to "relieve his mind."

"I believe," Julianna said haughtily, as she opened the door, "that certain of my relations make the idea of being born an orphan increasingly attractive."

Her mood was not improved when her great-aunt laughed.

❧ *Chapter 30* ❧

Really, Julianna thought as she made her way through the hall and up the stairs to her cousin's bedchamber, she was growing quite tired of having people tell her how much her cousin did not wish to marry her. Not that she wished to marry him, either, but still—it would considerably soothe her to have people worrying that Jonathan would be quite cut up, rather than buoyed, by her defection from the role of fiancée.

Determined to put an end to the charade as quickly as possible, Julianna knocked hurriedly on her cousin's door before rushing in. The words "Jonathan, we have to talk," died on her lips as she realized her cousin was not alone.

"Ah, Miss Cresston," the Earl of Marleton said, rising from his chair beside Jonathan's bed. "Won't you join us?"

Julianna looked from him to Colonel Higham, who rose expectantly, then to her cousin, who waved her forward with a, "Yes, do come in, Ju, and make us a fourth at whist!" He turned toward the colonel and said, "I'll take her for a partner. She's really quite good, you know."

Blinking, she looked from the smiling earl to her cousin to the colonel, and then at the cards resting on a board Jonathan was balancing on his lap.

"You're playing cards!" she said.

Jonathan gazed at her, surprised. "Well, of course we're playing cards, Ju," he told her, adding reproachfully, "weren't you listening? I just told you we need a fourth for whist!"

"You've been playing cards while I—while Great-Aunt Elizabeth—while we—oooh!" She frowned at her cousin. "Jonathan, you cow-heart—"

"Here now! I say!" her cousin interrupted, aggrieved. "How can you call me cow-hearted, when I've a bullet hole in my shoulder to prove I'm no such thing!"

"You left me to take Great-Aunt Elizabeth's scolding!" she charged, and her cousin regarded her with vague interest.

"Oh, well," he said, "as to that—nothing cow-hearted about avoiding the old lady's tongue-lashings! That's only reasonable."

"Noble, in fact," the earl suggested, enjoying himself. Miss Cresston glared at him as the viscount considered.

"No," Jonathan said at last, shaking his head regretfully. "Not noble. Just clever."

The earl bowed his agreement and Miss Cresston eyed them both smolderingly. Jonathan, the matter settled in his own mind, adjured her again to have a seat and to join them in a game of whist.

"I did not come here to play cards!" she snapped, her head up. Jonathan shook his own head regretfully.

"A pity," he said. "Because we need a fourth." His words trailed off as another thought struck him. "Why did you come, then?'' he asked. With difficulty Julianna refrained from stamping her foot.

"I came," she said, the words edging out around her clenched teeth, "to talk with you."

"Oh." The viscount considered this. "Well, then . . ." He waved toward the earl's recently vacated chair. "Make yourself comfortable, my dear, and talk. We're all ears."

Miss Cresston did not move. "I came," she said, "to talk with *you*, Jonathan—*alone*."

"Oh." The viscount's voice took on a note of caution. "You did?"

"I did."

The colonel, already on his feet, said hastily that they would go, so that the two lovebirds—er, cousins, he amended, catching a glare from three sets of eyes—could have their privacy. He bowed himself toward the door, linking his arm through the earl's when that gentleman showed every disposition to linger.

"I do wish I could hear this," the earl said regretfully from the door as the colonel, with another bow, disappeared through it.

"Well, you can't!" Miss Cresston told him, crossing the room to shut the door behind him with a decided bang before turning to her cousin again.

"Now Jonathan," she began, "about this marriage—"

At the same moment he said, "About this marriage, Ju—" and they both stopped to stare at each other before beginning again.

"Yes?" came from two throats, and Jonathan started to grin. Julianna returned his smile as she seated herself on the edge of his bed and took his free hand between her own.

"Jonathan," she said, "you know that I am very fond of you—"

He nodded glumly. "Very fond," he echoed. "Going to marry me. Don't understand it, but there you are."

The look on his face made her want to laugh, but she bit her lip instead and continued.

"The truth is, Jonathan," she said gently, "I am *not* going to marry you."

A look of hopeful astonishment lit his face. "You're not?"

She shook her head. "No. I never planned to."

"You *didn't?*" He was sitting up straighter now, and a wide grin broke across his face. "Well, of all the good news—"

She sighed. "I am sorry to have wounded you so deeply, of course—"

"What? Confound it, Ju, it was a highwayman, not you—"

"I mean to have wounded your heart, Jonathan," she corrected gently. "To have cut up your hopes—to have injured your tenderest feelings—"

He thought. "Oh. Of course. I'm quite cast down, but—"

Julianna burst out laughing. "What a terrible liar you are, Jonathan! You've never been so relieved in your life!"

"No, no, Ju," he protested, "I assure you—your most devoted servant—it's just that—well—" A rueful grin broke through. "I ain't the marrying kind, my dear—at least, not now. I wanted to tell you so, but there, after you'd accepted me it seemed a bit late." Another thought occurred to him, and he stared at her, his eyes narrowing. "Here," he objected, suddenly remembering what she'd said earlier, "what do you mean, you never meant to marry me?"

Julianna patted his hand. "I didn't know how else to get you out of London, my dear."

"*What?*"

"I was sure that if I could just get you out of London long enough to persuade you to accept a loan from me so that you wouldn't need to sell Bushy—"

Jonathan was staring at her in astonishment, his jaw working furiously, and she broke off, her eyebrows raised in question.

"Do you mean to tell me—" Jonathan started, "that we set off for Northumberland—that I got shot by highwaymen—to—to—"

"To save you from yourself," Miss Cresston supplied.

Her cousin goggled at her. "To save me from *myself?*" he repeated. "Lord, Ju—what I needed was someone to save me from *you!*"

"Now just a minute!" Miss Cresston cried, stung. "When I think of the shifts I was put to, trying to save your inheritance and keep you from flinging yourself into the river—"

"I told you I can swim—"

"Or put an end to your existence in some other way, and then to save you from that highwayman—"

"Save me from the highwayman?" The viscount's eyes grew larger. "You're the reason I was on the road, my good girl!" Seeing that that point had momentarily robbed her of speech, Jonathan pressed his advantage by adding the clincher.

"Besides," he told her, trying to adopt the air of authority that set so well upon the earl's shoulders but seemed to slip and slide off his own, "it's not like there was really any need, is it?"

"*What?*" Now it was Julianna's turn to goggle, and she rose to take a hasty step toward the door before turning back to stare at him again. "No need? When you were talking about selling Bushy?"

"Yes, well—" Her cousin looked smug. "It's not as if I'm going to sell Bushy after all, is it?"

"Of course not," Julianna agreed, "because I won't let you!"

"No, not because you won't let me," the viscount interrupted, "but because the earl and I have it all worked out."

Julianna stared down at him. "You do?" she said.

He nodded. "I am going to repay the debt as I can, over a period of several years. The earl tells me he was on his way to my apartments to see what arrangements we could work out the day you so ill-judgedly dragged me off to be shot."

"He was?" Julianna repeated, sinking down into the chair beside Jonathan's bed as if her bones had just turned to liquid.

"Yes," the viscount said with a smug satisfaction that made Julianna want to hit him. "So you can see, there was really no reason for you to meddle, now was there?"

At that his cousin fired up again. "Meddle? *Meddle?* Of all the—you ungrateful—rude—"

"Sticks and stones," Jonathan said loftily, raising his chin at her. "Sticks and stones."

Julianna rose and advanced upon him, and his superior pose deserted him.

"Here now, Ju—don't you go—what are you planning to do?" he asked uneasily as she picked up the water pitcher beside his bed and held it menacingly above his head. A splash of water on his forehead soon told him, and he tried to dodge, shouting, "Here—Ju—no!"

"I think, Jonathan," she said, "that this would be a very good time for you to tell me how much you appreciate my help."

"I do!" he said hastily, his eye on the water pitcher. "I do."

"And that while you would dearly love to marry me, you understand and honor my determination to do nothing that either of us would later regret."

Still watching the pitcher and hoping to avoid something he would regret extremely, he agreed hastily.

"All right." She poured a dash more water on him before she relented, and set the pitcher back on the table. Then she bent to kiss him lightly on the forehead. "I hereby declare us unbetrothed. You may kiss your former bride-to-be."

She offered up her cheek, and he placed a quick kiss there before settling back onto his pillows to watch her.

"You know, Ju," he said suddenly, "someday I hope I do meet a girl just like you—only not as much so." He was surprised when she laughed, and disappointed when she would not tell him why.

"I'll look about for someone for you," she promised as she bent to tuck the blankets in around his bed before leaving. As she walked to the door she was stopped by his, "Ju?", and turned back to gaze at him inquiringly.

"When you're looking about," he said, grinning, "I'd appreciate it if she wasn't quite as high-tempered—or as good a shot!—as you!"

When she closed the door, she was still laughing.

❧ *Chapter 31* ❧

"Men!" Miss Cresston stood in the hall, still smiling at the door she had just closed behind her. The earl, standing in the corner of the corridor disengaged himself from the shadows there and came toward her.

"I take it that means your engagement has come to an end?" he asked politely. Julianna, displeased to feel herself blushing, put her hand to her hair and said stiffly that it meant no such thing—that is, she and her cousin had agreed to end their engagement, but—what she was trying to say was—

The earl glided over her disjointed sentences and fell into step beside her as she moved down the hall. "I am glad to hear it," he told her. "You and poor Jonathan would have made a terrible mismatch."

"I wish," Miss Cresston said dangerously, "that the world would refrain from saying 'poor Jonathan' whenever it links my cousin's name with my own!"

The earl chuckled.

"And another thing," Julianna continued, glaring at him. "*Where* are you going?"

The earl smiled at her. "With you."

"Oh." Curiously, she found nothing really to dispute in that statement, and thought for a moment before asking cautiously, "And where, then, am *I* going?"

The earl smiled again. "With me."

A sixth sense told Miss Cresston that she ought to dispute *that* statement, but she realized rather bemusedly that she was quite tired of disputing. She tried again. "Where, then," she asked, "are *we* going?"

"To the morning room?" The earl suggested. "A new guest has arrived."

"Oh." The syllable did little to express excitement; Miss Cresston felt the house was quite full, already.

"Is it another of my relatives?" she asked.

The earl grinned, and did not return a straight answer. "It's someone you like."

Julianna thought. "Is it my Aunt Emilia? Jonathan's mother?"

The earl said it was not. She regarded him with suspicion.

"But it's someone I like?"

He nodded. "It's someone you like."

At the moment Julianna could think of no one who fitted that description, but did not say so; instead, she walked in silence beside the earl, showing little enthusiasm as he opened the door to the morning room and ushered her inside. There, with her mother, her Great-Aunt Elizabeth, Miss Marley and Colonel Higham was Lord Wafton, and she tilted her head to one side in surprise.

"Why, Edmund!" she said, moving forward. "Whatever are you doing here?"

Now it was Lord Wafton's turn to look surprised, and he gazed from her to the earl and back again. "I—I was invited, Julianna!" he stammered. "Don't you remember? To make up one of your betrothal party—"

"My what?" Julianna said, and she did not shake off the earl's hand when he thoughtfully placed it under her elbow to steady her.

"Oh." Lord Wafton's puzzled brow cleared. "You are thinking I put the cart before the horse, to be sure! I should have felicitated you first, shouldn't I, my dear? Well, I do!" He moved forward to kiss her cheek, and to smile at her. "I wish you very happy. When I read it in the newspaper I was delighted for you, and then, when the earl's kind letter came, inviting me to join you all here—"

He broke off as Julianna continued to stare at him. At last she found her tongue and stammered, "But I don't understand! This cannot be! No notice of my betrothal to Jonathan was sent to the newspaper."

"No, well, why should you?" Lord Wafton laughed, "when it is you and Richard who are to be wed—"

"What?" The word came out vehemently, accompanied by an incredulous glare as Julianna recoiled and stared at her friend in stunned surprise. "My dear Edmund, you are mistaken—"

Behind her the earl coughed apologetically, catching her attention. She turned toward him.

"It seems, my dear," he said, "that I forgot to mention this—"

"Forgot to men—" she repeated, and her eyes opened wider. *"Forgot to mention!* You—you—"

"Really, Julianna," Great-Aunt Elizabeth interrupted, prepared, as usual, to take charge of the situation. "Richard should be commended for his quick thinking in shielding you from the malicious gossip of the *ton*."

Miss Cresston did not have a commendation for the earl. The duchess continued. "I for one do not care to see our family name besmirched by tales of irregular engagements and wild flights to the border."

"There was nothing irregular about my engagement—" Julianna began but caught Miss Marley's eye and had, perforce, to remember the conditions under which her betrothal was contracted. Her sentence ended abruptly as she bit her lip and glanced toward the earl. His mouth twitched, and she glared at him.

"At any rate," Julianna began again, gamely, "we weren't fleeing to the border."

The duchess snorted. "As near to it as makes no difference, you foolish child. Driving north—"

"Northumberland," Julianna said stormily, "is *not* Scotland."

The duchess threw up her hands in disgust. "Northumberland indeed! Might as well flee to the wilds of America as—"

"We were not fleeing!" The force behind Julianna's words overrode even the duchess's commanding tones, and her great-aunt sniffed.

"Just as well," the dowager duchess pronounced, "because it would not have done. Wouldn't have done at all. And, thanks to Richard, it's all wrapped up in clean linen, and you're to be a countess.''

The strangling sound in Miss Cresston's throat made her great-aunt pause as Julianna whirled toward the earl.

''You—You—''

''Despicable—'' he supplied. She repeated it.

''Unscrupulous—'' he suggested. She nodded.

''Delightful,'' he tried. Miss Cresston ground her teeth.

''How dared you?'' she whispered venomously, growing even more uncomfortable under the interested eyes of their audience. ''You have the gall to send a notice to the newspapers proclaiming our engagement when you never even asked me—''

''But I did,'' the earl interrupted reasonably.

''You didn't!''

''I did. The night your cousin was shot—''

''In a *stable!*'' Miss Cresston shouted.

The earl conceded that the setting was somewhat irregular.

''I was covered with *blood!*'' she continued.

The earl nodded reminiscently.

''You are, my dear,'' he said, ''one of the few women I know who can wear red.''

Lord Wafton choked, hastily wiping the grin from his face as Miss Cresston glared at him. ''This is *not* funny,'' she said. Biting his lip, her old friend agreed. She favored him with another glare before turning back to the earl again.

''And you, sir,'' she said, ''to think that you can have the arranging of my life in this way; to think that you can run with your plans, without regard to the others involved—''

''Much as you ran with your plans for your cousin Jonathan?'' the earl suggested.

Julianna informed him that it was not the same.

''Oh?'' The earl affected polite interest. ''Perhaps you would like to tell us the difference?''

''Jonathan,'' she said, her head held high, ''proposed to me.''

''So did I!''

''But I *accepted* Jonathan's offer!'' Miss Cresston cried.

''Oh. Well. Formalities.'' The earl shrugged, and surprised them all by dropping gracefully to one knee before her. "Miss Cresston," he said, "will you do me the honor of becoming my wife?"

Glancing wildly around, Julianna did the only thing she could think of. She placed her hands on his shoulders and gave a mighty push, causing him to lose his balance and tumble into the small table at his left, to the imminent peril of the Sevres vase upon it.

"Julianna! The vase!" gasped her mother as Lord Wafton, with great presence of mind, dived for it, making a manful effort even as he tripped on the earl and collapsed upon him, the vase clasped determinedly to Lord Wafton's chest.

"Oh!" Julianna said, glaring down at the men, and then at the others in the room. "Oh, oh, oh!" Clenching her fists to her sides to prevent herself from pounding a certain self-important lord with them, she hurried from the room, ignoring the gentle pleas of her mother and Miss Marley that she not go away angry.

As the door slammed behind her the dowager duchess wiped the tears of laughter from her cheeks and shook her head. "Oh, yes," she said softly to herself. "Ain't love grand?!"

Miss Cresston was seated in a secluded corner of the garden, surreptitiously wiping her eyes on her sleeve, when a square of snowy linen floated into her lap, and she gazed up quickly into Marleton's sympathetic eyes.

"I am *not* crying," she said, snatching it up and applying it to her eyes.

"Of course not," the earl agreed, walking round the bench to sit down beside her.

"I never cry."

"No."

"And if I *were* crying, it would be because I am angry, and not because I am hurt. I am not one of those silly, weak women forever weeping because they do not get their way."

"But of course you're *not* crying, so it doesn't matter," the earl finished for her.

Miss Cresston gave an audible sniff and agreed.

"Of course," the earl continued, as if he were just

thinking aloud, "if you *were* crying, because you were angry, we both understand, it's no more than you'd have a perfect right to do."

Julianna gazed at him suspiciously. "I would?"

The earl nodded, and his face was quite sober as his eyes met hers. "My dear, that was badly done of me. I should have asked you before sending that notice to the newspaper."

"Yes," Julianna agreed, "You should have."

"But I was waiting for you to disengage yourself from your cousin, and I didn't expect Wafton for another day. I knew no one else would tell you—"

Here Julianna interrupted to ask incredulously, "You mean everyone else, *knew*?"

The earl nodded. "Knew and approved. Your mother, the duchess, the colonel, my niece, they all wish us very happy."

"Well, I don't know why they should," Julianna said, "when we are forever at each other's throats—"

The earl smiled. "But you have such a lovely throat to be at, my dear."

To her consternation she blushed, and bade him sternly to behave.

"You never even asked me," she charged.

"But I did!" he protested. "Not once, but twice—"

Miss Cresston snorted. "Once in a stable, and once in the morning room *filled* with onlookers! Do you really think that counts, my lord?"

He showed every disposition to rise and drop to his knees again, so she hurried on. "Besides, you have never said a word about loving me."

"I haven't?" The earl appeared much surprised. "Well, we must remedy that immediately, mustn't we?" He pulled her to him and kissed her—very thoroughly—rubbing his index finger over her lower lip when he was done, and saying, "I have been wanting to do that ever since we met."

"You have?" Julianna asked faintly, gazing at him. Her mind flitted back to their first meeting, and she straightened, pulling away from him. "Well, you certainly hid it well!" she said, looking into the distance.

He chuckled. "Believe me, my dear," he told her, "that day in the park you looked as if you would take my head off if I even so much as touched your hand, let alone your lips."

"Ah, yes." Julianna nodded her understanding. "Of course. I scared you to death."

The earl chuckled again. "Not exactly, my love. Of course, at that time I did not know of your penchant for pistols, or your accuracy with them—"

He broke off to gaze inquiringly at her as she sat, watching him wide-eyed.

"What—did you call me?" she asked.

He thought. "A crack shot?"

"No!" Julianna shook her head impatiently. "Before that!"

He thought again, and smiled. "My love?"

Julianna nodded. "Do you *mean* that?" she asked.

He grinned. "Yes, my love. My darling, infuriating, strong-willed, determined, courageous, sweetest love."

"I do not think," she said, regarding him with suspicion, "that all of that is meant to be flattering."

He chuckled. "Would you be flattered, my dear, if I told you that I know I do not wish to live without you?"

"Would you be *flattened,* my dear, if I told you I am not sure I can live *with* you?" she replied, her voice dry.

"But no! How can this be?" He held one hand to his forehead in mock protest before putting it down to grin widely at her. "Come now—confess—you would find life quite dull without me, after this season we have spent sparring together!"

Julianna tried to deny it; found she could not, and countered with, "There are worse things in life than being dull."

He regarded her in disbelief. "Name one!"

"I can name several!" she said, exasperated. "That is not the point! The point is—"

"The point is," the earl interrupted, "that I love you, and you love me."

"I do?" Miss Cresston asked.

"You do," the earl confirmed. "Ask anyone. Ask—" He looked out over the garden to where Miss Marley and Lord Wafton were strolling through the neatly kept flowerbeds. "Ask Wafton. Hey! I say! Wafton!"

Ignoring Miss Cresston's embarrassed plea that he sit down and be quiet, the earl succeeded in attracting the other couple's attention by the simple expedient of standing on the bench and waving the handkerchief he had so lately loaned Julianna. When the others had obligingly approached, the earl prodded Julianna with, "Go ahead! Ask him!"

"Ask me what?" Lord Wafton said when Julianna showed no disposition to do so, merely slanting a fulminating glance at the earl.

"It is the most ridiculous thing—" Julianna said. Marleton interrupted her.

"I told her to ask you if she loves me," the earl said.

Both Lord Wafton and Miss Marley appeared surprised. "But of course you do!" Edmund said, looking down at her. "Any fool can see that! I've known it for some time now! Half London knows it—and the other half is out of town!"

"Of course!" Miss Marley agreed, leaning impulsively forward to kiss Julianna's cheek. "And I am so glad!"

"You are?" Julianna said, surveying the faces smiling at her. The two nodded, and moved away.

"I believe," Marleton said, watching them go with satisfaction, "that there may well be a match there."

"What?" Julianna gazed at him in surprise. "Beth and—*Edmund?*"

The earl nodded, amused. "Really, my dear," he scolded her gently, "one would think you were not paying attention this season, to be sure!"

Julianna put a hand to her head, and agreed dazedly that one would. Watching her friends walk off, hand in arm, she said wistfully, "He is such a *good* man."

The earl agreed that he was.

"The kind of man every woman would be *lucky* to marry."

The earl was beginning to grin.

"Every woman wants to marry a *good* man," Miss Cresston continued.

"Ah, but my dear," he said, taking her hand and raising it to his lips, "there are just too few good men to go around."

Miss Cresston tried to ignore the way he was nibbling on her index finger as she sighed and agreed.

"And someone must marry the rest of us," he murmured, transferring his attention to her thumb.

She gazed down at his bent head. "Must someone?" she asked, faint but pursuing.

The earl glanced quickly up, and his eyes gleamed. "To save us from ourselves," he said.

"You certainly need saving!" Miss Cresston agreed. "But then the question becomes—who, my lord, will save *me*?"

The earl smiled the most devastating of his smiles. "We must think about that," he said. "We must think long—oh, years—and hard, and we must not stop thinking until we have hit upon the perfect solution . . ."

"I think," Julianna said with conviction, as he took her in his arms again, "that you are mad. Quite mad."

"Yes," the earl agreed, nibbling her left ear with the same interest he had shown in her fingertips only moments before.

"You need a keeper."

"Yes," the earl agreed again as his lips moved lower, and Julianna gasped as he found a particularly tender spot at the base of her neck. "And you, my dear, would be perfect for the job."

Julianna tried to sit very straight as his exploration of her neck continued. "Perhaps," she said, working to make her voice sound less breathless. "If I were asked."

The earl raised his head and gazed lovingly into her eyes, the flickers of light dancing in his own causing her to swallow deeply.

"Miss Cresston," he whispered, and this time the proposal was without any trace of flippancy, and for her ears alone. "My dear Miss Cresston, will you marry me?"